A WALKING SHADOW

SHADOW

PARADISE INVESTIGATIONS, BOOK 2

TEEL JAMES GLENN

Praise for *A Walking Shadow*

"Teel James Glenn has penned one of the finest literary mashups of our time. Part Hammett, part Shelley, and all heart. *A Walking Shadow* is a wholly unique take on the PI mystery genre, so well written it will leave you longing for the next installment in this Shamus nominated series. Brilliant!"

- Bruce Robert Coffin, bestselling author of *Crimson Thaw*

"This marvelous genre mashup was a fun read from beginning to end. Frankenstein's monster–true to the book, not the movies, is presented as a 1930s hardboiled detective written in a tight, strong pulp style. Elements of Eastern mysticism blend smoothly with the sci-fi character in this sweet detective soup in a suspenseful story that pulls you through the action to a satisfying finish that left me eager for a sequel."

- Austin Camacho, author of eight novels in the Hannibal Jones Mystery Series, five in the Stark and O'Brien adventure series and short stories featured in the Edgar-nominated *African American Mystery Writers: A Historical and Thematic Study*

"*A Walking Shadow* is compelling, exciting, yet deeply thoughtful. Teel James Glenn asks important questions about the human condition by giving us characters whom we care about—and one of the most human is Frankenstein's monster. Glenn weaves an action-packed story through multiple genres and ethnicities with care and respect. Jump on board. You won't regret it!"

- Carol Gyzander, Bram Stoker Award® winner and World Fantasy Award finalist

DEDICATION

To ET, who is a constant reminder that I am not fighting the fight alone...

And to P.N. Elrod who supported and encouraged above and beyond.

ACKNOWLEDGMENTS

My Group—Nancy, Lee, Wayne, and Jaime—who helped me to give birth to Adam and nursed him along all the way...thanks, guys.

CHAPTER ONE

Life's but a walking shadow, a poor player,
That struts and frets his hour upon the stage,
And then is heard no more. It is a tale
Told by an idiot, full of sound and fury,
Signifying nothing.

(William Shakespeare, *Macbeth*, act V, scene V)

I woke from darkness with no preamble and with no particular desire to exist, from a space between death and life. That was over one hundred and sixty years ago.

My creator, Victor Frankenstein, shunned me, leaving me to wander in search of meaning.

In the beginning, I had no desire to either be or not to be but was conscious only of a need to find my reason to exist. It was to that end that I returned to the world of man from the Arctic after many years and ultimately to the City of New York in the year 1936. That was three years ago.

I assumed the name of Adam Paradise after my favorite poem and set about finding my place within this new world I had entered in hopes of finding a place and a purpose. Names have power, so perhaps it was an unconscious attempt to will myself to a better place by using that name.

"You are going once more the movie with the Chinese woman, Mister Paradise, yes?"

The hunchbacked Romani woman at her desk startled me and drew me back from my ruminations.

1

"If you wish for dinner first, you have been staring out the window long."

"Yes," I agreed with both her statements. Of late, I had been aware of a deep unease, of something somehow wrong but in a way I could not pinpoint. This time, I had been staring out the window of my second-floor office on Fifth Avenue, watching the Friday afternoon parade of humanity from which I felt so apart. "I was lost in my thoughts." I turned from the window to smile at her.

"It is not good for one to look only inward, Mister Paradise." She didn't look up from the typing she was doing at her desk in the outer office and never missed a keystroke. "One cannot appreciate the flowers in darkness."

"Except by their scent, little mother, but that is why I am going out to be among people."

"Then you have better hurry," she said. "I have some pages to finish typing, then I will bring them to the magazine. I will lock up."

"As you wish." Vandoma Kalderash had been a client only months ago but now had become both ad hoc secretary and assistant to me. She was a Romani woman with a prominent place in her tribe, a position inherited from her recently murdered mother. She was in her mid-twenties and had not at all been limited by the malformation of her spine, which might have given another pause.

I think she felt a certain sense of responsibility for me as she viewed me as the fulfillment of Romani legends of the *gadjo mullo* (outsider revenant) who would not obey his creator and fled from this world.

"You have been spending much time with this woman." Her fingers kept flying on the typewriter keys as if they were separate entities, the clattering of her bracelets rivaling the keys for sound. Her gaze was focused on the page of pulp writing she was transcribing, but I detected a disapproving side glance at me.

"I can't learn Cantonese from a book." I grinned as I went to the coat tree and grabbed my leather trench coat, though the May weather was mild enough that I didn't belt it. "And John Dewey said, 'Education is life itself.'"

The music of her bracelets slowed slightly. "To learn things is good, this I know." When I did not react, she added, "And tomorrow you are here?"

"Yes, I'll be in tomorrow; even though things have been slow with no cases these last weeks, the routine of coming in is good."

"Yes, good. I will be here as well, I am sure they have more for me at the publisher today."

"Have a good night." I headed out to the stairs. "And say hi to your brother for me."

"*Latcho drom*, Mister Paradise."

"Good journey to you as well, Vandoma."

The air was brisk during my short walk to Fourteenth Street, where I elected to take a taxi to Chinatown. I was aware of the eyes on me during my walk, but being New Yorkers, the sight of a seven-foot-two-inch man striding down the street only drew a quick glance before they returned to their routines. It was one of the reasons I had located in the city.

One of the others was the diversity of cultures, such as expressed by my destination at the Florence Theater on East Broadway in Chinatown. It was built into the very arch of the Brooklyn Bridge to be a very unique structure.

The stonework of the bridge formed a vaulted ceiling high above the theater, giving it a cathedral-like feel. This helped with the acoustics of the large space. A hundred seats were set out in even rows facing a folding movie screen set up on the low vaudeville stage at the head of the room.

I only stopped long enough to get snacks for the movie, as I would go to dinner afterward with my host. I went in early to sit at the back of the auditorium also so as not to block someone else's view of the film. This also allowed me to leave my folded trench coat on the floor beside me.

The location helped me blend in as much as possible with my scarred Caucasian features. As I had been coming to these shows for months now, the regular crowd seldom took much notice of my unusual looks anymore—even in this sub-cultural pocket of the city, the "unusual"—or in my case, frightening—became commonplace and accepted quickly.

I appreciated films as a special window into the way the *vox populi* saw the world, for it was the only way I could see the world without the shades of the dead swirling around. The flickering light of the cinema made me feel closer to mankind in an odd way, allowing me to see the world much as they did.

Departed souls, attached to those seated around me by circumstance or blood ancestry, hovered above our heads. They were translucent, irregular shapes in many shades and colors with no discernible features; most would call them ghosts. In recent memory, I had confirmation that this seemed to be the case.

I thought about how some of the shapes floating around me were different, for they were not of my ancestors, not exactly. They were the souls of those who had inhabited the body parts I was assembled from. I had only recently had my suspicions confirmed that the amorphous shapes were indeed remnants of some part or whole of the consciousness that lingered on this plain. I had no way to communicate with them as of yet, but how to do so interested me. I intended to explore that possibility at some point when time and circumstance permitted.

I was there to enjoy a special showing of *Charlie Chan at the Opera*. The theater normally was home to Yiddish films and vaudeville shows, but the enterprising owners rented the space out on Friday nights, the Sabbath of the Jewish religion, to the ever-growing Chinese population of the area.

There, they held some Chinese Opera presentations and showed motion pictures, both silent and sound. In tonight's special film, a Swede played a Chinese-American detective, and an India-born Englishman played an American escaped lunatic. It was actually a product of Hollywood with the American print that had subtitles added in Cantonese and Mandarin for Far East distribution.

The audience around me, all Asian and mostly Chinese, were more than willing to forgive the Swede impersonating their race since, for once, the faux Chinese detective was the smartest guy in the film, and an actual Chinese-American actor played his Number One Son.

The oddity on the program that night was a second Hollywood-made Chinese detective film, *Mr. Wong, Detective*, this time with the Anglo-Indian actor Karloff playing a Chinese hero in a much more cartoon portrayal. Still, those around me enjoyed "one of their own" — albeit not played by one of their own — triumphing for once more over the "devil white man."

I had some fascination with the lead actor as he had, in a way, portrayed me — or at least the mythologized version of my story. The mythology of "our hero" fascinated me. Each group of the still tribal humanity had a desire to see some element of themselves raised to something "more." As Emerson said, "A hero is no braver than an ordinary man, but he is brave five minutes longer."

Yet each tribe from the dawn of time had found some archetype to admire and aspire to, from Gilgamesh to Galahad to the garish four-color fellows in the new comic books that had become popular in the last couple of years.

I personally had no archetype — no group nor real role model to aspire to, though with literary and academic pursuits, I did search for one. I stood outside all and every group, a singular being. I was so much so that I had to wear gloves to conceal the fact that my two hands did not match, for my creator had not really given thought to such niceties as symmetry.

I was passing, in my own way, as one of humanity under this assumed name of Adam Paradise. Names, they say, have power to conjure with, and I suppose subconsciously, I hoped to find such a place, at least temporarily.

When the second feature ended, the lights came on in a short break for the concession stand to make sales and local businesses to make announcements.

The break gave me a chance to stand and stretch my legs, which felt cramped in the folding theater seat. These seats were not fastened to the ground so they could be adjusted for different performances. This allowed me to quietly move my last row seat back to give me a little more legroom.

I still had some popped corn and sweetmeats left, so I didn't have to go out to the lobby for more. I had slipped my snacks into my upside-down fedora, which was resting in the wire frame below the seat.

It was good that I planned ahead. I could see through the doors that the concession stand was mobbed because the second half of the program was a fan favorite, a Hong Kong-made *Xuxia* film. It featured an adventure of Wong Fei Hung, a Chinese national hero, physician, and martial artist. He was a real man who was only recently dead, a historical figure in the birth of Modern China.

When everyone was settled again for the second part of the night's program, a short newsreel depicting the horrors of the war in Manchuria and China ran, changing the mood. The Han race was suddenly not heroes, but the victims of a vicious aggressor, and I could sense the undercurrent of anger in the room.

Even though Japan had begun its advance toward conquest seven years before, the Chinese-American community felt it as a fresh wound each day. Where I had been able to enjoy my anonymity among them and had been united with them in rooting for Chan and Wong, now I felt clearly apart from them—it was not my relatives, my ancestral homeland, my very heritage under assault. It was directly theirs. And I was once more "the other."

My connection to them, to all humans, was existential.

My only direct connection to the group in the theater was the woman who stepped up to make an impassioned plea after the newsreel when the house lights once again came on. She implored the crowd to dig more deeply into their pockets to aid their overseas brethren in the relief of the Manchurian people and to help against the Japanese occupation.

The young lady's name was Han Ku Lee, though she preferred to be called "Hank." She was Manchurian born but lived and thrived in New York as the owner of three restaurants and a pool hall up in Harlem, where I had first met her.

Physically, she was delicate, with a short-bobbed haircut and dressed in a green man-style trousers and jacket with a brooch on her lapel that had the flag of China on it. Her presence, however, was anything but delicate. Her persona filled the space of the room as if she was ten feet tall and again gave the people a new hero to look up to.

Hank also wore a green eye patch over her left eye that gave her a piratical, even swashbuckling air, which seemed to help her pitch. The patch served to make her good eye, a bright emerald green, almost glow with inner light.

In addition, the souls that hovered over her were golden shades, and it imparted a certain theatrical effect to my view.

"You have seen the news from Changsha in Hunan," Hank began. "Our brave brothers and sisters are repelling the horrors of the Japanese aggressor, but they need many things, things we can supply." She went on flowing back and forth from English to Cantonese with a very practiced and elegant plea requesting funds for food, medicine, and the purchase of weapons for the Chinese forces. I expect she had given the same pitch across the country, in any Chinese community she could reach, and in several sympathetic non-Chinese enclaves.

She had been doing so for five years, trying to arouse the sleeping giant that was America to the incursions in first Manchuria and then all of China. It was a hard task, as the United States had a strong anti-war faction that would have the country stay isolated from the troubles of the rest of the world. The American public was doing their best to ignore not only the war in China but the clouds of war from Europe, fearing a repeat of the remembered horror and death of The Great War.

Mankind continued to embrace tribalism as strongly as before I had taken myself to the Far North with initial, failed hopes of extinction. It was disappointing that so much remained unchanged since ancient times.

Hank spoke for some fifteen minutes, which ended with applause, and several even stood. People filed up and dropped little red envelopes in the bucket she had set out on a table by her.

I had understood about half of the Cantonese portion of her speech and felt proud of it. She had been tutoring me in the language for almost seven months since I had occasion to meet her while delving into a robbery case in my capacity as a private investigator. It was she who had invited me to the screenings at the Florence Theater once a week and I had tried to make as many of them as possible to further my education.

I would join Miss Lee for a late meal after the films but made no indication, at that time, that I knew her so as not to "taint" her appeal to her people with my outsider status.

Just as she was concluding her appearance, about to pack up the bucket so the second half of the program could start, the doors to the right of the auditorium flew open. Five masked men stormed in from the lobby. Above them, dark indigo shapes swirled and danced, an indication that these men had taken lives at some point. Violently.

"Everybody stay!" One of the masked men called out in Cantonese, "Pay tribute to Hip Sing tong!" He raised a gun into the air to silence the chaos when the crowd realized what was happening.

The startled exclamations stopped suddenly at a gunshot—these people understood the consequences of violence, having been preyed upon by forces inside and outside their community for many years— and everyone remained quiet.

Everyone, that is, but Hank.

The plucky woman stepped to block one of the men from reaching for the donation bucket.

"Keep your hands off that money," she said. "That is for our people back home."

The man ignored her and made to push her aside, but the moment he put a hand on her shoulder, she lashed out with a solid right punch that caught the man in the jaw. It rocked his head back, and he dropped unconscious to the floor.

"And keep your hands off me!"

The leader of the bandits who had fired his gun turned to her and yelled, "Bitch" in English as he leveled his pistol at her.

That was when I acted.

I rose swiftly, grasped the back of my chair, and swung it overhand directly at the gunman.

The wood and metal chair flew with such velocity that it hit the gunman in the chest and lifted him off the ground. He was catapulted back six feet to slam into the skirt of the stage before collapsing to the floor. He did not move again. I witnessed his shade rising from his body, a maroon blob of translucent light.

The amorphous dark shape hovered above the dead gangster, joining the dead he had made himself, then flowed across the room toward me. The essence of the murdered man joined the dark shapes that swirled over my head—all those whose lives I had ended. It was my own personal crown of thorns, or perhaps Jacob Marley's chains?

The theater erupted into pandemonium, the audience streaming for the exit doors with panicked yells of terror. This made it difficult for me to run directly to Hank's side. I had to weave around the fleeing crowd, all but knocking down several by accident.

At the front of the theater, a second of the masked men produced a knife and attempted to grab the donation bucket. Hank was having none of that. Abruptly, there was a small caliber pistol in her hand.

"Hey!" the bandit yelled. He slashed at her, but the woman fired twice, and the man fell back away from her.

The remaining bandits, including the now-revived attacker who had assaulted Hank, raced out the lobby doors to be lost in the concession crowd.

All at once, we two were the only living beings in the room.

Hank looked up at me and said with a crooked smile, "Nice pitching arm, Dizzy Dean. But I guess this means we don't get to see the second bill."

CHAPTER TWO

"His whole chest is caved in," Police Detective Pettruchi said in astonishment as he bent over the fallen leader of the bandits. "It's like he was hit by a freight train." The body of the masked thug was a bloody mess, a leg of the chair having penetrated through to his chest and out his back, bisecting his spine. The policeman looked up from the corpse to me with a mix of revulsion and fear. He took in my countenance, and I saw mirrored in his eyes what I had seen in many faces before.

My features were regular in that I had two eyes, a nose, and a mouth in the usual place, but all were cast in an angular mold that seemed to be harsh by all opinions. And there were scars that I passed off as from a car crash when an explanation seemed necessary. I also used makeup to minimize the starkness of the sutures against my skin. Tonight, I had opted not to use it.

Pettruchi held that appraising stare as he rose to his full five foot five in what I assume was an attempt to intimidate me to cover up his fear.

At seven foot two, I was not impressed.

"So, Mister…uh…Paradise," he began. He was a round-faced man of Italian extraction with a dark complexion and a five-o'clock shadow that I suspect required him to shave several times a day. He made an elaborate show of taking out a pencil and notebook and writing in the book. "Why were you here with the chow mein crowd?"

It was an odd attempt at a racial slur since I am sure his own Italian ancestors faced resistance in immigrating to America. I suppose he was trying to find a way to be on "my side" as an interrogation tactic since we both had Caucasian skin. The tendency of humans toward tribalism was always obvious but still made no sense to me.

I did my best to project docility despite the gory spectacle before us. I had developed that skill to make my interactions with people more comfortable for them.

"I came at the invitation of Miss Lee," I said. "The young lady your fellow officer is questioning."

He made a disgusted face and then asked, "And how is it that you, a licensed private investigator, had no gun, and the China dame had one?" Pettruchi looked sideways at the uniformed officers who had corralled as many of the patrons as they could to take statements. Another detective was questioning Hank near the back of the room.

"Simple," I answered, ignoring the insinuations he put into every statement, "I do not like guns, so I do not like to have them around. As for Miss Lee, she is a business owner and feels the need for protection—as this incident would seem to prove out."

"Soft-hearted are you?" He sneered and poked his pencil at the slain robber. "Shooting is too violent for you, but smashing a guy's chest to freaking pulp is okay? Your buddy Shane isn't around to give you a free pass this time, big guy, the DA is gonna want a murder rap on this."

He was clearly looking to prove his position in the "pecking order" was higher than mine, and he moved his hand near his belt-holstered pistol for security. I was used to frightened reactions to my size and countenance, but this hostile response from the policeman was completely unjustified. There had been more than enough witnesses that my actions and Hank's were made in self-defense.

True, I was a little angry with myself for not finding another solution than the fatal one. I had been a violent creature in my first days of awareness and had tried in this second sojourn amongst mankind to mitigate that. I felt no deep guilt, however, for it had been a split-second decision. And, on top of it all, my fedora was a blood-stained mess embedded in the man's chest. It had been my favorite hat.

11

Several dark shades floated around the detective's head, a sign he had taken lives himself, but whether it had been in The Great War or after in his capacity as a police officer, I had no way to determine.

For now, I pondered the correct course to take with the detective to mitigate the circumstances.

I depended on good relations with the police, yet there were times when my friend, Detective Tommy Shane, needed to smooth things over with the powers that be. There were a number on the force who did not like a civilian being involved in criminal matters, let alone one as unusual as I was. Two deaths—however justified—would be a hard pill for those sorts of officers to swallow.

The racial aspect would only complicate things. The police force often felt that crime that happens in Chinatown was none of the city's business, especially after the gang wars of the decade past where the criminous of the ghetto had "fed" on themselves. It was a closed-mouthed community, and the police were happy enough not to bother investigating most crimes within its borders.

Across the room, I could tell by Hank's body posture that she had reached a point of frustration with the policeman questioning her. She sat shaking her head, and the plainclothes officer wagged a finger at her like a teacher scolding a child. I knew that she would not sit well with that very independent woman. Her green eye blazed with fury like a fuse that had been lit.

"Detective Pettruchi," I said, "since I have nothing more to contribute to your report, I think I shall join my friend."

"I didn't say I was done with you, Paradise."

I gave him my most pleasant smile. "But you are, Detective. You can ask Commissioner Valentine just how done you are. You can remind him about Camp Siegfried if he needs clarification for my actions here." Commissioner Lewis Valentine was one of the few officials who knew of my involvement with some violence at that retreat for the Nazi Bund earlier in the year. It was an odd affair the city government wanted to keep from the public. I had helped the department considerably and was counting on them remembering to get me past the enthusiastic detective.

His eyes went wide, and he almost dropped his notebook, and I knew my bluff had worked. He knew that even mentioning the incident to the public was taboo, and if I knew about it and the edict from Valentine to keep it quiet, I might be well enough connected to be a danger to his position. His desire for a long career suddenly trumped his need to act tough.

He hemmed and hawed a moment, then finally found his voice. "So, well, just don't leave town." He abruptly turned from me and walked over to one of the uniformed officers holding the patrons at bay.

I walked to Hank's side, where a balding detective had been questioning her.

"I can't give you back the gun, lady," the cop said. "You killed a guy with it."

"But it's mine—" she insisted. She presented the image of defiance, standing with hands on hips and staring fire from her good eye. "What was I supposed to do, let him stab me?"

"I don't make the law, Dragon Lady," the cop said. "You have a receipt for it. You can pick it up after the coroner's inquest—or the trial if they charge you."

"Charge me? For what? He was trying to rob me and to stab me—"

"Look, calm down," the detective said, an edge coming into his tone, "I don't make the rules. The money is impounded until this gets sorted out, and you do not get the gun back." He lowered his voice and hissed out, "Not like you need it much with that attitude."

"Attitude?" Hank exploded, "A triad *bautu* attacks me and—"

"Thank you, Officer," I said, stepping up to partially block Hank from the startled detective. "Your superior has said the young lady and I can leave." He stared at me for a long moment, then looked to Pettruchi with a questioning expression and pointed to me.

"What—" Hank asked, her fury only slightly thwarted. I just smiled.

"Wait," I said. "Any moment…"

Pettruchi's face assumed a sour expression across the room, and then he waved a hand dismissively.

"Okay," the bald policeman said with an exasperated tone. "You two can go."

I took Hank by the shoulder and guided her gently past the clot of patrons and the annoyed Pettruchi, who was trying to get answers from anyone who had been in the theater. It was clear to me that most of the patrons had suddenly forgotten how to speak English or developed temporary blindness. I did not have much space to pity him and might have laughed at his frustration were circumstances less serious.

Once Hank and I were on the street, I answered her unasked questions.

"I informed the nice police detective in charge that we had nothing more to tell him," I said. "I am assuming you had nothing more to tell them, correct?"

She gave me a coy look. "Why, of course, Mister Paradise." And the truth of the closed Chinese community was never clearer to me. She definitely knew much more than she had told, so the question became, would she tell me?

"You know something about those gang members, don't you, Miss Lee?"

"I think we should skip dinner after all this, I've lost my appetite. You don't really have any interest in this."

"On the contrary, Miss Lee; to quote John Donne, '…any man's death diminishes me because I am involved in Mankind.' And in this case, I have already taken a life, so I am sure the fellows of those gang members will think I am indeed interested."

She laughed. "Okay, you asked for it, let's go to Wo Hop's."

CHAPTER THREE

Wo Hop's was a basement restaurant on Mott Street that I became quite fond of in the last year. I think the wait staff, now accustomed to my appearance, frankly, enjoyed the sight of the big *gweilo* squeezing himself behind the tiny table in a corner and having to duck below the low, tin-roofed ceiling.

They also seemed to enjoy my attempts at ordering in Cantonese. It was all worth it because the food was very good.

"So why here?" I asked Hank when we were tucked into a corner at the back of the small room. "You do have two restaurants down in the area."

She laughed. "Don't tell the world, but I like their cook better than mine. And I think it makes the staff of my places nervous if I show up too often."

We ordered a full meal, and she kept up with me as we ate steamed jasmine rice, soy sauce chicken, and stir-fried *bok choy* (with garlic). My mismatched hands are not so well-tuned for fine motor functions, so, to my slight embarrassment, I was always forced to use a fork.

It was only after we were in the last course of fresh tomato and tofu soup that I broached the subject of the attempted robbery. She smiled shyly and then fell easily into her lecturer's voice.

"The history of my people in this country has not been a happy one, Mister Paradise." She looked at the Han faces around her and then back to me. "Many were brought over to satisfy the cheap labor demands of the railroads when African slaves were not available after the Civil War. When the railroads were done, their numbers alarmed white men who came to fear being replaced. My people were herded into over-crowded areas that became Chinatown here and in San Francisco, and at the same time, they were derided for not mixing or assimilating. No effort was made to welcome them, and this fostered even more isolation. The federal government even passed a law in the 1880s specifically to block new Chinese arrivals and deny rights to the people already here. Conditions for immigrant laborers became more atrocious."

Her face assumed a pained expression. "Like other minorities, some of these immigrants joined together in the formation of benevolent societies—what you call tongs—based on such societies in the old country to help the people. They soon decided crime was the only way out of their poverty."

"Lord Acton, a British historian, wrote in 1887, 'Power tends to corrupt and absolute power corrupts absolutely,'" I noted.

"Yes," she continued, disgust seeping into her tone. "The tongs became about sustaining their own power and pursued criminal activities for gain. Slavery of women was one of the most profitable enterprises of the tongs, for my people here were mostly male Chinese brought over for their labor. Girls were smuggled in, and some tongs ran a thriving business in brothels. Others, like the Hip Sing tong, specialized in gambling to take the hard-earned wages from the men. The gangs became greedy and often fought over money and territory."

"That reputation colors the opinions of much of America about your people," I noted.

"Then there were the battles over opium sales that came about, a lingering effect of the opium the West forced on China and the hopelessness of my people."

"A true shame of the West," I observed. "But how does it have a bearing on what happened tonight? The thieves announced themselves as with the Hip Sing tong."

"They did. But I think it was not so. They were imposters."

"How so?"

"The Hip Sing have been supportive of my efforts. And the Cantonese of the thief you...uh...killed—I do not think he was a native speaker. I believe they wished to cast suspicion on the tong."

16

"To what end?"

"I don't know and cannot guess. Months ago, one of my lectures in California was disrupted in a similar manner, though they claimed to be of the Ghost Shadows. Several branch offices of my Manchurian relief fund were broken into some weeks ago in Los Angeles, San Francisco, and Chicago. Some minor damage done, and some funds stolen. It seems an organized effort, but by whom, I do not know."

"It is a curious puzzle, to be sure. Criminal gangs often fight or bully others for no other reason than to cause the other to lose face, so it is not the provenance of any race or tribal group, Miss Lee. And they were criminal organizations."

She nodded to acknowledge my attempt to offer some perspective to her statement.

"When the market crashed, and then the invasion in Manchuria happened," she continued, "the attention of the tongs returned to their original purpose. They turned their resources to helping the people, providing aid to the destitute, and helping to raise money for home relief against the Japanese."

"So, how do you account for these acts that appear to be against your relief efforts?"

"I can't. Except that someone is deliberately trying to sow discord between the Hip Sing and the On Leong tongs. They agreed to a truce brokered by Mock Duck some time ago in this city. There has been peaceful coexistence between the major gangs for years."

"Who would benefit from your losses?"

"Only the Japanese. If the shipments of food and war supplies are curtailed to our people back home, it could be disastrous. The money taken from my offices was inconsequential in the scheme of things, but after tonight, the word may spread and could discourage people from contributing…"

I contemplated what she had spoken about as I paid the bill and said thank you to the wait staff. When we stepped up to the street, the active Friday night crowds made it seem almost like a busy midday. Most of the faces were Asian, but there were some other races among the bustling crowd, so no one seemed to take particular notice of my companion and me.

"You see, Mister Paradise," she said, "I have nothing definitive to act on, so it seems pointless for you to spend time on this. I am sure the police will make no progress, so I will have to resolve it myself. It is not your problem."

"You intend to have Mister Chadeaux investigate?" I referred to the gentleman Miss Lee kept company with on a regular basis. He was something of an investigator and adventurer and fairly well known. She shook her head.

"As much as I like that tall drink of water, he's got his own problems." She must have realized her reply was too sharp and mitigated it with, "Actually, Anton is in the Philippines now, Mister Paradise." The two seemed well suited for each other.

"Adam, please," I said. "After all these months of tutelage and this evening's adventure, I think we can be less formal. And as I said before, I am part of this now—I have taken a human life. Whether tong or some other criminal gang, I fear my part in this will not soon be forgotten."

"In any case, Adam, there is nothing to do but add more security to any of my fundraisers—and get another gun."

We walked along Bowery Street toward Canal Street until we arrived at her parked roadster. She reached under the front seat and removed a small pistol. "In the meantime, can I give you a lift uptown?"

"No thanks, Miss Lee—"

"If I can call you Adam, you can call me Hank."

"Hank," I continued. "The weather is pleasant, so I think I will walk home tonight, but perhaps you can stop by my office tomorrow afternoon, and we will see if there is another way to approach this situation."

"Okay then. I will. And thank you for tonight."

"You did promise me an entertaining evening, and you certainly delivered."

She was laughing as she drove off.

The air was brisk for the time of the year, with a hint of rain to come, but I welcomed the chance to stretch my legs and walked up Bowery Street. The breeze off the river had a salty tang, just enough to make me miss my hat, left a wreck at the theater. Still, it was no discomfort by degrees from the cold I had experienced during my long isolation in the Arctic.

Since my return to civilization, first to Sweden, then Marseilles, and finally these three years in New York, I had looked to understand the motivations of the humans whom I moved among. It is why I undertook my manufactured identity and the profession of a private investigator. What better way to know mankind than to be the one to whom they bring problems?

In my time in the bustling city, I had found both anonymity and friends. Indeed, I had found such a community as I had not hoped nor expected. I had come to count Hank as friend, albeit one of my outer circle. Now, she was drawn into a more central orbit, and I into shadowed places such as my adopted profession often occasioned to lead me.

I mused on what I had learned from Hank about how the tongs worked; it was something I had not really thought much about before that day—another aspect of the tribalism of humanity that often perplexed me.

Nietzsche said that "human beings constitute a transitional, not final stage of development. Consequently, human beings cannot become too complacent about or satisfied with, their achievements without endangering their claim to be human." And it might never have been clearer as on the streets that I walked.

The Third Avenue Elevated Train ran along Bowery Street on a steel skeleton that looked like the survival of some prehistoric beast. It was on the eastern border of the old Five Points and was populated by cheap clothing stores, flop houses, and dingy eateries where formerly saloons had flourished before Prohibition. There were employment agencies and tattoo studios as well, frequented by many sailors, but the majority of those I passed were shattered husks of humanity.

Men and even some women clustered in the doorways and along the curbs, clearly intoxicated, many in a stupor. All looked to be in poor health and radiated a hopelessness that seemed a palpable thing.

A multitude of spectral shapes hovered over those streets, for it was clear that many had spent their final moments in the grimy shadows of the iron skeleton of the train tracks. Death walked those streets as regularly as the train rumbled above.

The very name Bowery had become synonymous with those on the downward curve of their lives to the point where there was a movement to change the name to Fourth Avenue South, but the name and reputation persisted.

I had not made Broome Street before I was aware of footsteps matching mine some distance behind me. I slowed my pace and then sped up to confirm my suspicion that the steps behind matched mine. I was being followed.

I paused outside a tattoo parlor to gaze into the window as if I was fascinated by the designs there. Behind my reflected image, visible through the phantom forms of my body parts, I saw that I was at the head of quite a parade.

There were four men half a block behind me that did not fit the character of the neighborhood. They were roughhewn, dressed as working-class men, for certain, but they were all healthy specimens, muscular in silhouette, and traveled in a tight group. They also moved beneath indigo clouds, and it was clear that, individually or collectively, they had caused the death of many individuals.

Before I could begin walking again, they must have surmised my ruse, for they hurried their steps, tied bandannas around their lower faces, and formed a semi-circle in front of me.

"You have offended the Hip Sing tong," the tallest of the quartet said in accented English—though he was several inches below six feet. "And for that, you must pay."

He produced a cleaver-like hatchet from under his pea coat, which was a signal for his fellows to brandish their own.

Here was a troubling situation.

"There is no reason for this," I said in Cantonese, but when I saw no reaction, I repeated it in English to the same result.

I slipped off my trench coat and wrapped it about my left forearm.

"I warn you, it is not in your best interests to pursue this," I said in full voice. "I will not hold back."

This seemed to amuse the four, as two of them laughed and then attacked.

I do not like violence; I have not studied it, per se, save that it seems such a part of the cycle of being for humans.

My creator, however, selected exceptional elements in his choice of component parts for his experiment. The fibers of my muscles, as well as

20

my healing capabilities, were robust. I was strong, even for my size and weight, and deceptively fast. Certainly, faster than my attackers counted on.

The first who got close enough to strike at me swung his cleaver at my left arm, but I batted the flat of it away with such force that the weapon flew from his hand.

A second darted in to slash at me, and I was able to deflect it, though my bundled coat took a deep cut before he darted back.

Their strategy was clear to me now; I had seen the same tactics when arctic wolves had harassed an isolated polar bear cub. They worried it, running in at it each time its back was turned to face another attacker. They eventually wore the cub down and killed it.

I hoped to avoid its fate by keeping my back to the glass of the storefront, but even that was only prolonging an inevitable outcome. Eventually, I would be wounded, and if they coordinated their attack well enough, they could end me.

I knew that for born souls, there was a survival, an afterlife of some sort, as evidenced by the "ghosts" I saw and by the one I had actually communicated with. As to my own fate when my consciousness in its current form ends, I have no idea. I have no model, no progenitor or mythology to give me a framework.

So it was that I decided to preserve my current state with action.

One of the attackers launched at my right side at the same time as a second on my left ran straight in on me. I suppose they assumed I would turn to face one or the other, but my peripheral vision was good; I saw both and shot a fist out to smash the one on my right directly in the face.

My blow lifted him off his feet to slam into the ground with a spray of blood from his broken nose. At the same time, his fellow slashed again at my left arm. This time, the edge of the blade sliced through the coat and into my arm, but I did not accept the attack passively. Instead, I lashed out to grab his swinging arm at the wrist and jerked hard.

His arm snapped with an audible cracking sound.

The man exclaimed, "*Akuma!*" and dropped to his knees in pain.

The tallest of the group, who had spoken initially, yelled, "*Damare baka!*" Then, he grabbed the wounded man by the shoulder and pulled him to his feet.

The man I'd punched staggered to his feet, and their leader yelled, "*Kaeru!*" and the four of the group all raced off as quickly as their injuries allowed.

CHAPTER FOUR

I waited a few moments to make sure it was no ruse, and then, stooping to pick up a cleaver that one of them had dropped, I continued. I deposited my now ruined trench coat and the cleaver into a trash receptacle and kept my senses on full alert for the rest of the trip. I'd recognized none of the attackers as those who had tried the robbery at the theater, so there appeared to be a plentiful supply of thugs involved in the incident.

The fact that I did not recognize the language of these four was troubling. I had a suspicion but didn't want to jump to any conclusion.

The cut on my arm did not feel deep, but it bled enough to color my suit jacket a muddy brown. I cradled it for the rest of the trip home.

My apartment was on the quiet block of Thirteenth Street off Seventh Avenue, not far from St. Vincent Hospital. I held the cut on my left forearm, but it had stopped bleeding by the time I arrived home. I concluded it was not deep and would not need stitches. I really didn't need any more.

My apartment was on the top, the third floor of an attached row house. I didn't relax my vigilance until I spotted that the hair I had stretched across the doorframe was still unbroken. I had been surprised once by Nazi thugs when returning home and was determined that would not happen again.

Inside, my apartment loft was humble but comfortable. It consisted of a main room with a wide artist's window that gave me a view of the Empire State Building. It had a bookcase, a comfortable reading chair, a lamp, and an easel near the window. The easel held my latest attempt at a painting, a still life of some books and fruit set up to take advantage of late afternoon light.

Across the room was the extra-long bed I had built myself, and a small counter with a hotplate and a few odds and ends on it.

The room had no closets, so I had a large wardrobe and a dresser for my clothes. I went to the small washroom off the studio and, after stripping off my gloves, jacket, and shirt, attended to the injury.

As I had expected, the cut was long but not deep, and I was able to wash it and close the wound with a styptic pencil and some surgical tape. I knew from experience that it would be healed in a day or so completely, leaving yet another scar to add to my body's art gallery of existence.

The shirt and jacket were both ruined and that was as annoying as the loss of the overcoat. I had to have all my clothes, including my shoes, custom-made, so losing all three pieces was considerable. I had only two suits left, so would have to order some more soon. I needed lightweight suits for summer in any case.

I would miss that fedora, however.

I donned a lounging robe and settled down to finish reading a new book my friend Digger had obtained for me. It was a children's fantasy by some English professor drawing on old Norse and Celtic myths. I found it soothing with its positive view of the world and was amused by the constant mention of the tiny size of the hero.

The adventure set me thinking about an issue that often occupied my mind: the nature of not just good and evil but of life itself.

Ex nihilo is the idea that matter was created out of nothing by a divine act. It is in contrast to *Creation ex Materia*, which means that all things were formed *Ex Materia*, from preexisting things. So, the question I wrestle with is the philosophical dictum can something come from nothing? Did my creator Frankenstein stumble upon some arcane secret that gave lie to the Genesis narrative?

The Hebrew bible begins with *Bereshit bara Elohim et hashamayim ve'et ha'aretz*. *"In the beginning, G-d created the heavens and the earth. Now the earth was unformed and void and darkness was upon the face of the deep."* It could have multiple meanings—there was either nothing, or there was pre-existed matter that was then "formed" by an external power.

Most have a preconceived view of this based on the rituals they have been raised with. The Egyptians, Indians, and many native animist religions followed the *creatio ex nihilo* view that the Almighty caused all to suddenly appear. And, of course, the Hebrews and the other People of the Book—the Christians and Muslims—follow that interpretation.

The opposing view that there was "something" before the universe we know aligns with the newer Big Bang theory proposed by the Roman Catholic priest and physicist Georges Lemaitre.

I often wondered which view my creator held or if, as I seem to, he wandered blindly into his discoveries and had no vision beyond his own hubris.

I sought clarity on the issue each day.

Having taken yet another life that night at the Florence Theater, the concept was even more important to me. I knew from my own experience that there was survival—the essence of individuals did continue—the conventional concept of ghosts.

As before, I wondered if I had the right to take life, to end the continuance of an individual's path in the "living" form and send it to the beyond.

Yet I felt little guilt for the man at the theater, for did not Hank deserve to continue her current life? It was a concept I would continue to wrestle with. Still, I was determined to help her, and I suspected I would face more tests of my views on the issue before her problem was solved.

I tried to put it all aside to enjoy the satisfying conclusion of the book about the little Hobbits, which allowed me to drift off to sleep thinking positive thoughts. Still, the fact that I had taken a human life cast a shadow, even on that light fare.

I rose early Saturday, donned a blue suit, my remaining overcoat, and a teal Tyrolean hat I had, and headed out. The threatened rain of the previous night had not manifested, so the walk was pleasant.

My usual breakfast spot was on my way to my office on Fifth Avenue off Twentieth Street. I kept to a fairly regular schedule six days a week, so enjoyed the anonymity of being a regular there. I took my lunch from the store below my office most days and ate dinner at any number of places for variety.

Despite several attempts, I was not a very good cook, even if I had the facilities in my room. Since I had subsisted on raw seal meat and fish for many years, it was no surprise that my palate was not well educated.

Since expense was not an issue for me, having the treasures I found in the ice-locked sailing ship where I resided for so many years, I had started to explore the different cuisines that New York offered, such as eating at Wo Hop, to expand my experience.

I had also recently purchased the building that held my office after the previous owner died suddenly. I'd done so because I'd become accustomed to the regularity of my office there and was not ready to move yet. There was a storefront pharmacy/soda fountain on the first floor with a new tenant (who did not know I was the landlord) so I was able to continue my life as I had before.

I stopped inside the pharmacy, said hello to the teen boy behind the counter of the soda fountain, and picked up several of the morning papers. I also picked up a hot tea to bring up with me because I knew someone would want it.

I went back outside as my access to the second floor was via a separate staircase by a street-level door.

I ascended to the comforting machine-gunning sound of typewriter keys, and I had cause to smile.

CHAPTER FIVE

The sound of the typewriter meant that Vandoma Kalderash was already at work in the anteroom outer office, which she had claimed as her own space.

She had recovered remarkably from the shock of her mother's murder only three months ago.

It was from the elder Kalderash's shade that I had my first confirmation of human survival. It was she who had communicated with me after her death that allowed me to rescue Vandoma and her older brother Nico from Bund killers at a summer camp on Long Island.

Vandoma assumed her current position as secretary and aide and proved herself invaluable, not only in keeping records but also in making calls. She insisted I have a phone installed, though I am not fond of the devices. In addition, her brother Nico had extensive contact with the shadier side of society, which was useful for my investigative work.

There was an added fact—she knew my secret. Like her mother, she had a gift of "the sight." She was a female *chovihanis*, a *drabami* who was a healer, and a *drukker*—she who sees the future, at least in a limited degree. The facts of my creation that had become a legend, which Shelley based her fictitious book on, had been known to her people for a long time and were believed to be true.

Once more, I thought about my choice of Paradise as my last name in this incarnation and what had truly influenced me to assume it. So much wishful thinking.

She viewed me as a *Martja,* a spirit of the dead that walked among the living but which she saw as a *pajivalo*—a good person.

I was glad she believed me so, for I tried to be.

"*Jo reggelt,* Mister Paradise." The Romani woman looked up from her typing and smiled as I entered. She wore a green dress that almost concealed her hunched back and had her dark hair pulled back into a ponytail with a blue ribbon. Combined with her petite size and the fact that she wore no makeup, the effect made her look younger than her twenty-five years.

"And good morning to you, Vandoma." I set the tea down on her desk for her, which she accepted with a shy smile, then hung my hat and coat on a tree by the door and stepped back to her desk to see what she was working on.

"*The Blue Brother's Revenge?*" I dramatically quoted the title of the front page of the manuscript she was typing. Since I had relatively little work for her, she still took in regular work for the pulp magazine company Thrill-Street, which had offices a few blocks away.

She giggled at my reading. "Just the usual silly things," she said. "They are increasing the magazine to twice a month so there will be more work. Is alright?"

"Yes, of course. I don't have much work currently, though I suspect we will be busy soon." She raised an eyebrow and paused while putting a new sheet into the machine.

"There is a new, as you say, case?"

I told her a bare-bones version of the events the night before. When I finished my recitation, she rose and came to me, shaking her finger like an old crone. It was then that her hunchback became more visible. While it was the first thing most people saw about her, I had come to barely notice it.

"You should not take such a chance, Mister Paradise, you should've taken the ride from the Chinese lady."

She came to stand at my side, barely coming to my chest, but as from when I first met her, my size seemed inconsequential. She never showed any fear of my appearance at all, which was remarkable in my experience interacting with people.

28

"You take off your jacket, I will look at cut." I could do nothing but comply as she treated me as if I were a junior and she the senior even though I was, technically, seven times her age. She had appointed herself my guardian, and there was nothing I could do about it.

Nor did I have a wish to escape her ministrations. In the few short months she had come into my orbit, she had somehow become not only indispensable to my business but, I suspect, to my mental health. And I looked forward to the occasional home-cooked meals she made me.

She had me roll up my sleeve, then pulled back the bandage and looked at the wound. She made *tsking* noises.

"Can you have the dress-man look at this?" She referred to my cross-dressing neighbor Dottie (whose birth name was Daniel), who was the nurse at St. Vincent and had taken care of me when I had medical issues from wounds. I was reluctant to go before doctors for fear of arousing questions, so avoided such visits whenever possible. Fortunately, except for stabbings or such, I had little reason to need a physician with the robust health my creator had built into me.

My clumsy hands had not done a very good job with the bandage, so she undid it completely, studied the wound for a moment longer, and then pulled out a first aid kit from her desk. "I can make good," she said. "You wait."

She ran down the hall to the washroom, filled a small basin, and returned to wash the wound, cleaning it thoroughly, dusting it with sulfur powder, and then re-wrapping it.

While she worked, she asked me questions about the night in detail, as my description had been sparse. We spoke, our words flowing from Romani to Hungarian and English much as she had with her mother, who had been old-country-born Hungarian. It was how she still spoke at home to her brother, and I'd picked up the habit when the two of us spoke.

It was a surprisingly comfortable arrangement, which made me reflect on how much I had indeed found community as I spoke with her.

"There, this should heal well now," she said when she was done. She put away the first aid kit as if such a service was a daily occurrence. "I will make call to the tailor, yes? You will need more clothes?"

"Yes, little mother." I smiled. "I need a new trench coat as well as a replacement suit. But might as well get two summer-weight suits as the weather is about to change."

"I will make appointment for you." She reached for a phone book on the corner of her desk. "Yes?"

"Yes, and I'll stop by the haberdashery about a new fedora; I feel silly wearing a Tyrolean hat in the city."

She grinned up at me and then went to her task as I headed into the inner office feeling well taken care of.

Before I had sat down, she was already typing. I unlocked the bottom door of my desk and removed the journal where I had taken to recording my feelings and the events of my days. I took some time writing up the occurrences of the night before, then looked them over again to see if I could find any relevant facts.

I kept coming back to the words the attackers had uttered that I did not think were a Chinese dialect. "*Akuma, damare baka* and *kaeru*!" I repeated the words over again to be sure I pronounced them as the attackers had.

When I was done with my recording work, I settled in to read the newspapers before I really began my day. The events were both new and very much the same as the days before.

There were some bodies found in a garage in the Bronx attributed to a mob killing, another corpse had washed ashore near the Manhattan Bridge in Brooklyn that had been beheaded, and assorted celebrity scandals.

According to an article by a columnist I followed, Moxie Donovan, a poll said eighty-four percent of Americans believed the country should stay out of the European war. The writer exhorted America to "wake up—the wolves are at the door!" The article did not mention if America even noticed the ongoing war in China, but I suspect Mister Donovan was well aware of the menace.

Britain and Turkey announced a mutual aid agreement in the event of aggression and war. Spain withdrew from the League of Nations.

Both events would complicate the European issue.

The King and Queen of England were in transit to Canada to show both they were not worried about things to come and to bolster confidence in the Commonwealth.

Meanwhile, New Yorkers were delighting in the World's Fair in town and going about the business of forgetting the ills of the world.

It seemed to me that one of mankind's dubious talents was the ability to deny impending disaster as long as they could find distractions. The old bread and circuses of Rome brought forward to the modern world.

It put me in mind of those Hobbits again with their preoccupation with their stomachs and attempts to ignore the rest of Middle Earth. The pain of the "over-the-hill people" meant nothing to them. All but one little hero.

I set down the papers as it occurred to me that America was the Shire and the clouds of war both in the Far East and Western Europe were imminent. The question would be, how long could the country ignore the gatherings of wolves? I was put in mind of Rome with the Visigoths.

My musings were useless, however, as I had a real case to work on, and it was ten-thirty already, so it was best I get to it.

"I'm going to get the street working on the extortion case, then walk over to the Tome Tomb," I said to Vandoma as I came out of my office. "I don't expect to be long—shall I bring you back up some lunch?"

"Yes, please," she said without looking up from her typing. "You know what I like, you may surprise me. Thank you."

"Will do," I laughed. She was a creature of habit, too, so I knew her three or four sandwich choices.

She would not accept a salary from me, saying the use of the office for her to do typing instead of having to take it home was enough, so I bought her lunches and occasionally dinners and made her take taxicabs that I paid for if she worked later than five. She protested at first, but I told her I was older, so she had to listen. She laughed but knew it was true, so accepted it as a compromise.

"Oh," I added as I headed out, "Miss Han Ku Lee is supposed to stop by in the afternoon, but if she comes early, tell her I won't be very long." She nodded silently, but I thought I detected a slight downturn of the corners of her mouth as she went back to typing.

I headed over to Seventh Avenue first and the impressive rail hub that was Pennsylvania Station. It was a massive Beaux-arts-style building that covered over eight acres and dominated the neighborhood around it. Thousands streamed in and out of the train station, which was one of the largest public spaces in the city. They came from all over the country to the madhouse of New York.

I used the western entrance but stopped short of the vast main room, which was on the scale of the St. Peter's Basilica in Rome. Instead, I stayed in the arcade, where there were shops, food stalls, and a shoeshine stand.

The stand was my destination.

"Hi, Mister P," the black man at the last of the row of raised seats said. He was a fit man in his mid-forties with a shaved head and a pencil-thin mustache that gave him a dapper look despite his working-class attire. "Looking for a shine?"

"Hi, Leroy," I said as I climbed up into the chair. "Yes, among other things."

When I said "other things," I saw his gaze dart around to be sure there was no one sitting in any of the chairs near us. Leroy Dumas had contacted me two years before when his brother had been arrested on trumped-up charges, and I had been able to find the real culprit. Since then, I stopped by regularly, and he had been a reliable source of information on many levels of society.

The very setup of wealthy white men sitting in a chair while a "working" man did the menial task of shining one's shoes was a snapshot of the racial hierarchy in modern America, even in a cosmopolitan city like New York. Even the demeaning name most were called, "shoeshine boy," showed how language creates a cage to reinforce societal norms.

But Leroy, like so many in the divided nation, had found a way to work around the "limitations" of his enforced station. The relaxed interface of the two races meeting at the shine stand meant many of the customers felt free to talk, their positions reinforced and magnified by the physical arraignment. Leroy was a good listener. And to special friends—among whom I felt honored to be—he was an informed talker.

"What's the word on a new extortion racket in Chinatown?" I asked as he began to apply the paste to my shoes and buff them.

"Ain't just downtown, Mister P," he said. He had a slight Southern drawl but a well-modulated voice. "Word is that somebody been pushing in on Queenie's territory."

"Seriously?"

"A couple of houses hit. Runners roughed up but not enough for the police to get wind of it."

Queenie, or Stephanie St. Clair, was a woman who ran the numbers game in Harlem, taking bets on sporting events, running a lottery and other enterprises, including a bank for those of African ancestry when many white banks would not take their money, further excluding them from the "system." Queenie was active in promoting her race and educating her people, and she had something of a Robin Hood reputation despite her criminal roots.

She and her enforcer, Ellsworth "Bumpy" Johnson, had also successfully resisted Mafia intrusion in her territory, and so there was a general truce between her and the Italian gangsters, much like that between the various Chinese tongs.

"Any idea who is making the moves?" I asked.

"No, but might have an Oriental flavor."

"Hmmm," I mused, "that is interesting."

"You okay after your little celebration in Chinatown on Friday?"

"Yes, thanks. It's why I'm asking."

"I'll keep my ears to the ground," Leroy said. "We don't need any more shooting wars like before Repeal."

"I agree."

We chatted amiably about his family and aspirations—his son, Waylon, was at Morehouse College down south—the first in his family to attend higher education—while he finished the high-gloss shine on my shoes.

When I hopped off the stand, I handed him a large amount, which he always tried to refuse for the regular fee, but I always argued, "You're working overtime on all this real estate on my feet," and he accepted the money.

I walked east to Third Avenue and then uptown to the mid-twenties to the bookstore of my friend Digger Tome.

The Tome Tomb was a long, narrow oasis of literature, cluttered with shelves overflowing with new and rare books. It was never very crowded with customers, though four at a time in the dark store would feel like a mob.

I'd discovered the store my first week in the city, and the remarkable man who owned and ran it had become a friend. Digger Tome was a man who appeared to be in his forties, balding and overweight, with thick glasses, a pallid complexion that implied he'd never been out in the sun at all, and the most remarkable recall I had ever encountered.

Rumor had it that he had done a memory act in a carnival at one point and that he had a photographic mind. I certainly had not found that false since it seemed he had read every book in his store and many more and recalled all he'd read.

Digger—the only name anyone knew him by—looked up from reading when I entered and said, "Without remorse drive out the sinful Pair From hallowed ground th' unholie, and denounce To them and to their Progenie from thence Perpetual banishment."

It was a game we played, trading quotes as a test.

I shot back, "If patiently thy bidding they obey, Dismiss them not disconsolate;   reveale To Adam what shall come in future days, As I shall thee enlighten, intermix My Cov'nant in the woman's seed renewed; So send them forth, though sorrowing, yet in peace.' Arch Angel Michael was a little dismissive, I think, in this passage, eh?"

Digger shook his head. "I have to try harder."

"I have the advantage. It was almost too easy this time. Milton's *Paradise Lost* is a favorite of mine." I had read the twelve books over and over in my Arctic isolation—I had not only adopted my current name but others before because of it.

"Try this," I offered in return. "Say how I loved you, speak me fair in death; And when the tale is told, bid her be judge."

He blinked owl-like for just a moment. "Shakespeare, *Merchant of Venice*, Act IV Scene I. Too easy for me as well."

We two chuckled, which startled the single customer at the back of the store, who looked up from the book he was examining to do a comic double-take when he saw me. He replaced the book and made his way out of the store without looking back.

"I'm sorry," I said when the man had left, "I seemed to have chased out a customer."

34

Digger made a dismissive gesture. "He thinks this place is a library—he never buys. I think he just looks at the pictures anyway. So, how did you like *The Hobbit*?"

"I liked it. It was hopeful. We need hope these days."

"That is true." He adjusted his glasses. "To what do I owe the visit?"

I explained briefly my adventure of the night before and concluded with, "So these words are what the attacker yelled: '*damare baka, kaeru,* and *akuma.*'"

He asked me to recite it again. "Are you sure that's exactly what they said?"

"Yes, I have a good ear." In fact, I have two good ears, mismatched like my hands, but which give me exceptional hearing. My creator did strive for the best parts—just not for bi-symmetry. It's why I kept my hair long to hide them.

He smiled slyly. "I think I may have an idea." He moved from his chair behind his counter and rummaged around, then, with a cry of triumph, pulled out a leather-bound volume whose title I could not make out.

"I thought that word *baka* sounded familiar." He set the book on the counter before him. "It is Japanese for 'idiot'!"

"Japanese? Why would a Chinese thug curse in Japanese?"

"More than that." Digger sat back and closed his eyes, and I knew he was picturing the pages of the book as if it were a movie screen. "*Damare baka* means something akin to 'Shut up, idiot,' and *kaeru* is 'we must go' but an urgent version."

"So those men were communicating with each other in Japanese?" I was a little surprised by that and the implications.

"The last one will interest you, Adam." He opened his eyes to peer up at me. "*Akuma* means 'demon.'"

"Really?"

"Yes, demon."

It was my turn to laugh. "I'll add that to yet another opinion of me. That's good to know."

CHAPTER SIX

I returned to the office after my visit with Digger, equipped with two sandwiches, some soda pop, and a copy of the British pre-publication edition of *Arms and the Covenant* by Winston Churchill from the bookstore.

Digger apparently had an "inside man" across the pond and knew I would be interested in the Parliamentarian's views. He'd previously praised both Hitler and Mussolini but had become a strong voice warning of the German chancellor's aggression. On the other hand, he had also allowed the Japanese occupation in Manchuria to proceed unopposed in the League of Nations, so his opinions interested me.

There was an ominous silence from my office as I ascended the stairs. I steeled myself for some danger, but when I reached the landing, Vandoma was seated at her desk reading the manuscript she'd typed, and Hank was seated quietly across from her, hands folded.

"Good afternoon," I said as I walked through the doorway. I set Vandoma's sandwich and soda pop by her typewriter. "You came early, Hank."

"There has been a—development," Hank said, rising. "Perhaps we should head inside to discuss it." She cast a wary look at the Romani woman.

"You can say anything with Vandoma present you can say to me. She knows all my secrets."

My statement caused the Romani to show a ghost of a smile, though her eyes stayed on the manuscript she was reading. I took a seat across the office from the two women.

"Very well then," Hank continued with another quick look to Vandoma. "Overnight, two of my restaurants were burglarized and damaged considerably."

"Was anyone hurt?"

"Not badly, fortunately," she said. "One was after closing, and the other was near to that with only staff. A busboy was roughed up, but not badly."

"That is troubling. One might have been a coincidence with regards to the Florence Theater incident, but two is another thing."

"And in one case, the Hip Sing took credit for writing on the walls. In the other, the Jade Dragons claimed credit. And both said they would return to collect tribute."

"It seems that affairs are escalating," I said. "Is there a chance it could be actually from the tongs?"

"I know at least one—the Jade Dragons—was false. I personally know the leader of that tong. He assured me this morning that his people had nothing to do with it."

"I might have an idea who did." I proceeded to tell her about the attack on myself. When I was done, Hank slapped a hand on her thigh in an angry gesture.

"This is terrible," she exploded. "All the work to help my people will be destroyed. When the word gets out it could spark another tong war."

"There may be a clue that can help us find out who is doing this. I discovered at Digger's that my attackers were not Chinese, they were Japanese."

"Japanese!"

I told her what the thugs had yelled, and she nodded.

"Yes, yes." She paced the small outer office. "It makes sense, the Japanese would want me to stop the supplies going home, but why would they become so open about it now?"

"Perhaps these criminals felt you were being too effective," Vandoma offered. Hank looked at her in surprise.

"I…uh…yes," Hank **replied**. "We have raised more in the last months than ever before. And I've heard that the *Kempeitiai*—the Japanese Secret Police—in Manchuria have stepped up their looting, kidnapping wealthy White Russians and Chinese for ransom. Japan seems to be desperate for money."

"That could be a factor," I **said**. "Yet for them to reach this far into America, they must have a large organization."

"Yes," Hank hesitantly **agreed**. "They would have to have men here and on the West Coast—even Chicago."

"That is many men." Vandoma was leaning forward, her dark, intelligent eyes focused on the other woman who did her best not to look at her.

"Yes," Hank **said**, "but they would not all have to be part of any such group. Many desperate types would hire out."

"Like the ruffians who accosted me," I **noted**. "Though if they were Japanese…"

"How is that so?" Vandoma **asked**. "For them to pretend to be Chinese? Are they not very different-looking peoples?"

Hank shrugged. "Very much so, but just as say, an Italian may be mistaken for a person from Spain purely by look—dark hair, perhaps olive skin, etc.—some Orientals may have features that look like others. It's not like the movies where they just make a white man squint and talk pigeon-English and become an all-purpose Asian."

This caused Vandoma to laugh. "Like all the time when they make Romani, just silly accents in movies."

"Yes." Hank seemed to reluctantly agree with Vandoma.

"I imagine immigration and intermarriage also contributed to certain features being common," I **offered**. "Some Chinese features may show up in some portions of Japanese society."

Hank **nodded**. "Yes, it can be looked down on by Japanese as their society is very stratified, but some may look that way. I have no doubt the Empire would take advantage of it for spies." She was standing now, her fist balled in anger. "But how can we fight this, Adam?"

"By being calm and making a plan. The ones doing this have thought it out carefully—destroy your credibility with the community and create confusion and chaos with the appearance of predatory tongs. We should explore how to keep them from destroying your credibility. We must talk to the tongs, set up a summit to forestall trouble in advance."

"As I mentioned, I know the head of the Jade Dragons, a small local tong here in the city," Hank said. "He is young but well respected. I can see if he will set up such a summit as it is in his best interests."

"We must also try to find out where the finances of such an organization we theorize exists could come from."

"You have a clear head, Adam." Hank moved to the outer door. "I will see if the Honorable Chung Lee Fu of the Dragons can set up a meeting with the other tongs and let you know if we can make it happen." She stopped and looked back at Vandoma. "Thank you for the help," she said to the Romani. "Nice to meet you." She looked up at me and smiled. "Adam." Then she left.

There was a long moment of quiet in the room as Hank's heels clicked down the stairs. Vandoma's expression was unpleasant, with pursed lips and narrowed eyes.

"What is it, Vandoma? You seem upset."

"She makes rash decisions. Be careful, you should be wary of her judgment."

I was taken aback; it seemed to me that the Romani woman was judging Hank harshly. "You have just met her. How can you say that? You make her sound like a *Coxani*?" I used the Romani word for witch, half-jokingly.

"She talks fast."

I laughed before I could stop myself. "Is that bad?"

"Am I not a *drukker*? I see that she will bring you much trouble in the future."

"I will be cautious." When her expression did not brighten, I added, "I listen to your advice, always, little mother, but I have taken on her case, so I can't let fear cloud my vision."

"Fear no, caution, yes. You have purpose in this world, Mister Paradise." She spoke quietly but with such conviction that I was speechless.

Purpose was what I sought. A place in the world and a reason to exist. Here was someone I respected who had senses beyond the "norm" and saw my existence as meaningful. I felt myself moved.

"*Solax*," I said in Romani, "I give you my oath to take all care, Vandoma. I will not leave this plane casually."

She stared at me hard, and then her stern expression softened. "Good," she said in a firm tone. "Is good." Having said that, she then rolled another piece of paper into her typewriter and went back to work.

I went into my office, still a bit off kilter by her statement. I sat at my desk and took out my journal again to try and set down what had just happened and to plan.

Nietzsche said that "He who has a why to live for can bear almost any how." I swiveled my chair around to look out the arched window to Fifth Avenue below, studying the humanity I had come to live among. The city bustled with cars and pedestrians, the people always moving quickly, going to and fro at a frantic pace.

It was a place like no other I had been, where no one wandered—they all moved with purpose toward whatever goal their life path dictated. Work, play, and education all compelled the denizens of New York City forward with an abruptness that was not a reality in other places. Not that they were rude or even unhelpful as they were often perceived—the opposite, in fact, for in a crisis, native New Yorkers would leap to help, but Nietzsche also said, "The doer alone learneth" and they were all hungry to learn.

As was I.

In general, in my existence, I was hungry for knowledge, for answers, but now, specifically, I had a real puzzle to unravel. The thing for me to contemplate: what was to be my next step now that the first move had been made? Like in chess, the opening gambit might determine the outcome of the game. Had I not already met the pawns of my phantom opponent on the Bowery the night before? How to counter that?

I wondered what contacts I had that could help me look for the finances behind such an organized "player." The thought of chess put me in mind of my friend Tommy Shane. I would meet him on Sunday afternoon for our weekly game of chess; perhaps he would have an idea. He was a detective with the New York City Police and might be able to give me a direction. In my time in the city, I had been able to assist him in a number of criminal investigations, and he with some of mine.

"Can I help you?" Vandoma's voice raised in inquiry drew my thoughts from my musings.

I swung my chair around to see two dark shapes squeezing through the doorway from the hall.

"Paradise," the tallest of the new arrivals said. His voice was deep and coarse. "We're here for Adam Paradise." Both men were rough featured, in their twenties, wearing suits and overcoats with dark shapes hovering around them like a black mist. They were killers.

"I will see if he—" Vandoma rose to step around her desk to block their way.

One of the two men moved forward, grabbed her by the shoulder, and pushed her out of the way. "Step aside, hunchbacked freak," he barked.

I was on my feet immediately and racing for the door.

"Unhand her!" I yelled.

The man who had touched Vandoma must have seen my silhouette backlit by light from the street moving toward him, for his eyes widened in shock. His right hand reached into his coat.

I could not allow that.

I sprang through the doorway and collided with him, clamping my right hand to pin the arm in his coat and my left on his shoulder. He yelped in surprise as I spun him away from me. He was disoriented by the move, and the gun dropped from under his coat to clatter on the floor.

His partner was also stunned by the sudden action but recovered quickly and drew his own revolver.

I swung my left hand to slap the gun out of his grip, sending it careening off the wall. He quickly produced a switchblade, but I grabbed him by his coat with both hands. I shook him until he dropped it, then lifted him off the ground and slammed him down on the other

41

man who was trying to rise. The violence of my action knocked the wind out of the pair.

Both men stayed on the floor in a cursing heap.

"Are you alright?" I asked Vandoma.

She looked shocked but nodded. "I am fine, Mister—behind you!"

CHAPTER SEVEN

A third man stood in the doorway to the hall with a revolver pointed at me. "Calm down, big man," he said in a thick Brooklyn accent. "I apologize for these two mooks, but don't mistake me being polite for being soft." He was older than the two on the floor, his thick black hair with some streaks of gray at the temples and a sported an old-style handlebar mustache.

"I would never conflate the two." I stepped in front of Vandoma. "What is this about?"

"Mister Anthony Manzetti would like to see you. Now."

"Of course," I said. "I'll just get my coat." When he saw I would not resist, he slid his gun back under his coat, but I had no doubt he could draw it quickly if needs be.

The two men on the ground were moaning and crawled to their feet. The one I had first thrown looked up at me and snarled, "Shoot him, Enzo, I think he broke my arm."

"Shut up, Angelo," Enzo said. "You were impolite."

"Mister Paradise—" Vandoma began.

"It's alright, Miss Kalderash," I said in a calm voice as I donned my overcoat. "Mister Manzetti is a gentleman. He and I are acquainted." I took my hat but stopped to look into her eyes, which were narrowed with concern. "Please don't worry, Mister Manzetti is a professional man. I will be fine."

I stepped around the two underlings, who were now on their feet and staring daggers at me. I addressed Enzo directly. "Thank you for being polite."

He nodded congenially and gestured for me to precede him.

"She is not part of this," I said.

"Of course not," he answered. "Sorry to bother you, Ma'am."

"I will wait, Mister Paradise," Vandoma said with tension in her voice.

"It might be some time."

"Maybe not," Enzo offered. "I don't think this is that kind of trip."

The two soldiers followed us out into the hall. One of them snickered, but Enzo shot him a cold look, and he quieted.

We rode in a dark touring car, Angelo driving, and Enzo and the other gunman seated on either side of me in the back seat. All were silent.

Anthony "Guido" Manzetti was a powerful crime lord in the city. He and I had crossed paths only months before when I was on a case, and he had given me some information. It happened at the same time a series killer had murdered a priest, among others, and the gang boss had reached out to me to find the guilty party. I had been able to reveal the criminals to him. Manzetti had taken it from there.

I thought we had discharged our "debts" to each other, so why he would summon me with such a sense of urgency was a mystery.

His ad hoc headquarters was the Caffé Algeria, a "private club" which was a storefront off Mulberry Street in Little Italy. It had several tables outside, where the neighborhood oldsters ate and sipped espresso and talked of the good old days.

A little bell above the door rang as we walked in. There were half a dozen tables without customers and a jukebox playing classical music against a back wall.

Two young men in dark suits were seated at a table by the door with the obvious bulges of their shoulder-holstered guns visible.

Manzetti was by himself at a table alone with a commanding view of the room. He was physically a little man with a large nose, a balding head, and intense, dark eyes. Nonetheless, his presence filled the room.

When he looked up at the sound of the bell, he fixed his dark gaze on me.

My entourage paused just inside the door, and Enzo stepped forward to have a whispered conversation with his boss.

The two standing beside me and the two seated in the café were nervous, eyes focused on me and their hands hovering near their holstered weapons.

The air was thick with translucent purple and crimson shapes of the many souls that had died at the hands of the men in the room. However, the shades that hovered over Guido Manzetti were the thickest and darkest.

Those ghosts that had their lives being taken violently either by his hand or his word were different from others I had seen, their pulsing color somehow seeming angrier than others. They swirled and eddied like a violent surf, going closer and further from the gang boss's head as if repelled and attracted alternately.

When Enzo finished talking with Manzetti, the crime lord looked over in my direction again, but it was clear he was not happy with the two men on either side of me. He gestured to them with a crooked finger.

The two soldiers shifted position uncomfortably and then walked to their chief.

"I asked you to invite Mister Paradise to visit me," Manzetti said, his voice a hoarse whisper. "Not to inconvenience him."

Angelo cast a sidelong glance at me, then started to speak, "We…uh, I didn't—"

But Enzo cleared his throat, and Angelo choked back his unspoken words. He snapped to attention.

Manzetti then shifted his focus back to me, and it was clear the two men had been dismissed. They glanced at Enzo, who indicated with a jut of his chin that they should move, so they walked to one of the empty tables to sit with grim expressions. Angelo looked as if he was grinding his teeth.

"Mister Paradise," the gang boss said, "please, have a seat."

I removed my hat, walked to the chair opposite Manzetti, and sat.

"Espresso?" he asked.

"Yes, thank you, that would be very nice."

Enzo stepped away.

Manzetti smoked a hand-rolled cigarette. He inhaled deeply and breathed out through his nose, adding to the clouds of the undead that circled him. His eyes were heavy lidded and reflected only the outer world from their black surface, letting no inner life escape.

We waited in companionable quiet until Enzo returned with two small cups on saucers, which he set down on the table before stepping back out of earshot.

I let Manzetti drink first.

Only after I had sipped did he speak again.

"You have a good rep, Paradise," he said. "After that thing in February, I asked around."

"A man is only as good as his word."

"True." He sipped again. "They say if you give your word, you keep it."

"When I can, yes."

"Yesterday, some of my boys were done up in the Bronx. Done good."

"I read a bit about it in the paper. Shot in a garage in Fordham Road?"

"Yeah," he said. "Done St. Valentine's Day style—six of them. Good boys. But they were leaned on first."

"I'm sorry. I presume you know who did it? And why?"

"No," he said. "And that is the issue. No one who knows me would be crazy enough to kill my boys. And if they don't know me, I don't know them. As to why—doesn't matter. Needs to be dealt with."

"And you would like me to make inquiries?"

He nodded and set down his empty cup. "You have sources I don't. Your Gypsy friends, the cops I can't buy, and those Chop-Suey kids."

"You heard about the Florence Theater?"

He let his face assume a mirthless smile for a moment. "Not much happens in this burg I don't know."

46

"Except this."

"Except this," he agreed with a reluctant nod.

Here was a situation to consider. Manzetti and those who served him were men who would kill dispassionately as easily as they would say hello. Yet, Manzetti, at least, had a moral code that was as strict and simple in its way as the heroes of the pulp magazines or radio's Lone Ranger. He and his ilk prized loyalty and the bond of one's word above all things.

His underlings would obey orders and would do what was necessary to accomplish the mission of the boss, no matter how horrific or morally repugnant, but such morality was a thing of relativity. The one sin that they would not forgive was the breaking of one's oath to their boss and organization.

How could I deal with these people? Only by understanding them and that all moral codes are relative. While people might resort to their animal base when pressed, if they were not, then they could be reasoned with. It's what I had to do, to reason with this man and do what he asked must be done.

My time among the various levels of New York meant I had to navigate the various moral strictures of many different subsets of society. As Shakespeare said, "Let every eye negotiate for itself And trust no agent." If I made a bargain with Manzetti, he would keep it. And I must keep it, even if it meant he would revenge himself upon the killers of his men. It was the most basic form of "justice" one could imagine.

To not deal with him could impede me in my other investigations. Or worse.

So, I followed many others in my deal with a devil. I would have to be as optimistic as Faust.

"I will look into it," I said. "I can't promise results, but I will make my best effort."

"All one can do."

"Shall I report to you here?"

"Enzo will give you a number, day or night, when you know something."

"Excellent," I said, rising. "A pleasure to deal with a professional."

He nodded to Enzo, who moved to stand by the door.

"Enzo will drop you wherever you want."

"My office, if you don't mind," I said. "But wait, just a moment."

I moved slowly across the café to the table where Angelo and his partner were seated and leaned down over him to whisper in an even tone.

"If you ever speak disparagingly to Miss Kalderash again, I will make sure you will lose the ability to speak. Understood?"

His eyes went wide, his chin began to quiver, and his face drained of all color as he stared up at me.

When I returned to Enzo, I said, "We can go now. I suspect my secretary will be a little anxious."

I cannot be sure, but I thought I detected a slight smirk on Enzo's lips.

CHAPTER EIGHT

Vandoma was indeed anxious. She must have been pacing in the outer office, for when I returned, she raced out to meet me.

"Mister Paradise," she blurted out when I got to the top of the staircase, "Is—" She saw Enzo at the bottom and stopped.

"It's alright," I said. "Things worked out just fine." I turned to look back down the stairs. "Thanks for the lift, Enzo," I called down the stairs, "You'll be hearing from me shortly."

He had already given me a number, which I had committed to memory.

He touched his hat brim, nodded, and then left.

I joined Vandoma in the office, where she did her best to interrogate me about the meeting. When I had disclosed what had transpired, she shook her head.

"He is a bad man, Mister Paradise."

"I know, Vandoma. But he will keep his word, as will I. For me to work in this town, it is impossible to avoid Manzetti and his ilk, but there is an old saying: keep your friends close but your enemies closer."

"You take too many chances." Her lips were pursed, her eyebrows knit in worry. It was not a good expression on her.

"I promise always to be cautious, little mother," I said in a calm voice. "But I can only do this with your help. Yours and Nico's."

She made a blessing sign. "Tell what I can do."

I sent Vandoma home in a taxi and took myself out to dinner at a French restaurant in the East Thirties.

Afterward, I went to a late movie. It was a varied program with a newsreel, a serial about a comic strip illusionist named Mandrake, an amusing short *A Ducking They Did Go* with a trio of buffoons that made me think of old *Comedia* players, and a double bill of what was referred to as B pictures. One was a rather typical Western morality play, *Spoilers of the Range*, about crooked gamblers and a cliché hero named "Strong," but the second film, based on a stage play, was *Blind Alley*. That was interesting.

It told the story of a criminal who took a psychologist and his family hostage while waiting for an escape boat. In the course of the night, the criminal and his motives are analyzed, and the root causes of his criminality exposed.

Its explorations of the themes of repressed guilt, dream symbolism, and repentance intrigued me—albeit reduced to a melodramatic formula.

It was late, and I found myself weary after walking home. I opted not to read, instead falling into a sleep without any dream images, though before I drifted off, I had a final image of Guido Manzetti's frozen smile. I wondered if I had gone a bridge too far with my deal with a devil.

I hoped it was not one that I would regret.

Sunday was bright and a preview of the summer to come. I obtained a quick breakfast from a street vendor, walked across Thirteenth Street to Fifth Avenue, and then walked down to Washington Square Park.

The park was at the foot of Fifth Avenue and had been a parade ground long ago till it was turned into a rustic oasis with curvilinear paths and small lawns of grass and shade trees. It was an open space with no fences and a center of a bohemian collection of artists, musicians, and college students. In warm weather, there was always someone playing guitar and students reading on the lawns, playing catch, or just relaxing on blankets.

I saw the park differently than most, of course, for the park had been a cemetery for the poor, a potter's field in times past, and so the dark shapes swirling over the space were thicker than in most of Manhattan.

In one corner of the park stood the Hangman's Elm, where traitors were hung during the American Revolution. The shapes that circled that tree were black as pitch, and I could feel the anger and pain emanating from them.

There was a fountain that sprayed a cooling mist in the spring and summer months and a marble triumphant arch designed by Sanford White in the center of the park. It was on the edge of Washington Square North, aligned east-west. One could stand under the arch and look directly for miles up the avenue through the corridor of concrete. It was quite an impressive sight.

My friend, Detective Lieutenant Tommy Shane, was seated at one of the chess tables that were a permanent feature on the edge of the park in the shadow of the arch.

Now that the weather was more pleasant, we had a standing Sunday afternoon game after his family time at church. On nice days, we met in the park and in inclement weather at Caffé Reggio, a couple of blocks away.

"Adam!" he said, rising to extend a hand. His grip was firm, and his smile genuine.

He was square jawed, of Irish descent, with a warm smile and blue eyes that complemented his intelligence. He was an inch over six foot and just a little soft with middle age, but still had a full head of dark red hair.

He already had the chess pieces out, so we sat. This time, I was playing the black.

"How was your week?" I asked after he had made his opening gambit.

"Brendan lost his last baby tooth," he said. "It's oddly an important milestone, you know? My little guy is on his way to being a young man."

He fairly beamed with pride whenever he talked about his son or wife, Mary. He had come to marriage later than many of his contemporaries, so he still was filled with awe at the life he was able to lead. He was a good cop and an honest cop, so that made him one of the ones Manzetti didn't have in his pocket and who could not be gotten to.

I could not ever have the life he had, but I could appreciate it. And in some ways envy it.

"You've given him a good role model."

He laughed. "Well, I hope he only sees the good stuff." His smile transformed as a memory flashed across his eyes. "I hope he never has to fire a gun."

Tommy walked with a slight limp, shrapnel from The Great War. He had run away from home to enlist even though he was too young legally. Though he never spoke of the experience, I knew it affected him deeply.

"The price of living is taking the good with the bad," I said.

He nodded. "How are you and Vandoma getting along now that she has civilized you and brought you into the twentieth century by making you get a phone?"

"She is a hard task mistress; she's organized my files, keeps me on a regular schedule, and even gets me to return calls."

"It's good, Adam. We guys need a civilizing influence."

Civilization. Henry Bailey said, "The origin of civilization is man's determination to do nothing for himself which he can get done for him." Had I ceded control of my office out of laziness? Or was I simply smart enough to know my limitations?

We played in companionable silence for a time, enjoying the intellectual combat. His ability to sit in silence was one of the things I enjoyed about him.

When we finished the game he won, it was time for me to ask him for his help.

"I can't tell you my client, of course," I said when he sensed I was moving out of polite conversation into a more professional realm. "But I wondered if you knew anything about a new wrinkle in the protection racket that has popped up recently in the Oriental community?"

The corners of his mouth tipped up, and he chuckled. "I was going to ask you if you'd heard about something similar."

"How so?"

"A pal out in a Queens precinct said that some local store owners had a rash of vandalism about two weeks ago and then suddenly clammed up and blocked his investigations. Suddenly it was 'no understand English' and rubbish like that."

"Now in Manhattan as well," I said. "At least two restaurants. And rumors that Queenie is having new problems with, perhaps a Far East tinge." I told him a slightly edited version of the events at the Florence Theater—not because I did not trust him, but so that his position as an officer of the law would not be compromised.

"It is sure as shootin' wider in scope than those incidents, because if we heard about these, there must be dozens or more we don't know about." He stood to stretch his wounded leg, rubbing his thigh. "Immigrant communities have always been easy prey for gangsters. It happened to my Irish ancestors, and the Black Hand did it to the Italians not long ago."

"Tribalism: always suspicion of 'the other.'"

"Yes," he said. "Gives a lie to the melting pot we are supposed to be." He registered his disgust with the dilution of the ideals he had risked his life to protect and continued to work for.

"But the Black Hand you spoke of still holds sway over the Italian community?"

He shrugged. "Some form of it, yes. They gained enormous wealth with Prohibition, and even after repeal, they are a power." He ran up against the "on the take" cops in Manzetti's employ. As an honest cop, it was almost as dangerous as encountering street thugs. Despite Tommy's principles, he had a family to protect and negotiated daily to balance the scales of duty and practicality. Much like my deal with the devil-in-Manzetti's-form.

"Do they still engage in this sort of activity?" I worked to get around to the shooting in the Bronx.

He was walking back and forth now to stretch his leg. Behind him, some college sweethearts who had been holding hands underneath the marble arch looked around and then embraced. Tommy saw the two and could not help grinning.

"Funny you should say that. I heard there was a gangland massacre in the Bronx like the old days, two in Brooklyn and Queens each. The guys at the station are afraid a full-scale battle is about to break out."

"Were they all the same gangs that were killed?"

"No. That is the strange thing. The ones in the Bronx were Guido Manzetti's boys, but Brooklyn was the Gambino's guys, and Queens were an Irish gang, Dooly O'Halloran's bunch. You can see why it looks like the beginnings of another gang war."

This was a new development. If the Japanese were behind the restaurant extortions in an attempt to spark a tong war, is it possible that their organization was also working to get the other ethnic gangs involved? To what effect?

Sun Tzu, the Chinese general who wrote on the philosophy of conflict in his book *The Art of War*, stated, "Every battle is won or lost before the battle is fought," which meant that it was all about planning. This disruption of the peace was well planned.

The effect could cause chaos in America, leaching resources from the government and destroying confidence in the authorities akin to the worst, lawless days during Prohibition.

It might even cause those advocating intervention in external conflicts to turn inward like the isolationists.

Sun Tzu also said, "To know your enemy, you must become your enemy." I had to think like these phantom gangsters if I was to defeat them. And that meant I needed more facts.

I could not offer this conjecture to my friend, however, for fear of tainting his official objectivity. Instead, I was about to ask him for the name of one of the extorted restaurants when I noticed a car starting up on Washington Square North.

It didn't seem unusual—a black four-door late-model sedan like any other, but what drew my eye was the cloud of swirling indigo shades that eddied above it. Then the back door opened slightly as the car sped up. And out of that forward opening door, a figure crouched, leaning over a dark object.

I realized what it was and pushed Tommy to the ground. I yelled, "Gun!" just as the flash of the Thompson submachine gun exploded like a miniature sun.

The roar of the weapon had a surreal quality in the quiet Sunday afternoon scene and at first, no one reacted. The couple embracing under the arch parted with sudden shock as the bullets began chipping marble off the arch. They had no chance at all to respond before their bodies exploded in a spray of gore. Then the screams of others began.

The sedan slammed to a stop directly across from Tommy and me and sprayed a barrage of deadly lead in our direction. The dirt and paving stones around us were kicked up into a secondary cascade of particles.

My suit jacket was torn in several places, and I felt something—probably a ricochet—tear across my cheek. Tommy exclaimed loudly, "I'm hit!" just before I heard a secondary explosion from beside me, which I realized was his service revolver returning fire.

The car started up again but immediately sideswiped an oncoming roadster in a minor collision where the bumpers locked.

The machine-gunner stepped out onto the running board to scream at the driver of the roadster. His shouts were mostly incoherent with anger, but the few words I could understand I realized were Japanese. The gunman turned his wrath on the startled driver and almost literally cut him in half with gunfire.

The sedan driver backed up with a grinding of gears that tore the bumper off the roadster trying to get around the car blocking the street.

I was up on my feet by this time and raced at the attackers.

"Get out of the way, Adam," Tommy bellowed, but I could hear pain in his voice. I could not stop to check my friend for the quick reversal of the sedan unbalanced the gunman so he could not aim to fire at me. If I was fast enough, I might get to him before he could recover.

If I did not, I was almost certainly the proverbial sitting duck.

CHAPTER NINE

The action of backing up the sedan to pull clear of the roadster unbalanced the gunman on the running board. It was enough that he had difficulty aiming his weapon at me. When he did, it clicked on empty as he had unloaded the last of the drum at the roadster's driver.

He tried to reload to point at me while his arm was looped inside the open window.

I was out in the open. I had no choice but to press my legs to run faster than I have ever moved. I had to reach him before he could chamber the gun to fire.

Fortunately for me, I could see a sudden terror in the gunman's face, which caused him to fumble in drawing the bolt.

The driver of the sedan had seen me, as well, in the rearview mirror. It apparently unnerved him. Rather than correct the car to go on North Washington Square to get around the stopped roadster, the driver just hit the gas. This panicked reaction sent the car lurching straight up Fifth Avenue against the traffic flow.

The jerky movement of the car unbalanced the gunman, who tumbled from the running board just as he got the bolt back to re-cock the Thompson. The man hit the ground, rolled deftly, and came to his feet, ready to raise the weapon to fire at me again.

But by then I had reached him. I grabbed the smoking barrel of the weapon with my gloved hand and yanked it away. I flung the gun off to my left and seized him by the collar. I growled in anger as I violently threw the man up in the air. I tossed him behind me with all my might, with no care if he lived or died.

I heard him slam into the ground with a painful cry.

The sedan started to race up the avenue going the wrong way, swerving wildly to avoid a head-on collision with a coupe. That slowed it long enough for me to catch up to it before it gained enough traction to put on speed.

Just as the sedan's tires straightened out to move forward, I jumped to the running board on the driver's side. The man at the wheel was desperately trying to avoid oncoming traffic, hitting his horn hard at the same time he was weaving back and forth. He spotted me and swerved the car hard in an attempt to throw me off.

I grabbed onto the car frame at the open back window with my right hand and smashed my left fist through the driver's closed side window. Fortunately, my glove mostly protected my hand, though the jagged glass shredded my jacket sleeve.

The driver screamed invectives in a mix of languages, some of which I recognized as Japanese. I grabbed him by the tie and used him to steady myself. That stopped him screaming.

There was another thug in the front passenger seat who pulled the pistol but could not get a clear shot past the driver's head. He shoved the revolver in front of his compatriot's face and fired twice. I dodged out of the way.

The shots startled the driver, who yelped each time, but the bullets went wide and shattered the rest of the window. The car continued to careen up the avenue.

It was amazing that the driver managed to avoid a head-on collision as several cars that came at us swerved as we passed. We left a chorus of horns and crashes behind.

The car reached Fourteenth Street, leaving a trail of vehicles that had skidded out of the way. The driver had the presence of mind to turn the wheel sharply and had us racing across Fourteenth, going east in the correct lane.

The passenger tried one more time to shoot me and leaned forward with his gun to push his arm past the face of the driver. I was having none of that.

I couldn't let go of the driver's tie with my left hand while my right hand was holding onto the frame of the car, so I yanked the driver forward hard. His face smashed into the gun, which drove the weapon directly into the steering wheel. The pistol discharged with the bullet going wild into the side panel of the door.

These actions caused the driver to jerk the wheel hard to the left. The speeding car drove up on the sidewalk with a violent lurch, scattering pedestrians in all directions.

The sedan rocketed into Union Square Park at Fourteenth Street on two wheels, swerving across the grass and kicking up huge clots of dirt. The driver tried to regain control, but before he could, one fender clipped a tree. I jumped off the running board just before the car crashed into the trunk. I hit the ground, tumbling several times.

The sedan turned over on its side and was all but destroyed with a horrendous shriek of metal, and the impact felled the tree.

I gained my feet just in time to see the passenger climb from the car and stumble shakily to his feet. He'd lost his gun in the collision. He was a sturdily built Asian in an expensive suit, and his expression was one of pure hate. Blood plastered his scalp from a wide wound.

When he saw me standing, the gunman cursed and ran across the park toward the kiosk of the IND subway station.

I glanced at the driver, but he was going nowhere as he had been impaled on the shaft of the steering wheel. It was a hideous and gory sight. His shade was already rising from the corpse.

I ran after the fleeing man who entered the kiosk and descended into the subway not far behind him.

After the bright afternoon sunlight, the gloom of the underground platform was like twilight. It took a moment for my eyes to adjust to the darkness while I ran down the stairs. Several commuters who were on the way up the stairs literally jumped out of my way.

I must have looked a fright. I'd lost my hat, could feel blood on my cheek, my coat was in tatters, and I was angry. The callous disregard for the people these thugs had endangered—or killed—gave rise to a rage I had not let myself feel often in my existence. It was a part of me I fought so hard to suppress, that atavistic anger that had been so part of my early life.

The image of that couple under the arch who had their young lives ended for some foul, arcane purpose was emblazoned on my mind's eye and would stay with me for many years.

When I reached the platform of the station, I could see the figure of the running gunman far ahead of me. As I chased him, someone screamed, and several people dove out of my way with exclamations and curses.

I ignored them and called ahead, "Give up, there is nowhere to go!"

The gunman ignored my yell and proved I was wrong, for when he reached the end of the platform, he jumped off it to the track bed.

I had no choice but to follow, putting the thought of a train somewhere in the dark maw of the tunnel out of my mind. With no idea if the gunman I'd left behind in the park was alive, this man might be the only chance to question an attacker for a clue to those behind the attack.

My quarry was shorter than me, but he was a good runner and might have outdistanced me in an even race had he not stumbled on one of the wooden track ties.

This fumble broke his stride, which allowed me to catch up with him.

He sprang to his feet but was wise enough not to try to keep running with me so close. I was upon him with great bounding leaps, prepared to grab him, but he spun, producing a six-inch, single-edged blade. He flailed at me, slashing my coat, and then he tried to stab me.

I slapped a knife out of his hand with enough violence to knock him to his knees, then reached down to grab him by the front of his coat.

"Why did you—" I began in a tone that was more a growl than speech, but the man looked up at me, not with fear, but apparent contempt. This caused me to pause.

The man had wide cheekbones and close-set, dark eyes that were full of hate. He smiled and yelled, "*Hakkou ichiu!*" He then deliberately reached over to grab the electrified third rail that ran the trains.

I had no chance to pull free of him before everything suddenly arced blue-white, and I had the sensation of moving through a long, white-walled corridor at tremendous speed.

Then, all went black.

I heard myself reciting the words of Coleridge's "Ancient Mariner" as if from a distance.

> *Like one that, on a lonely road,*
> *Doth walk in fear and dread,*
> *And, having once turned round, walks on,*
> *And turns no more his head;*
> *Because he knows a frightful fiend*
> *Doth close behind him tread.*

The waves once again bore me away, and the ship I had fled from was lost in darkness and distance. As far as I could see was arctic white and bone-chilling cold, colder than the emptiness that swirled within my heart, that lashed my eyes until they teared.

Some years ago, when the images which this world affords first opened upon me, when I felt the cheering warmth of summer and heard the rustling of the leaves and the warbling of the birds, and these were all to me, I should have wept to die; now I knew not if death would claim me.

I blinked. The arctic white of my memory was not what I beheld now; rather, there was a vastness of a featureless vista before me.

I stood in tattered clothes on a flat, level plane, the horizon blending to a pale sky that shimmered with what first I took to be the Aurora Borealis. I realized that the flickering illumination was not the northern lights but the swirling shapes of a thousand, thousand souls floating in echelons across the sky. The spirits of the departed seemed to flit around and to cast a shadow, which was felt but not seen.

"This cannot be," I said, my words etched in a frozen mist before me. "I am hallucinating this, or is this the land beyond the veil of death?" Perhaps I could die? Had I crossed over? Gone from consciousness and flesh to whatever came beyond?

I held my hand before me. It seemed still substantial, the scared knuckles of my hand that showed through the torn glove streaked with blood. I flexed my fingers and made a fist, then turned it over to look at the palm.

No phantom shapes swirled around the arm, and I was aware for the first time that the shades who had been the souls that made up my body parts no longer orbited me. It was a new experience for me, but what did it mean? Had they moved on to the "next" phase of existence, or had I?

"I think, therefore I am," I breathed, the frozen mist of my words falling to my open palm. It seemed as eloquent a statement as any to describe my conundrum. If I could still postulate what form I was, substantial or otherwise, I still was. As long as I still had coherent memories of my existence, then I still existed.

I, the miserable and the abandoned, that was an abortion to be spurned at, and kicked, and trampled on, still thought. My blood boiled at the recollection of those injustices.

But it was true that I was a wretch. I had murdered the lovely and the helpless in my time before my arctic isolation; I had strangled the innocent as they slept and grasped to death his throat who never injured me or any other living thing.

Could anyone expiate such crimes? Was I so different from the Manzettis of the world? Though I was innocent when the crimes were committed, striking out like a child in a tantrum who, feeling hurt, could only reply in kind, was I still not responsible?

Kant suggested that each person was responsible for self-redemption, that the human experience was purely subjective. But I was not human, so was I capable of salvation? What did that mean?

Even the Sumerian Gilgamesh found redemption after his friend Enkidu's death, which was caused in part by his hubris. He only discovered his atonement when he came to terms with his mortality.

Was I less worthy? Was I less willing to find a way to expunge my transgressions? Was oblivion so bad? Would I even know it?

I pondered this all as I walked across the frozen waste for what seemed an endless time until I abruptly heard a voice behind me that told me I was not alone.

The voice spoke. "Miserable wretch!" I knew the voice. "You have determined to live, and I am not satisfied."

I knew not only that voice but those words, for I had said them to my creator in the frozen wastes when I had first hoped to die.

I turned to see him, Victor Frankenstein.

CHAPTER TEN

There, before me, stood my creator. He was as he had been when last I saw him on the ship in the Arctic, save animated and apparently alive. Then, he who had called me into being had been dead. Could it be, now I was no more, that the very remembrance of us both would speedily vanish? Had we come to the same place in the beyond?

"You shall no longer see the sun or stars or feel the winds play on your cheeks," the image of Frankenstein said. "Light, feeling, and sense will pass away; and in this condition must you find happiness."

"Yes," I agreed. "But how is it you are here?"

"How could we not be connected, Adam? The thread of your life is connected directly to mine, an abomination in the eyes of God. Hateful day when I gave you life!"

These words struck me as a knife to my heart. I had read his journals of the four months that preceded my creation. He had minutely described in these papers every step he took in the progress of his work.

"You doubtless recollect your references to my accursed origin? The whole detail of that series of disgusting circumstances which produced me was set in view; the minutest description of my odious and loathsome person was given, in language which painted your own horrors and rendered mine indelible."

The figure before me in the endless plain laughed, a dark sound that chilled.

I exclaimed in agony, "Accursed creator! Why did you form a monster so hideous that even *you* turned from me in disgust? God, in pity, made man beautiful and alluring, after his own image, but my form is a filthy type of yours, more horrid even from the very resemblance."

"In a fit of enthusiastic madness," Frankenstein said, "I created a rational creature and was bound toward him to assure, as far as was in my power, his happiness and well-being. This was my duty, but there was another that was still paramount: my duties toward the beings of my own species." He waved a hand at me in accusation, which I noted was pale, almost skeletal.

"Satan had his companions," I yelled, "fellow devils, to admire and encourage him, but I am solitary and abhorred."

This brought another laugh from my creator. "You urged me to change that, but I refused, and I did right in refusing to create a companion for you, creature. You showed unparalleled malignity and selfishness in evil; you destroyed my friends, devoted to destruction to beings who possessed happiness and wisdom; nor do I know where your thirst for vengeance would end."

I cried, my tears cold on my cheeks. "And do you not dream? Do you think that I was then dead to agony and remorse? I, too, suffered in the consummation of the deed. My heart was poisoned with remorse. My heart was fashioned to be susceptible to love and sympathy, and when wrenched by misery to vice and hatred, it did not endure the violence of the change without torture such as you cannot even imagine. Nietzsche said, 'To live is to suffer, to survive is to find some meaning in the suffering.' I have suffered, and I search for that meaning each day."

My legs weakened, and I dropped to my knees so that the cold of the snow lanced up my body, and I shivered. "In those murders, my crimes are consummated; the miserable series of my being is a wound! Oh, Frankenstein! What does it avail that I now ask thee to pardon me?"

Yet he was colder than the snow and did not answer. His intelligent eyes bore down with unspoken accusations that drove a spike through my heart. Since my return from the Arctic, I had attempted to expiate my crimes, to live a positive life, and contribute to the world.

Teilhard de Chardin, the Jesuit priest and scientist, believed that man was evolving, mentally and socially, toward a final spiritual unity, an Omega Point. He opined that each positive act added to the energy sphere around the world, and a quantum event would occur when enough positive energy enveloped the earth.

That priest believed that the most satisfying thing in life is to be able to give a large part of oneself to others. I had tried to do this. Yet, could any positive act level the scales for my early existence? Did I even qualify as being alive? A thing of discarded remnants assembled to prove my creator's theories with no thought to what came next. With no thought of what real benefit such an act could mean.

"Why have you come to torment me?"

"You must pay as I have," the image of Frankenstein said. "The gate to the next world is open to you, and you must go through it."

My knees were numb from the snow, but my soul was more so, as the words of he who brought me into being flogged me. I wished at that moment for oblivion, to end my pain and move on to the great outer dark.

"I am here to help you move on," Frankenstein's image said. "It is my duty."

He stepped forward with hands extended, then placed his fingers gently on my neck.

"It is better this way, my creation," he said. His fingers tightened on my throat.

Numbness rose in my body, and somehow, I knew that when the numbness of the cold reached my neck and his fingers tightened enough, I would fall into that oblivion I craved in my darkest moments. I would end then, perhaps not die as I was never so sure that I lived, but my consciousness would be no more. My sins would be erased as I was, and I would be at peace.

Frankenstein stood impassive, his slim, handsome form with a grim, judgmental expression. His gripping fingers slowly tightened. Red spots filled my vision while dark joy filled his eyes.

"Do not believe this *Booja!*" A frail female voice cut through the cold as if it were a winter wind. "It is a trick of the universe, Adam Paradise." My creator released me and stepped away. I tore my gaze from him to see Mother Kalderash.

Vandoma's mother was much as I had seen her last when she died in my arms three months before, save with the blazing light in her eyes stronger even than when she had lived.

She was a small woman dressed in an old-fashioned, high-necked dress, her grey hair piled on her head, her eyes an older mirror of Vandoma's. Her hand was extended to point at Frankenstein in accusation, and her expression was angry.

"I see you for what you are, *beng*," she accused my creator, calling him a devil in Romani. "I am a *drukker*—she who sees the future—but I also see the past."

"Mother Kalderash," I gasped, "my sins—"

"Hush," she said, not taking her piercing gaze from Frankenstein. "I know you are a *pajivalo Martja*, an honorable spirit of the dead. This thing before you is a *gadjo beng*, an outsider devil. He is not what you see."

I tried to find the words to tell her, to explain that he was the one who had made me—who brought me to the veil of tears and who, by withdrawing his creator's love, had made me a monster—but before I could speak, Frankenstein laughed.

"You have no power here," the image of my creator said. "Here I am strong, your ways are weak."

"What do you mean?" I shuddered. "Are not all equal here?"

"See his deception," the Romani woman said. "Know the truth, he would eat at your soul's doubts, Adam Paradise."

Frankenstein hissed then, his face a grimace. "Leave this, mongrel bitch."

"I do not fear you, *beng*," the woman said. "You are *marime* by your own people. An outcast."

The image of my creator began to waver then, to shift as if he were somehow a heat phantom in that frozen place. His features lengthened, and his eyes widened and darkened, the whites shrinking as the black pupils expanded till all were entirely as dark as night.

"Your interference will only prolong the misery of this monster," the transforming figure said. "He is an abomination, and I will not allow him to vex me more."

Now his face became ruddy, and the nose elongated and hooked so that it was a beak. His dark hair became feathers, and he was no longer a human but a strange hybrid thing.

"What are you?" I asked.

This creature laughed now with a strange squawking noise. "Your destruction, monstrosity."

"It is you who are a monster," Mother Kalderash said. "You wish chaos, you would punish this good one with his own doubts." She stepped between me and the bird thing as if to stop him attacking. "It is you who has no right to be here. You are from across the sea."

Again, the strange thing made his odd laughing noise, then hissed at her. "My time will come; I will always win; I, Daitengu, swear it."

Then, the apparition faded, evaporating until it was gone.

Mother Kalderash turned to me.

"I don't understand," I said.

"You are young, *Baba Fingo*." She used the Romani term for savior. "Even though you are old on the earth, in the other worlds, you are young. The demon is a thing that despises the living and the things you have seen. It would trick you."

"Why? Am I not—not dead now? Is this not the beyond?"

"You are no *stafie fantoma*, Adam Paradise, no ghost," the Kalderash matriarch said. "You are not yet to be in this place that is between the worlds, not yet. You have purpose in the world of man."

"That—that thing, what was it?"

"A *beng* from across the sea, who would destroy. An agent of chaos and death. He knows you are a force for good, so he knows you are his enemy."

My limbs were all numb now; no longer did I feel cold. Indeed, I felt a sort of warmth spreading over me, and I realized, from having read accounts of people dying from the cold, that it meant death was coming. In all my time in the Arctic, I had never felt such a sensation.

Mother Kalderash reached out and cupped my face in her delicate hands. She looked directly into my eyes. "You should have no *ladz*," she said. "No shame for what has been. You are *pajivalo Martja*. To you, I have entrusted my Vandoma and Nico, and I know I have not been wrong in this trust."

"You are a *Sara e Kali*, a saint who knows many things."

This brought a smile to her gaunt face. "I learned many things before I died, and more even now, it is true."

"But I die now." I felt nothing, not even the touch of her hands.

"No. You are returning from this between place. You have work to do, my son."

Then, there was a flash of brilliant blue arcing, white light.

Then blackness.

CHAPTER ELEVEN

I opened my eyes to see the worried face of Tommy Shane. It took me a moment to realize we were in some sort of moving vehicle. When he saw my eyes open, his worried face brightened.

"Adam! Thank God," he said with great joy in his voice, "I thought we'd lost you."

I realized I was strapped down on something, and I recognized what must be the inside of an ambulance. The spectral shades of my body parts once again swirled around me. I was back in the world of the living.

Tommy was seated beside me, his right leg elevated with a bandage on it. He saw me looking at it.

"My luck," he said. "They got me in the other leg, maybe now it'll even me out and I won't limp."

"What happened? I'm not clear…"

"I'm not surprised, Adam. We thought you were dead—you got a major jolt of juice."

"Oh, yes," I said, "I remember. The subway."

"We figure you must have been thrown clear at the last moment when he grabbed the third rail."

I knew that was not true. I had been holding him when he touched the electrified rail. It should have killed me. I made no comment.

"You were out for ten minutes," Tommy gave a soft laugh. "Took four of our guys to get you up out of the station onto this gurney."

"The arch?"

"Yeah." His expression darkened. "The one with the machine gun you cold-cocked was alive when the uniforms got to him, but he yelled something I couldn't understand, and then"—he hesitated for a long moment as if recalling something that revolted him—"then he bit off his tongue and died. Choked on his own blood."

I thought about it for a moment and remembered the assassin in the tunnel. "Could it have been *Hakkou Ichiu*!?"

"Might have been. How did you guess?"

"The one in the tunnel yelled it."

He thought about that and shook his head. "Fanatics? What could it mean?"

"We'll find out. I'm sure Digger will know what it means."

"I want the guys behind this, Adam," he said with more anger in his voice than I'd ever heard.

"We'll get them. How bad was it at the park?"

"Four dead from the shooter. A dozen wounded, and three others hurt from car crashes. That it wasn't worse is a miracle."

"Yes," I said bitterly. "A miracle."

I thought about what had happened to me—or had it? Was my time with the image of my creator and the shade of Mother Kalderash a hallucination? Could it have been my subconscious, my inner mind reaching out to me? Was I recalling the plot of the *Blind Alley* film and applying it to my life circumstances?

I had never had such an experience, even when I suffered fevers and debilitation for months after a fight with a polar bear in the Arctic. And if it was not the result of electrocution or a concussion, what did it mean? Was it the confirmation of so many religious traditions, so many shamanistic views of reality?

There *was* survival beyond life, for I had seen and spoken to Mother Kalderash three months before when she was murdered. I had seen the shades of many as they passed over the barrier between life and death. But if my recent experience was real, it implied more—that there was a whole other level to existence.

The ambulance arrived at St. Vincent Hospital, where I resisted being wheeled in and was finally allowed to stagger in on my own power with the help of two attendants. The hospital was in complete chaos as victims of the massacre in the park still flowed in, some brought by patrol cars, as there were not enough ambulances. The halls were a frantic madhouse of gurneys with bloody civilians, crying women and children, and grim-looking medical personnel.

I was brought into a small examining room where a harried nurse insisted on taking my vital signs. I kept insisting I was alright, but she was having none of it and was backed up by a young intern doctor.

The confusion allowed me an excuse to refuse to remove my shirt all the way. I only opened it enough so the examining doctor could listen to my heart and take my blood pressure, which he noted was extremely low.

"Like an athlete's," he said. He looked into my eyes and tapped my chest and seemed satisfied that I was in no danger of cardiac arrest from my shock.

When the harried doctor remarked on my scars, I told him my usual lie, that I'd been thrown through a car windshield in an accident. It also helped to explain the graft marks on my left wrist when he treated my wounds from punching through the car window.

"There are others more serious you should attend to," I told the physician when he'd bandaged my left hand. "I will be fine till later, sir."

He looked at me as if his first instinct was to argue but then nodded. "At least let me get some salve on those marks on your neck."

"Marks?"

"Yes, here—" He angled a mirror on the table near me to show me my neck.

I was stunned to see that there, on my throat, were clear and distinct welts that looked like finger marks where the image of my creator had throttled me. The fingertips of the marks were pointed like bird talons.

So, it was real. The spectre of the elder Kalderash had been real, and so it followed that what she said had merit. At that moment, all I understood or speculated about the very nature of reality shifted.

My mind was awhirl—this was not only confirmation that an afterlife did exist but that some other phyla of beings existed besides humans and their shades. I knew that I would spend much time pondering this very thing later, but now I had to justify the old Romani's faith in me.

"I shall be fine. They are of no discomfort at all."

"I guess you're right, sir." He nodded. "You do look pretty sturdy."

I thanked him, and he went off to deal with the seriously injured. That left me alone in the small examining room, but I was not alone for long.

"Adam," my friend and neighbor Daniel, who was a nurse at the hospital, rushed in, his expression worried. He was a slight man with dark hair and kind eyes, which were full of concern at that moment. "I just heard they brought in a big fella, and from the description, I knew it had to be you. Are you alright?"

"Easy," I chuckled. I rose from the examination table, stretched, and accepted a hearty handshake. Then he noticed my bandaged left hand, the scratches on my face, and the state of my clothing.

"My gosh. You look like you wrestled an alligator."

"Really, I'm okay. It looks much worse than it is. My clothes took the brunt of it." I held up my tattered suit jacket. "You've sewed me up from much worse wounds."

"There are armed police all around the hospital," he said. "The news of a massacre at the park is terrifying. The wounded are still coming in. What is it all about?"

"I'm not really sure. But I'm going to find out." I saw him looking worried and added, "I am fine, Daniel. Go take care of the people who really need you."

"I'll stop by later when things calm down a bit."

"I'm leaving now, heading home." I redonned my torn jacket. "I really am fine, and the resources here are best used for others."

He shrugged. "I'd argue with you if I didn't know how fast you heal. But at least go rest. I'll stop by your place in two hours when my shift is done to check up on you, okay?"

"Mother hen. Yes, straight home. I promise."

When he'd left, I finished dressing and then looked around the hospital, making my way through the confusion of the crowded chaos until I found an orderly who knew which room Tommy was resting in.

"What are you doing up and around?" he asked.

"I'm good enough to head home."

"Is the doctor sure of that?"

I shrugged.

He chuckled and then shook his head. "I know, you didn't ask him."

"Did you call Mary?"

"I did." He propped himself up on the bed. "As soon as they got the wound closed—fortunately, it went through clean, and there was no major damage. She will be here in a little bit. Thank God she hadn't heard about it. She has no idea how serious it could have been."

"Yes," I said soberly.

"Did you call your Gypsy mother hen?"

"I suspect I'll be in for a scolding if she hears about it on the radio." The thought made me feel somehow better, and then I remembered the violence and felt anger. "The forces behind this attack care nothing for human life."

"That gang war we feared looks to be starting."

"I still don't think it is that, in the conventional sense. I think this is the beginning of a greater war on America itself."

"How can you say that?"

"The attackers were all Japanese as far as I could determine, but those gang killings were Occidentals. If the tongs and the gangs all start shooting at each other, then today will be like nothing."

He contemplated my words, and his expression clouded. "You're scaring me."

"It scares me as well. I've found good in this city, and I plan to protect it."

"Don't go off half-cocked, Adam."

"You know I don't even carry a gun," I said to lighten the mood. He was not having it.

"These people are ruthless, Adam, worse than the bootleggers. We have to assume they targeted you this time. They will do it again."

"Then I need to be where they can get to me, Tommy. How else to bring them out into the open."

"You're not a Judas goat."

"It seems I have to function as one. But trust me, I am not going to take unnecessary chances...I...I have reason to think I'm supposed to be here."

"At least let me have the department post a guard on you."

"I'll be fine," I said. "My place is only a block from here—and I'll need to write up a report of all that's happened for your official records anyway. I'll stop by tomorrow morning to visit you here, and we'll take it from there."

I could see our conversation was taxing him, so I put a hand on his forearm. "I'll be alright. I promise."

"You'll do what you want anyway," he said. "I give up. Just—"

"I know, I'll be careful."

I left him then, and with all the confusion that still gripped the hospital, I managed to slip out without being challenged by any uniformed officers.

The lasting image of the day was of a young girl, no more than ten, sitting in a hallway by a gurney on which a bloodied woman, her head covered in bandages, lay unconscious. She was holding the hand of the woman, and her eyes were swollen from crying, though it looked as if there were no more tears left.

I headed to my apartment on Thirteenth Street, but on the way, I had to pass The United Methodist Church of the Village on the corner of Seventh Avenue. It was less than a decade old, though it had the feeling of great age. Religion might be the opiate of the masses, but it also was a glue to hold many societies together.

I often paused before it, watching the swirling golden phantoms that orbited the building. I had never entered, feeling myself an aberration, a soulless simulacrum unworthy to stand in a sanctuary. Now, I had Mother Kalderash saying I was here for a purpose, that nothing that happened under the heavens was not meant to be.

Even the hubris of my creator that resulted in my existence was for a purpose. I was not the lone thing I had seen myself to be—not now that I had found Tommy and Daniel and Digger. And Vandoma.

They and others accepted me as part of their community. And that community was threatened by some malignant force, and my reason to be seemed to be to oppose that force. The people who hurt that little girl's mother were now my mortal enemies.

I stopped by the church and touched the ornate wooden doors but still could not summon the courage to enter. Not yet.

There was a phone booth on the corner. I entered it, fished in my pocket for change, and called the number I had for Han Ku Lee.

"Hello?" she answered.

"This is Adam Paradise."

"Oh, I'm glad you called. I was able to arrange a summit with the tongs for some time this week. I'll hope to know when soon."

"Good."

"And I forgot to tell you that I have another lecture this week," she added.

"Where?"

"At the Forty-Second Street Library. Wednesday evening, to a group of educators."

"Is that wise?"

"I can't let these thugs stop my work."

"I know, but you should know there have been some disturbing developments." I related the attack and its aftermath, though I omitted my experience with the Elder Kalderash and the strange transforming being. I was still not sure I believed that part myself.

When I was done with my recitation, she gave a very un-lady-like curse, then added, "*Shinobi*."

"A what?"

"The man who bit his tongue off..." She sighed. "That was a common way for the *shinobi*—a cult of spies in ancient Japan—to commit suicide. They were sworn never to be taken prisoner."

"The one in the subway?"

"I suppose he intended to take you with him. It would have been a bonus to complete his mission to kill you."

"Yes," I said. "I was the brass ring for today, I suppose."

This brought a chuckle from her. "You seem a durable sort, Mister Paradise."

"So I have been told. But this all means you have to be doubly on your guard. Today proves they will stop at nothing."

75

"I knew that about them already, Adam, but your point is well taken. I always go armed now. You should."

"I still prefer not to use guns."

"Stubborn is one of your best qualities," she said. "Mine too."

"Would you like me to be at the lecture?"

She was quiet for a moment, and then, "Actually, yes. I'll have some of my friends there, but…"

"Give all the details to Vandoma, I'll be there."

"Okay," she said. "I'll call you at your office tomorrow around two?"

"I will look forward to it. We have been playing catch up until now. We need to try and get ahead of these killers."

"You take care, Adam. 'Night."

"'Night."

I hung up and called the number that Enzo had given me. The conversation was short.

"Today's attack on me at Washington Square Park was most likely connected with the attacks on Mister Manzetti's men. I will call when there is more concrete progress."

"I will give the message to Mister Manzetti," a male voice on the other side said. "Thank you for calling." Then, the connection was broken.

I considered calling Vandoma, fearing she might hear of the events from the newspapers or radio, but I could not decide on a way to relate to her what had transpired in the vision that had been the world between.

Being Romani, she believed in such things, but I was still confused, both skeptical and frightened that such a thing could exist. I needed more time to evaluate and absorb what had happened. The nickel for the phone call remained in my pocket.

I walked down Thirteenth Street to my apartment, my senses alert but no danger manifested.

My apartment door was still undisturbed, so I entered, suddenly feeling exceptionally tired. For the second time in two days, I stripped off ruined clothing. If this kept up, I would be wearing bedsheets in the street.

CHAPTER TWELVE

Daniel kept their word and stopped by my apartment after their shift at the hospital at dinnertime, bringing sandwiches and pastries. I heated some tea, and we enjoyed an evening meal as Daniel informed me about what had happened in the hospital after I'd left.

"Two more died from gunshot wounds," my friend said. "And everyone is on edge. The police said not to talk to reporters that already started to besiege the hospital."

"There is no way Mayor La Guardia can downplay this. The public will start to lose confidence in government."

"Start?" Daniel laughed.

After we ate, Daniel insisted they look at the bandage that the doctor had applied to my left hand.

"Sloppy work," the nurse *tsked*. They'd brought medical supplies as well and fussed over me like a mother hen. Daniel was one of the few people who had seen both of my mismatched hands without gloves. They never judged nor pried at all about my "condition," accepting me as I was. They had also seen the many suture scars on much of my body. Daniel had added some stitches themselves, as I was reluctant to see physicians who might ask too many questions.

Fortunately, I seemed immune to most diseases—all their medical care had been for wounds. And I healed at an accelerated rate, at least so far.

When Daniel was satisfied that my hand was well taken care of, they stood to take their leave.

"After today's excitement, I'm turning in early," they said. "Dottie had a rough night last night."

Dottie was the alternate life that Daniel led when they enjoyed the company of men. It was a part of their life they kept hidden from most of the world, though everyone in the neighborhood knew about it as Dottie liked to sun themselves on the stoop of their apartment building when in that persona. It was how I had met them.

"I think I will be retiring early myself." We stood by the door. "And don't be worried if you don't see me around for a few days; I may stay at my office."

"It's that serious?"

"Yes," I said. "I might attract more unwanted attention like that at the park, and I'd rather not endanger anyone here if they come for me."

"You take too many chances," Daniel said. "Be careful, this neighborhood would be pretty dull without you."

When my friend had left, I locked the door and, because I was feeling extra cautious, I lodged a chair under the knob.

I sat in my reading chair but not to read. The city was laid out before my window, the office lights in the buildings that worked at night blinking on as twilight graded to darkness. The constant hum of the city changed into its nighttime tempo. The city was never really silent, like a massive, sleeping entity. Alive with the thousands who thrived there. A community.

Most nights I felt myself as separate from that life out there, more alone in the midst of the crowd because I was an outsider. Not that night.

I saw Mother Kalderash before my mind's eye. "*You have work to do,*" she had told me, and whether it was her shade or my wishful thinking, I now felt that.

What's more, the one who had worked on my inner weakness, who called himself *Daitengu*, called me a sworn enemy.

He was right. Now that he threatened the community I had found.

I slept in the chair, still in my dressing gown. When I woke to the rising sun, I was stiff, my bandaged hand ached, and I could feel the marks on my throat, which now looked like a sunburn.

I washed and assessed my remaining wardrobe. If I became involved in any more physicality, I would need something sturdy. I had a dress shirt, tie, heavy trousers, and a short leather jacket that would have to do. I added a silk scarf to cover the marks on my throat.

There was only one suit left and I decided to keep it in abeyance until I could have new clothes made. I would have to buy a hat during the day. I admit I did not feel completely dressed without one.

I took the account of Sunday's events to the hospital, where I gave them to Tommy.

He was feeling much better and told me they would discharge him later that day. I told him about the coming summit and that I could be found at my office if the authorities needed more information.

He once more admonished me to "be careful," and I left.

I picked up breakfast on the way to the office and tried to figure out how to tell Vandoma of my encounter with her mother.

At the haberdashery on the way to my office, I found a suitable fedora. Feeling complete again, I strode a little more confidently toward the office, picking up the daily papers on the way. I found myself always conscious of my surroundings, more so than usual. After the attack in the park, I felt that whoever my enemy was, they would not hesitate to attack again without regard to any innocents that might be affected.

When I arrived at my office, I heard the comforting sound of Vandoma's typing upstairs.

As I hit the top of the stairs, she stopped and came running out from behind her desk.

"Mister Paradise." Her expression seemed concerned. "I saw the papers this morning—" Her eyes went to my bandaged hand and the scratches on my face, and she gasped.

"I'm fine, Vandoma. The doctors and Daniel checked me over." She followed me into the office as I hung up my hat and coat, but when I removed the scarf, gasped again and made a Romani blessing sign.

"Mister Paradise, you have met a *beng*!"

79

I saw first fear, then understanding in her eyes. I knew that her life and her culture had conditioned her to know that something extraordinary had happened. I wish I had her certainty of belief system on which to frame my existence.

"You must tell how this happened," she ordered.

I had her sit back at her desk and, as best I could, tried to describe to her the events of my experience. I was surprised that I had such a hard time expressing the whole of it. She listened with intense concentration, and when my words finally faltered, she spoke calmly.

"This is as it should be, Adam Paradise." She made a blessing sign.

"I didn't mean to upset you, Vandoma."

Her jaw tightened then, and her eyes were close to tearing up, but she pulled her focus back inside by effort of will.

"It is good that you tell me of this," she said. "It is good to know, not just to believe, but to know that Mama is content. She is a *Sara e Kali.*" She smiled and then said quietly, "I knew she would be."

"Yes, she is."

"These men of the guns," she asked after a time, "they are like the *gadjo* gambling man?"

"I don't know, but I think in some ways, yes."

"They will try more times to kill you?"

"It seems likely. That's why it might be better for you to work from home—"

"This is not so," she said. "My place is here. Mama said so."

I knew that arguing with her might be more difficult than facing down a Tommy gun again, so I acquiesced.

"Okay, I know that look." I said, "Miss Lee will be calling by later, but I want to go over to Digger's place before then with some questions I need answered. From now on, when I leave, I'll lock the door downstairs."

"It is good. I will keep this door closed as well."

"Good," I said. "I just want to make some notes first."

"All will be well." With that prediction, she put another sheet of paper into her typewriter and set to copy another pulp story.

I went into my office, entered the events of the day before in my journal, and gave a cursory reading to the newspapers. This occupied me for an hour, by which time I knew Digger would be opening his store.

"I won't be long." I redonned my coat. "Keep the door locked. I will call from the drug store downstairs when I come back to see what you want for lunch."

"You—"

"I know," I cut her off. "Be careful."

"I won't even ask if you heard it correctly," Digger said as he picked up the leather-bound volume on language and even before he opened it. "*Hakko Ichiu!*" He closed his eyes, and I could almost see him visualizing the page in the book. "It is Japanese and means literally, 'eight crown cords, one roof,' but the rough meaning is the divine right of the Empire of Japan to 'unify the eight corners of the world.'"

He blinked and gave a lopsided grin. "Pretty clear declaration of a world-conquering agenda, wouldn't you say?"

"Yes," I said. "Not the least equivalent."

He set the book down, adjusted his glasses, and looked serious. "It's that other word, the word that you gave me, that is problematic."

"How so?"

"Well, it is not really a person's name."

"What do you mean? He announced himself by that name." I thought back to my encounter with the strange shape-shifting individual—now convinced it was not a hallucination—and he was very specific.

"Read for yourself." He pointed to the back of the store. "Grab the thin red book from the bottom shelf."

I walked to the narrow space and crouched down, where I found a slim volume titled *Religions of Japan*. I flipped to the index in the back of the book.

"*Daitengu means 'greater* tengu.' *A tengu (which literally means 'mountain dog') is a type of demon of Japan, a more general term being Yokai.*

They often are the ghosts of angry, vain, or heretical priests who had fallen into the 'tengu realm' Tengu are famous Buddhist mischief makers, in some ways similar to the trickster gods of many pantheons around the world or the leprechauns of Ireland.

"These tengu may be either good or bad, though generally, one does not benefit from dealing with them. They were also legendary swordsman, thought to teach martial skills to samurai and are often harbingers of war."

"This is incredible," I said from where I was crouched.

"I thought you'd think so," Digger said. He closed the comic book he had been reading, smiled his gargoyle smile, and began to recite. "Accounts tell of many *tengu* causing trouble in the world. Possessing people and speaking through them, and abducting young boys as well as priests. *Tengu's* victims often came back in a state near death or madness. The expression *tengu ni naru*, or becoming a *tengu*, is still used to describe a conceited person."

Digger adjusted his glasses again. "So, you see, whoever called himself that was pulling your leg. It's not really a name at all."

Or it was, I thought. *Arrogant of him to announce with whom I was dealing.*

This was startling to me. Demons? Demi-gods? Had my experience in that between world been falling into this *"tengu realm,"* using the term that the Japanese called it? From what I learned when Mother Kalderash died and I encountered the Golem afterward, I knew there was a world beyond what was called "the natural" world. Indeed, my own existence was outside that definition. Now, it seemed I was encountering an even wider universe.

Before I straightened up, just as I slipped the book back on the shelf, the door from the street opened, and two men entered. One was a tall blond, and the second a broad-shouldered Oriental. The shades of the violently dead floated around both men.

They took no notice of me and walked directly to stand before Digger.

"So, Four-eyes," the blond said. "We told you we'd be back. You consider our proposition?"

"I told you before, Mister Smith." Digger had an edge to his voice I had not heard before. "I don't need any of your protective association. Get out of here."

Mister Smith made a *tsking* sound. "Now, that is not a smart way of thinking. Mister Jones?"

The Asian he called Mister Jones grabbed some books on one of the shelves and pulled them out to throw on the floor.

"Hey," Digger yelled.

"This place is a fire hazard," Smith said. "Lots of clutter." He struck a match, held it up in front of himself, and smiled. "Bad things could happen if you don't have protection. Very bad things."

CHAPTER THIRTEEN

I was about to rise, intending to come to Digger's aid, but my friend surprised me and the two thugs by producing a pair of ancient-looking flintlock pistols from somewhere behind the counter.

"You get out of my store," Digger said as he cocked the hammer on one of the massive weapons. They looked to be the type used as coach guns in the time when I was brought to consciousness.

The blond made to laugh, but Digger cocked the second one. His expression was as stone-cold as could be. He never resembled a true gargoyle more than at that moment.

"One for each of you," my friend said. "And at this range, there is no chance that I will miss. And in case you wonder, they are fifty-caliber balls. They make quite a hole."

The two men stared at him and then looked at each other, confused. Mister Smith yelped as the match he was holding burned his fingers. "You're crazy."

"Could be," Digger said. "But crazy people can still pull triggers the same as sane people. Maybe even more readily."

The two men hesitated for a moment, then slowly backed toward the exit.

"You're making a mistake, Four-eyes," Mister Smith said. "Our security is what you need, or bad things can happen. You'll see." When they reached the door, they took a last look inside. Mister Smith made a rude gesture, then the two left at a quick walk.

Digger uncocked the pistols and put them down behind the counter. He then picked up his comic book and went back to reading it, apparently unperturbed.

"What was that all about?" I stepped up to the counter.

"Oh, nothing. Those two jerks came in here a couple of days ago pushing protection."

"And you didn't think it was interesting enough to tell me?"

"Nothing to tell," he said. "That kind of extortion has been tried on me before. I heard they've hit a couple of the other bookstores down the block as well."

"But this is something I need to talk to you about it." I went on to tell him about the apparent extortion pattern in Queens and that it seemed in some way related to the tong problem.

"Wow, Adam. It does sound like this could be connected." He reached down behind the counter and rummaged around, producing a business card. "That Mister Smith—as he calls himself—left this two days ago. I meant to throw it away, but now I'm glad I didn't."

He handed me a card that read, "Shinobi Security," and had a phone number on it, but nothing else. I noted that it was cheaply made.

"This is most definitely connected, Digger. Mind if I keep this?"

"Sure, Adam, no problem."

"And do you mind if I tell Tommy Shane about this? He can tell the local precinct to have a patrolman stop by from time to time."

"Sure," Digger said. "Bobby Cooper is the regular beat cop. He must have heard about this anyhow." He gave me his gargoyle smile again, then held up one of the flintlocks. "In the meantime, I've got these."

I left Digger's store with many thoughts racing and was so preoccupied that I almost missed seeing Misters Smith and Jones exiting another store down the block and across the street. They were not looking in my direction, so I joined the flow of pedestrians heading toward them.

Despite my height, I have been successful in following people before, which I think is more a function of the busy streets and the fact that New Yorkers are conditioned not to gawk at the unusual as much as to any skill I displayed.

I stayed close to the storefronts and was not concerned about getting close, preferring to let them get more than a block ahead of me. The pair were easy to spot, and stopped in two more stores, spending some time in each. This allowed me time to squeeze into a phone booth at a corner drugstore to call Vandoma.

"Paradise Investigations," she answered.

"I have a couple of tasks for you." I spoke while keeping a watchful eye on the last storefront the thugs had entered. I gave her the Shinobi number and Tommy's home number and asked her to have my friend use his official contacts to run down an address for the company. I told her that I was following the two thugs.

"Do not take such a chance," she said. "You are too reckless."

"I'm just doing a little shadowing." I had to smile at the number of my friends who had expressed concern for my safety. It only reinforced my desire to preserve the existence I had built as Adam Paradise.

"What do I tell the Chinese lady when she calls?"

In my excitement about the hunt, I forgot Hank was phoning me about the lecture on Wednesday. "Her number is in my office, ring her and let her know what I am doing and get the information she'll have for me. If she says she heard about a tong summit, say I'll make it, whenever it is."

Vandoma tried once more to caution me to be careful, but I had to hang up as the mismatched pair of extortionists exited the business they were in. They continued their tour of stores along Third Avenue, and I followed. I made a note of each address for a later report to Tommy. This went on for over an hour, and they stopped in a dozen storefronts.

I was able to observe some of their interactions with the merchants. It was clear that a previous visit had cowed most of those they approached, as some actually handed over envelopes, which I assumed were payoffs. It made me wonder how long they had been working this scheme.

At the end of the hour, the two men went into a bar on the corner of Thirty-Fourth Street, and when I peeked in, I saw that they had ordered a meal. Apparently, their morning shift of extortion was at an end.

I think I've gotten enough information for Tommy. Let's see what sort of fellows they are when pressed.

I entered the bar and paused to let my eyes adjust to the interior gloom.

The bar was along the left wall of the long, narrow tavern, with some small tables on the right and larger ones in a room in the back. That was where Smith and Jones had settled for a meal.

There were only a few patrons in the establishment, two at the bar and a couple seated at one of the small tables along the right side.

An overweight, balding man stacking glasses behind the bar looked up when I entered, did a double-take at the sight of me but then assumed a professional demeanor and asked, "What'll it be, sir?"

I gave as non-threatening smile as I could muster and a vague wave toward the back room. "Here to meet some friends," I said. "I see them." Then kept on walking toward the rear of the establishment.

The two extortionists were enjoying beers and had hamburger meals before them. When I walked into the back room, the Oriental, Mister Jones, was facing me and almost spit out his drink.

He said something in a *sotto voce* voice to his partner, which caused the blond to turn in his seat.

I didn't wait for them to react further but strode quickly to their table, grabbed a chair from nearby, and sat.

"Good day, gentlemen. Is the food any good?"

Mister Jones, who I noted was missing the first joint of his left pinky finger, set his mug down and moved to slip his hand under his suit jacket.

"No need for that. I just want to have a little talk."

He hesitated for a moment and looked to his companion, who gestured for him to pause any action.

"What do you want to talk about?" Mister Smith asked. I could see he was engaging me in hopes of distracting me so his companion could be free to draw whatever weapon he had under his coat if it was needed. It was easy to see he was the "mouthpiece" for the pair and Mister Jones was the muscle.

"Your boss," I said.

"Boss?" Smith gave a pleasant smile and tried to look dumb. "What do you mean?"

I gave a forced laugh and launched a straight right punch that took Mister Jones by surprise. The punch connected to his nose with a cracking sound, rocking his head back and rendering him unconscious. He fell forward on his hamburger.

The blond gave a startled gasp, and I clamped the same right hand around his throat before he could scream.

"Socrates said, 'Be of good cheer about death and know this is truth.'" I spoke in a calm whisper while smiling. "I would advise you to tell me only the truth, or your good cheer will be assured."

Mister Smith's mouth quivered, and he blanched, but his eyes stayed cold.

"I want your real name and the name of the person who employs you." I lifted him from his chair to a standing position as I rose, my hand beneath his jaw. "I will not ask a second time."

He swallowed hard, clearly thinking over my offer and perhaps considering whether he was in more danger from me or his boss. His gaze darted over to the unconscious Mister Jones.

"Gustave Schulz," he finally said, "I'm Gustave Schulz." I suspected he was just frightened enough to be telling the truth, at least about his identity.

"Excellent, Gustave." I let him sit back down but stayed standing, looming over him. "My name is Adam Paradise, and if you or any of your people enter the Tome Tomb again, I will be very upset. Understood?"

"You don't know who you're dealing with."

"So, enlighten me."

Silence.

"Your boss's name," I repeated softly. "Who is *Shinobi* Security?"

The unconscious Japanese snored loudly and made a moaning sound.

"I don't know." Gustave was less emphatic with this pronouncement, so I knew he was lying.

"You do, but I am not in the mood to beat it out of you." I reached into his suit jacket and trousers pocket and pulled out his wallet. When he made to protest, I cuffed him across the chin with the back of my right hand, just hard enough to daze him.

"Tell your boss or bosses that I will come for them," I said. "And know from this moment forward you and Mister Jones here are marked men as

88

far as I am concerned. If I see you again, I will be very angry." I gave a smile that had no humor in it. "And stay away from the Tome Tomb."

I could have pummeled him, but he was the sort Tommy would call a hard case. He would not tell me anything useful. Torture had been proven to give as much false information as true, as in all those poor souls who confessed to witchcraft in ages past.

In any case, I had his particulars and would let Tommy and his boys in blue follow up.

As I strode through the main room of the bar, I heard Gustave curse and slap his companion in an attempt to wake him. He was apparently unsuccessful, because Mister Jones fell off his chair from the blow.

It made me laugh.

CHAPTER FOURTEEN

"The *baulo* called back," Vandoma said when I called in. She used the Romani vulgar slang for police.

"Tommy?"

"Yes." Her people had a very low opinion of the *gadjo* police, and even though she had met and liked Tommy, some prejudices linger. "Mister Tommy gave me the address of the place of the bads men from the card."

"Shinobi Security?"

She gave me the address in the Turtle Bay section of Manhattan on the East Side. It was not too far a walk.

"How did Tommy sound?" I asked. "Did he sound alright?"

"He said he was feeling good, he told me to tell you to be careful."

"Is that all that anyone says to me anymore?" I laughed.

"Do not make light," she scolded. "I have seen danger ahead of you, Mister Paradise. You should fear the shadow of the raven."

My first impulse was to brush aside her warnings, but I had no doubt she had inherited abilities from her mother. Of anyone, I knew that reality was a multi-layered thing, and so my answer to her was simply, "I promise to be careful, Vandoma."

"The water is your salvation. I have seen it. You must mark this."

"I will. I promise."

"*Latcho drom*," she signed off in Romani. "Good Journey."

90

The Shinobi Security location proved to be a warehouse on the East River, built partially over a wharf. It looked disused, but as I watched it from across the street for an hour or more, several pairs of men went in and out of it. They were always an Occidental and an Oriental in tandem.

So, you have a winning formula for extortion, eh? There has been considerable thought to this criminal scheme.

I debated what course of action to follow then, thinking for a moment about the legalities of closing down this extortion ring. There was no phone booth nearby to call either Tommy or the police station, but even then, the question was whether they had enough information to act on the place by getting a search warrant. Everything was circumstantial so far as any court would be concerned.

As I watched, a closed van drove up that bore the legend "Black Bird Moving." Several men got out and went into the building, coming out a few minutes later with some boxes.

That made my mind up for me. They must have heard from Mister Smith that they were in someone's crosshairs and were making to skip.

If I were to find out who the mastermind of *Shinobi* Securities was, I would have to confront these men.

Having made up my mind, I crossed the street swiftly, going past the moving truck and into the building. I passed two men coming down the stairs from the third floor carrying open boxes that looked to be heavy like they were filled with files. They were muscular Orientals who paid no attention to me as they descended. The *Shinobi* offices were located at the end of the hall and had a frosted glass outer door that was open. I stepped into the outer room without announcing myself.

The office had two desks with phones on them and several file cabinets. There were also a number of boxes in which two Asian men were loading files from the cabinets.

When I entered, the men looked up with curious expressions that quickly turned angry.

"What you want here?" an Oriental asked. "You no belong, get out."

I went to one of the phones without speaking and picked up a receiver, dialing when I heard the tone.

"Here, stop that," one of the packing men commanded. He made a grab for me, and then I grasped his shirt and pushed him off hard enough that he flew across the room.

"Hello, Detective Pettruchi?" I said when he answered. "If you are interested in capturing some of the gang who held up the Florence Theater, I need you to send a squad to come get them."

A second of the men jumped at my back, but I shrugged him off, so he fell onto some of the boxes. I gave Pettruchi the address where I was and added, "I would hurry, they are a pretty lively bunch."

Just as I finished speaking, another of the packing men yelled, "You leave!" as he clamped a hand on my right wrist. I hung up before the startled Pettruchi could comment.

I wasted no words and simply punched the grabber with my left hand and knocked him out cold. The action made the wound on my left hand sting.

As the man hit the floor, his mate called out, *"Tasukete!"* and two more Asians came out of the inner office. One of the new arrivals had a handgun.

"I know you, freak!" the one with the pistol said. "You killed Yoshi!"

From his build, I suspected he was indeed one of those who had held up the Florence. My wild plan to give Pettruchi an excuse to rush a squad to the address seemed to have been correct.

The gunman stepped up to all but shove the gun directly into my stomach.

"'Our will and fates do so contrary run,'" I quoted Shakespeare. When he looked at me without understanding, I explained, "I made a lucky guess." While he was distracted trying to decode my statement, I slapped the pistol out of his hand. It discharged, the bullet shattering the transom over the open door.

The other three men in the room charged.

The one who had pulled the gun on me was in arm's reach, so I grabbed him and used him as a battering ram against the others, smashing him bodily into the first two and then flinging him at the third.

While I was dealing with the men in the office, Gustave Schulz from the bar stepped in from the hall, a semi-automatic pistol in his hand.

"Oh, this is too good," Gustave said. He laughed and pointed the gun at my face. His muscular, Asian companion, Mister Jones—his nose bandaged and with two black eyes—stood beside him.

I froze; there was nothing else to do. He was across the room from me, and the pistol was aimed directly at my head.

The four men lying around the office moaned, and one of them yelled, "He called the cops."

Gustave cursed profanely. "Grab the rest of those records and get out of here fast." Then he commanded me, "Into the other room, freak. Move it!"

I had no choice but to comply. There was no point in arguing, so I moved ahead of him, keeping a keen eye out for an opening.

The inner office had a broad window that overlooked the river, a desk with several phones on it, and a single, now empty file cabinet.

"I'd like to take a long time with you," Gustave said. "Make you really suffer, but you've screwed things pretty good for this operation, so I'm gonna have to just cut and run."

He raised the weapon to aim directly at me.

I faced the barrel of the gun, wondering if this was my time to exit this existence again. It seemed that of late, and despite the protestations of my friends, I faced oblivion more than ever before on a regular basis.

Will I exit this way? Will I join Mother Kalderash now?

Gustave laughed and squeezed the trigger but there was no explosion. The hammer clicked. The weapon had jammed.

"Damn!" Gustave cursed and grabbed the slide to try and clear the gun.

Mister Jones, beside him, had no patience for him to try shooting at me again. He charged forward like a bull, pulling a six-inch blade and lunging at me.

I seemed stuck between the proverbial rock and a hard place, but thought of Vandoma's words and knew what to do.

I let the Asian get close, so close that the blade sliced into my leather jacket. When it did, I seized his leading arm to pull him past me, grabbing the back of his jacket at the same time with my other hand.

Swinging Jones around in front of me and then summoning all the power of my legs, I propelled him before me so that he crashed into and then through the window like a battering ram.

As we went through the frame, I kicked off from the building to push us as far out into the water as possible. Jones and I flew away from the building, arcing over the pier and plunging into the cold water of the East River.

The man screamed all the way down so that when we hit the water, he swallowed a good deal of the murky fluid.

We smashed into the cold surface hard, the force of the collision rendering Jones unconscious.

I held onto Jones so he would not drown, but when we surfaced, there were several explosive geysers in the water around us that I realized were gunshots. Gustave fired from the window. Two of the bullets struck Jones in the head and chest, and I saw his shade leave his floating form.

After releasing him, I dove under the surface and swam with the current away from the building. When I'd swum as long as I could that way, I came up and moved toward shore at the foot of Thirty-First Street.

Police sirens wailed in the distance, and I hoped it was them getting to the Shinobi offices. In any case, I had now made my declaration of war with the forces of Shinobi and, in the process, lost another hat as well as ruined a good leather jacket.

My office was closer than home, so I walked there, my shoes squeaking the entire way. To add insult to injury, a light rain began, wetting the city. At least I would not look completely out of place with my soaked clothes.

With luck, Pettruchi found something of use at the offices, but I doubted it, suspecting that the extortionists had been able to flee. The body of Mister Jones would complicate things when it was discovered, but it would just be a "John Doe," and there would be no way to connect him to the extortion.

I felt like I had fumbled the case as far as they were concerned. At least I could recreate the list of stores that I'd observed them visiting that had been waterlogged by my swim. The courts would require physical proof, and that would be gone with the thugs in the office.

Still musing over my failures, I trudged up the stairs to my office just in time to run into Vandoma, who was leaving.

"Mister Paradise!" she exclaimed when she saw me. She dropped her papers on her desk and ran over.

"I do seem to have made a mess of myself again."

When I removed my jacket, she gasped. "*Dordi!* You have been shot!"

While Gustave was shooting at us in the river, he had not only killed Mister Jones but apparently also shot me. There was a bullet wound on my left deltoid muscle. I had been so full of adrenaline that, apparently, I had not noticed.

"Off the shirt," she commanded, and I complied. The action of removing the garment made it smart, so I suddenly felt it.

Out came the medical kit from her desk again, and she examined the injury. "The bullet has made in and out." She held a mirror to show that the bullet had passed just below the surface of the skin without penetrating too deeply. Essentially a long graze, but under the skin.

"I can still move the arm." As I did, though now it hurt more. "So, it can't be too bad. I can have Daniel look at it."

"Yes, so. But I will clean the wound so it does not become *marime*." She got to work, bandaging it and sprinkling on sulfur powder.

When she finished, I donned a clean shirt I had in my office, though I left it open. I did not have spare pants, so would wait for the Rom woman to go before I stripped to let my trousers dry properly.

"You are in danger." She gathered her things to leave. "I have been having dreams—"

"Visions?" I asked. I had learned even before I had encountered her mother in the Realm Between that Vandoma's instincts were good. Now, I knew they were more than whims.

95

"You must beware of a *szelhamos ordog*" — she used the Hungarian for impostor devil. "This *beng* will oppose you in this world as well as the other."

At this point, careful was beyond attaining so I stopped her from wishing me to "be careful" again. I had initiated a battle with forces not just corrupt but evil by all civilized standards, and there was no going back.

"I promise I will be fine here tonight," I said at the top of the stairs. "And I think it will be safer for you to work from home tomorrow and maybe the day after." When she made to protest, I added, "I will heed your cautions, Vandoma, but I want to be sure you are safe as well. I worry my enemies would strike at you — as I am concerned they would strike at Daniel. They have already hurt Tommy."

She listened to my reasons with a serious face and nodded. "What you say is true. But my place is here. I will return in the morning. I will bring needles to sew the leather of the jacket. *Latcho drom.*"

Before I could argue, she was down the stairs and gone.

"Good Journey to you as well," I said after she had left.

I do not think I have felt more helpless or more proud at the same time ever before.

CHAPTER FIFTEEN

After washing in the restroom, I went and got sandwiches from the drugstore downstairs, then settled in for a night in the office. It would not be the first time. I steamed my trousers in the washroom and washed the shirt with the bullet hole because I was beginning to believe I wasn't done with destroying my wardrobe.

I sat up late that night, first recording in my journal and then reading from *Amuletae boni et mali*, or *Amulets of Power; Evil and Good*. It was a rare book written in the 1700s for the Vatican and listed many occult items from around the world. Included in it was the *Koshti Bok*—the good luck necklace owned by Vandoma through her family. It was the reason that she had come into my life.

Plutarch believed "Fate leads him who follows it and drags him who resists." Mother Kalderash seemed to think I was fated to be on the path I was to oppose this *Daitengu* and his efforts to destroy Hank's aid for Manchuria. And more.

But was it right to endanger my friends? I had become a nexus for violence. Violence, which I abhorred, yet which seemed to swirl around me as much as the shades of the souls who had inhabited my component parts.

Selecting my favorite poem, *Paradise Lost*, by Milton, I read myself to sleep. I viewed it, as I had read the other volumes that had fallen into my hands, as a true history. It moved every feeling of wonder and awe that the picture of an omnipotent God warring with his creatures was capable of expressing.

I often referred the several situations, as their similarity struck me, to my own. Like the Adam in that book, I was apparently united by no link to any other being in existence, but his state was far different from mine. He had come forth from the hands of God a perfect creature, happy and prosperous, guarded by the special care of his Creator; he was allowed to converse with and acquire knowledge from beings of a superior nature, but I was wretched, helpless, and alone. Until now.

Now, I had people who depended on me, who believed in me. People who were more than just objects to study, a means to finding my place and my purpose in the universe.

I seemed to have found that place.

And perhaps even my purpose.

With those thoughts circling in my mind, I went to sleep in my office chair.

I do not dream often; indeed, lying down to close my eyes and opening them to wake often feels like a blink between, yet I feel rested as I suppose anyone would from a full night's sleep. It was as if I was so hungry to experience existence that my body rejected sleep as nothing more than an inconvenience, and I didn't want to miss a moment of reality.

That night, however, I did dream.

I saw Mother Kalderash standing alone again in that strange between worlds…but behind her loomed a large black bird, a raven, its wings spread wide to send a cold shadow across me.

"You must look with your heart," she said, "not just your eyes."

In the dream, I tried to speak, but my words were lost in a sudden rush of wind, and I heard a laugh, that same laugh that *Daitengu* had laughed, and his voice became the sound of thunder.

Then I snapped awake.

There was a knock on the outer door of my office.

I rose, stiff from how I slept. My left shoulder was still painful, but I knew it would be healed in a day or two. I pulled the bandage off my left hand; the stitches were already healed. I flexed the fingers.

The knocking on the door continued.

"I'm coming." I threw on my trousers and a shirt and a tie and went to the door.

"Who is it?" I could see two vague shapes through the frosted glass.

"You in there, Paradise?" I knew that voice. "It's Detective Pettruchi. Open up!"

I did, and the detective, accompanied by a uniformed officer, pushed in past me.

"Good morning, Detective," I said. "How can I help you?"

The uniformed officer stood a bit off to the side, his gaze on me with the usual mix of fear and suspicion. I was used to it.

Pettruchi looked no less rumpled than he had Friday night, his chin still shadowed with a beard he could not fully eliminate. The little man walked once around the outer office and then went straight into mine. He made a circuit of the room, pausing at my desk, where he used a pencil to poke at the papers on it.

"Is there something specific you want, Detective?" I asked.

"I've been asking questions about you, Paradise."

"So?"

"So, you show up in this city three years ago, get a PI tag, and suddenly you're working."

I felt a chill up my spine. What was this exposure of my fragile history going to mean? Did I have to leave the life I had built? I had worked hard, I thought, to build a convincing backstory. I had hoped to stay in this city for a decade or more.

"Is there something wrong with my profession, Detective?" I kept my voice calm.

"I'm a professional." He sat in my desk chair, opened the top drawer, riffled through it, and then looked up. "I don't like amateurs."

"Do you have a search warrant?"

Pettruchi stopped his ministrations with his hand on the bottom drawer, the locked one where I kept my journal. "No need for that," he said. "I just want to ask you a few questions."

I had a sudden jolt of horror that if he'd a search warrant, my innermost secrets would have been exposed. That had been an issue before I had kept the drawer locked; now it was clear I would have to find an even more secure place.

Time to install a hidden safe.

Detective Pettruchi stood and made a production of lighting a cigar, shook the match, and dropped it on my office floor. I almost snickered at his mannered attempt to play the tough guy.

"About what?" My fear of him jeopardizing my situation now made me realize he was just attempting to unnerve me. It had to be connected to the Florence Theater attack…or…

"What do you know about a robbery on East Twenty-Eighth Street yesterday, Mister Paradise?" He made my name sound like an insult. "Or the body of a Japanese man found in the East River this morning?"

"Why would I know anything about either occurrence?"

"I'm asking the questions. I got a call yesterday directing us to that address. When I got there, it looked like a hurricane had hit it. I think you were that hurricane."

"Mark Twain said, 'Never tell the truth to people who are not worthy of it,'" I quoted.

"What the hell does that mean?" He walked right up and waved his cigar at me like a pointer. The scent was pungent.

"Just that your insinuations are not welcome."

"You may have friends in high places, Paradise. But you're just another Joe who has to abide by the rules."

"I always try to, Detective."

We exchanged stares, but I kept my features neutral. I could see frustration in his eyes. It was clear he was sure I was involved at Shinobi Security but had no direct evidence to connect me. He could do nothing to compel any statement, and that galled him.

"Keep your nose clean, big guy," he said. "I've got my eyes on you."

He stormed past and gestured to his subordinate. "Come on, O'Leary."

I could not help but smile as both of them made a point of stomping down the stairs, their attempt to establish dominance failed.

"'The truth has no defense against a fool determined to believe a lie,'" I said aloud, once more quoting Twain.

I chided myself for my reaction to Pettruchi's blind prodding about my history. I had been unsettled since my excursion into the Realm Between and thus more emotional than I could remember. I felt unmoored from the few concepts of reasoned reality upon which I had built the frame of my world.

I was reminded of Hamlet's statement, "There are more things in heaven and earth, Horatio, than are dreamt of in your philosophy." Indeed, there were.

"Mister Paradise?" Vandoma's voice called up from the bottom of the stairs.

"Up here, Vandoma," I called back.

"I saw the *baulo* leaving the building." She bustled into the outer office. "Is all okay?"

"Yes. Just some unfinished business from the Florence last Friday. As Tommy would say, 'a fishing expedition.' It is nothing to be concerned about."

She made a *"humph"* sound but seemed satisfied with my explanation. She carried a carpet bag beside her usual briefcase with her typing work for the day. She removed her coat and hung it by my leather jacket.

Today, she was dressed in a yellow flower print dress, anticipating the summer to come. She had begun to dress, as she put it, "more professionally" as she thought a secretary to "an important man" should. I was glad the additional typing she was able to take in while working out of my office had allowed her to upgrade her wardrobe.

That day, the dress made the hunch on her back more prominent, but I had long since failed to take special notice of it. She was more than her stature, proof to me that the human spirit was not confined to any single mold or model. It sometimes gave me hope for the flame that burned within me.

Vandoma gestured for me to hold my hand out to check the stitches on my left hand and gave a satisfied nod.

"Is healing well?"

"Yes." I flexed my hand to show her. "See?"

101

"Is good." She opened her carpet bag to pull out a set of long needles.

She took my leather jacket off the coat tree and brought it to her desk. She smoothed out the area on the coat that the knife had sliced and where the bullet hole had damaged it.

"I can fix," she said as she examined the tears. "Then I will oil this to make like new."

I had to smile. "You are amazing, Miss Kalderash."

This got an answering gentle grin from her.

"I'll head downstairs. Would you like some breakfast?"

"Yes, please."

"Good, I'll get today's newspapers while I'm at it."

She nodded again and then bent to her task at the leather jacket.

I donned still-damp shoes and headed downstairs to the drugstore in my shirtsleeves. I made a promise to myself to purchase another hat, or perhaps two, as my luck with headgear was running in the direction of my wardrobe. I did not want to make a liar of Vandoma's working for "an important man"—I should at least dress the part.

While I was there, I got us both hot tea—I had never adopted the American habit of coffee—and fried egg sandwiches.

The newspaper headlines made much of a policeman saving a would-be suicide in the Hudson River, but there was no mention of Mister Jones's body in the East River. There had been another gang killing in Brooklyn (I was sure I would hear more about it from Enzo).

Scandinavian nations met to shun a non-aggression pact with Germany. It seems they had a clearer image of the Nazi threat than America—where, on Long Island, they allowed a Nazi Parade, waving foreign flags. There was also a Nazi Bund that held festivals in Andover, New Jersey.

This country does not want to see the danger. I had dealings with the Bund only months before and knew that their fascist ideology was a knife in the heart of the so-called "American experiment." They despised democracy and touted an imagined Master race.

They were also in search of occult forces to help them gain power. And occult objects such as Vandoma's *Koshti Bok*.

102

In Europe, Pope Pius was stalling any condemnation of Berlin for actions against Poland.

Britain was prepared for action with all their armed forces and reserves held at their summer posts in preparation for combat.

Berlin was to be decorated by order of Hitler and his underling, Goering, all in celebration of the one-year return from Rome and the announcement of the Axis of Italy and Germany. It was not a big extrapolation to believe it would not be long before it became a triad with Japan. The same Japan that had fought and defeated the Chinese National Revolutionary Army in the Battle of Nanchang just recently. They were reported to have used gas warfare against the under-equipped Chinese.

It seemed that the Sons of the Rising Sun would stop at nothing to attain their goals of absolute power.

The Norse religion believed in three Norns who spun the threads of each one's life to determine their fate. So many threads of fate seemed woven into the tapestry I was a part of that my head was spinning.

When I reached the top of the stairs, that weave became even more complicated.

CHAPTER SIXTEEN

When I opened the door to the office, I froze. Vandoma sat at her desk with a look of fear on her face, while behind her stood a well-dressed Japanese man with a single-edged tanto-style knife that he tapped on the side of his chin as he smiled menacingly.

"Come in," the Japanese said, gesturing with the blade like it was a wand. "Do not make any moves that are fast."

I stepped through the doorway to see a Japanese on either side of the jamb, also armed with knives. They were dressed more casually than their leader, with leather jackets and hats pulled low over their foreheads, but their thuggish faces were set in grim lines, their gaze focused on me with animal intensity. They all but salivated with feral hunger.

"*Daitengu* has had enough interference from you, large man," the leader standing by Vandoma said. "It is time for that to stop—*Ima!*"

When he said "now" in Japanese, the two beside me stepped forward simultaneously.

Dark shapes hovered around all three men, which confirmed they could be ruthless, so there was no chance to make a move for fear of danger to Vandoma. I allowed them to move directly to me, each holding their blade up to press against my neck. They compelled me forward, closing the door.

"You must know that the destiny of your decadent country is to surrender to our Emperor and the superiority of the Nipponese way," the leader standing by Vandoma proclaimed. He moved around the desk, ignoring her, and walked to face me. He held his blade up to press it under my chin. "The Emperor demands obedience."

"Your Emperor's demands mean nothing to me. You know the war you propagate is the desire of your General Tojo and his Kwantung Army."

My recognition of the political situation in his country angered him, and he pressed the point of the knife till I felt it break the skin.

"We will leave your rotting corpse as an example to all who oppose the glory of the Empire."

It was clear that there was no negotiating with these fanatics and my patience was not going to stop their violence. My fear for my Romani friend made me search for a solution that might allow her to be free of any repercussions.

"Your plans are doomed to fail, and they can only bring ruin to your country—bullies always pay in the end."

"Your Western ways have proved powerless in Manchuko," he said, apparently delighted to gloat before his *coup de grâce* to me. "Soon all will know the superiority of Nippon."

"Then leave my secretary alone to be witness to your strength. My death alone will bring you no success if no one knows you did it or why."

He laughed then and stepped back. "It is true an artist must leave a signature. And fame can only come with notoriety." He drew his weapon back, intending, I am sure, to drive it into me.

There was no alternative to him shooting me unless I fought the three men and that I could not do. I only hoped that they would keep their word that they would not harm Vandoma. I prepared to enter the greater dark outside of life with some new understanding that there might be more than my conscious existence. At least for those born of man. As to what I might return to, to perhaps nothingness, I could not tell.

Before the Japanese could act with a fatal thrust, however, there was a sudden deafening explosion.

The leader of the thugs jerked forward, a look of shock on his face, before he dropped to the floor, dead.

The two knifemen to either side of me were as stunned as I was to see Vandoma holding a smoking revolver.

I shook off my surprise quickly and smashed a fist into the thug to my left with enough power to feel his skull crush beneath my blow.

The knifeman on my right slashed, his blade cutting through my shirt just as the gun in Vandoma's hand fired again. The second gunman spun as a bullet slammed into his side. He dropped to his knees, blood pouring from a wound under his arm.

He looked up at me, spit, and yelled, *"Hakkou Ichiu!"* Then he took his knife and slit his own throat.

The knifeman dropped to the floor in a spray of his life fluid, gurgled once and his indigo shade left his body.

There was a long moment of silence, then Vandoma hissed, *"Du-te-n Pizda Ma-til!"* —as foul a Romania phrase as I have ever heard. She dropped the revolver to the desk and raced across the room to throw her arms around my waist.

The shades of the three dead men in the room swirled up about us while she squeezed me with all her might. I put a hand on her curved back.

"Vandoma," I said, "where did you get that gun—"

"Nico gave to me. To be protect."

I could not stop myself from giving a short chuckle. She pushed away.

"You laugh?" She looked hurt. "I am joke?"

"No, little mother, you are certainly not that. You are amazing."

Her smile returned, and then she abruptly walked back to her desk to sit down heavily in her chair, her breathing ragged.

"Are you alright?" I went to her side and held her tiny hand in mine until she was breathing easily again.

"I am good," she said after a time. She looked around at the carnage in the office as if it had suddenly appeared. "Is a mess."

"Yes, it is. But now we must make to clean it up." I reached for the phone, but she stopped me.

"No. It is for me to make the call. To the *baulo*?"

"Yes. You should ask for Detective Pettruchi. I suspect he will show up here as soon as he hears of this anyway."

While Vandoma called the authorities, I looked through the pockets of the dead men in hopes of finding some clues. There was only small change but nothing that could lead me to where they had come from — no wallets or other documents.

I heard the sound of a siren approaching downstairs just as I found a small matchbook in the leader's pocket. It was for the Rising Sun Restaurant. On impulse, I pocketed it.

Heavy footsteps pounded up the stairs and a uniformed officer entered the office, gun drawn. When he saw the bloody carnage, he stopped short and pointed the gun at me.

"Hold it right there," he ordered.

I held my hands up in an attempt to look as non-threatening as possible. "This is my office, sir. These men attacked us."

"Is so," Vandoma said. She stood by her desk. "I had to shoot the bads mans."

He looked from her to me and the bloody corpses, then said a very bad curse word in astonishment.

"You're a special kind of monster, Paradise," Detective Pettruchi barked at me through a cloud of cigar smoke. "You keep your lily-white hands clean while you have all the women around you slaughter people for you with guns."

I was seated across a table from him in an interrogation room in the Tenth Precinct police station and had been enduring the harangue of the Italian detective for a half hour.

It was useless to mention that my hands were not lily-white either in color or guilt, as I had killed one of the assailants with a punch. Still, I had endeavored to explain the attack, detailing the order of occurrence to a stenographer earlier.

"I told you and the others how it all happened. In great detail."

He snorted and jabbed his cigar at me.

"You told me a cock and bull version that makes you look like a hero and blames the dame."

"I told it as it happened."

"Well, I'm telling you how it really happened," he insisted, clamping the cigar in his mouth again, "You suckered these rubes into your office and your hunchbacked Gypsy moll popped them for you."

I slammed a hand down on the table between us with enough force that it shattered the wood of one leg, so the table leaned. "You will not refer to Miss Kalderash in such derogatory terms again." I spoke in a very calm voice.

The detective jumped back, his face pale, and bit through his cigar so that the burning end dropped to the floor while he swallowed the other and coughed.

A second officer, standing near the door, also jumped back against the wall and pulled his pistol.

"You crazy SOB," Pettruchi yelled. "I will see you and your freak do time for this—"

"Stand down, Detective," a harsh voice called from the entrance. The man in his late fifties who spoke had a high forehead, a somber face, and was lean with piercing eyes. He was not tall, but his presence filled the doorway. "I've read the transcript of this case, Pettruchi," he said, "and your statements are not warranted."

Police Commissioner "muss 'em up" Lewis Valentine stepped into the room and walked directly past the startled detective to stand before me. He wore his uniform tunic, but his tie was askew, and his whole attitude was one of "get things done."

"Good to see you again, Mister Paradise," he said. He thrust his hand out for me to shake, and I rose to do so.

"And you, Commissioner."

He had taken over a corrupt department from John O'Ryan and worked hard under Mayor LaGuardia to root out criminality, not always with a gentle hand, but with, for the most part, a fair one. I had spent time with him and the mayor after the violence at the Bund camp in February and been instrumental in helping them suppress the details of the deaths involved.

"But Commish," Pettruchi protested, "This guy killed a guy and his dame—"

"His secretary," Valentine said, "shot two of the attackers. And he killed a third." He threw a file on the crooked table. "And fingerprints on two of them allowed me to pull the jackets. Very bad men—one is wanted in several killings in Boston and the other for drug offenses on the coast."

"But Commish—" Pettruchi tried to protest. "The Gypsy had a gun—"

"That is not a crime under the Miller Act," Valentine said. "And he is licensed as a PI in this state."

"But she—"

"Is his under his license as his secretary," the Commissioner said. "Mister Paradise was a citizen protecting himself from the same kind of killers who attacked him and Detective Shane last Sunday in the park."

Pettruchi's face colored red, but he bit back any further protests when Valentine added, "And we can release him and Miss Kalderash. I am sure they will both be available if we need them for anything."

"Most certainly," I said. "I have a good number of things to do here in the city and no reason to leave at all."

I walked out of the interrogation room with the commissioner under the withering gaze of Detective Pettruchi and found I quite enjoyed his discomfort. But I didn't have any more time for him, as I decided to broaden my dietary education and have a meal at a Japanese restaurant.

It was about time I seized the initiative from my opponent and took the attack to them.

CHAPTER SEVENTEEN

"They yelled at me a lot," Vandoma said as I escorted her away from the police station. She was accompanied by her brother Nico, a tall, handsome Romani dressed in a stylish, flashy checkered suit who was even more uncomfortable around police than Vandoma.

"*Baulo* always yell," he agreed. She'd called her brother, and he'd come running with plans to bail her out if required. Fortunately, they had not actually booked either of us, choosing instead to grill us relentlessly—and separately—after taking our statements. Pettruchi turned the screws extra hard on me, so to speak, in keeping me isolated longer but had not counted on my previous service to the city.

"You had better take Vandoma home." We were on the street. "I fear those who did this thing will not be content with only one attempt on my life"—I looked at her, her jaw locked and her expression still defiant—"and she will not be safe around me until this is resolved."

"Yes," he said. "She should come home." Our relationship was a rocky one, with him at first resenting me as an outsider, but after his mother's death, he had come to realize our fates were intertwined.

"No," Vandoma spoke quickly, "My place is—"

"Being safe, little mother. We know these men will come after me now."

"Yes, and more than men." She held out her hand to her brother so that he reached under his checkered jacket and presented her with a small chamois-wrapped package. "You must take this for your protection."

She held out the package to me. I knew without opening it what it was.

"No, Vandoma, I can't—"

"Yes. The Luck of the Kalderash is for protection. You are to face that *beng* which is not right. You will need."

The Luck of the Kalderash she spoke of was her family's *Koshti Bok*, a necklace of white gold with a ruby of some size in the center. It was not only an heirloom passed from mother to daughter over many generations but was a symbol of her status in the Romani tribe as well as a powerful occult talisman.

"This should be with you." I knew what the import of her offering it to me was.

"You are fighting for Kalderash now. Mama would want it so."

There was no arguing with that pronouncement; it was as definitive as a Romani—especially Vandoma—could say.

I unwrapped the necklace and it felt oddly warm in my hand, the power of it almost palpable.

"I accept this and promise to keep it safe for the family Kalderash," I held the wrapped necklace in my hand and turned to Nico.

"Be sure to stay close to her, Nico. These men are ruthless."

"I will stay by her," Nico **said**. "This, I promise. The tribe will also watch." He flashed a smile and opened his jacket to show a holstered pistol. "No one hurts Kalderash."

"No; no one does."

Vandoma stood proud and took up the necklace. "Down," she ordered.

I bent so she could close the clasp of the necklace behind my neck. Even through my shirt collar, I felt a strange tingle from the piece of jewelry. I loosened my tie and opened my shirt to ease the necklace beneath the collar.

"You must take care," Vandoma **said** when I stood back up. "This you will promise?"

"I will take no chance I do not have to." I put a hand on the necklace beneath my shirt and felt its warmth through the fabric. "This, I promise."

I hoped I was not lying to her.

The Rising Sun Restaurant was located on Thirty-Sixth Street off of Sixth Avenue. It was on the second floor, accessed by a narrow staircase with elaborately decorated walls with dragons painted in gold and scarlet.

The restaurant itself was simply laid out: a large room with conventional Western-style tables but with a back section that had raised platforms with traditional tatami mats for more formal dining.

There were only a dozen customers at that time of the afternoon, and all of them Orientals. All turned to look at the Caucasian giant that entered.

"Can I help you?" the Japanese *maître d'* who met me at the entrance asked. He was dressed in Western clothes but wore a brightly colored cotton *happi* coat over his suit jacket and made a show of bowing. "I think you are in the wrong place."

"Oh no." I bowed back. "I am exactly in the right place. I came for a meal."

I ignored him and moved to sit at an empty table.

The *maître d'* looked confused and quickly sent a Japanese woman dressed in a silk kimono over to where I sat. She was delicately featured, with pale makeup and lustrous black hair done in an elaborate hairstyle. She bowed deeply. "We have no menus in English. So sorry you—"

I had prepared myself for that moment by stopping at Digger's to consult a book on Japanese cuisine—it was always good to expand my knowledge and experience, even if I were not pursuing villains.

"I will have some of that vinegared rice, fish, and vegetables I have read so much about," I said, catching her off guard. "*Sushi*, I believe it is called?"

She was bewildered now and looked to her boss, who had recovered his composure quickly. He nodded to her.

"I will bring *miso shiru* first to begin your meal," she said quickly. "You wish *sake*?"

I had heard of the rice wine, and though I had no real desire for oblivion, I decided to taste it.

"Yes, I believe I will try some." She bowed again and hurried away.

The *maître d'* regarded me with suspicious eyes from his standby the door while most of those at the tables studiously avoided looking in my direction, though I knew they were very conscious of me. I noted that all were rough-looking sorts and saw a tattoo peeking out from the shirt sleeves of two of them. At least one was missing the little finger of their left hand. It was fairly clear they were criminal types.

The dark shapes swirling around most of the guests gave me confidence that I was indeed in the lair of the killers.

I had placed myself in the midst of enemies, a Daniel in the lion's den, but I had to make sure I did not become a sacrificial lamb or lose clues like I had at the *Shinobi* offices. Perhaps I had erred in keeping this restaurant from the police, but I felt that the realms that this *Daitengu* was operating in were beyond the ken of the regular authorities.

The waitress returned in a few moments with a small bowl and ceramic bottle, pouring some of the rice wine into the bowl. She stepped back and waited while I tentatively sipped it.

It reminded me of some dry wines I'd had in Marseilles. I gave a slight smile, which she returned and then headed away only to come back a few minutes later with a bowl of the salty soup.

I had the soup and my meal, which I found quite tasty without any interruptions, but at the end of it, a small plate was placed before me with a crunchy pastry shell on it.

"What is this?" I asked.

"It is a fortune cookie," a slender Japanese gentleman in an elaborate kimono said as he stepped up to my table. "You should open it."

I cracked the small shell-like shape to find a tiny piece of paper within. There was writing on it that said, "The curious cat often ensnares itself."

I looked up to see the thin man smiling. "You should heed warnings, false man," he said. "And treasure the false life you have." His head was bald, and his right cheek jumped with a muscular spasm as he smiled so wide as to be grotesque. His teeth were blindingly white, and pupils so black that they appeared to have no whites. He resembled nothing so much as a skull.

Most remarkable about him, however, was that no phantoms swirled around him. None. It was a void space as if he did not even exist, certainly as if he were connected to any human dead. Or perhaps living. I knew then that I had met him before, in a very different form.

"Please be seated. It is good to meet you in this world, Mister *Daitengu*."

The smiling man sat and signaled to the waitress, who brought him a cup of tea. She presented it to him with exaggerated gestures, and he took it, turning the bowl slowly in his hands before sipping it.

I waited in quiet while watching his ceremonial consumption. I knew he was counting on the prolonged silence to build tension in me, to work on my nerves, but I had waited for days alone on ice floes for seals to come up for air. Time and solitude were not my enemies.

After a time, he set the tea bowl down and spoke. "You are foolish to come here, one called Adam Paradise." His cheek twitched at a steady rate, like the slow beating of a heart.

"One pursues knowledge where answers can be found," I said.

"And what answers do you seek?"

"Why you have marked this society for destruction."

The man's smile widened, enhancing his death's-head-like appearance. "This Western mass of confusion is no society. Fools and barbarians that are little more than children, with no guiding principles, no unifying center."

"Like your emperor?"

"Yes," he gave a slight bow of his head. "The sun source of our people."

"But America is not at war with your country."

"Not directly," the smiling man said. "But he who aids my enemy is my enemy. They deny the raw materials such as fuel that we need to expand our divinely ordained destiny on the mainland."

"Similar to the *lebensraum* policy of the Nazi regime in Germany," I noted, "the search for living space that supersedes the needs and wants of your neighbors for your own selfish desires?"

I saw a hint of discomfort pass across his features. "Inferior races are only impediments to be brushed aside."

"A very cavalier attitude that explains why you are allied with the Bundists—you have much the same worldview."

"Even some of our own people who have emigrated to this decadent wasteland have been seduced by the shallow ways of the whites; they have forgotten the honor and tradition of the old country."

"All people desire to grow, to learn, sir; is that not the human experience?"

He sipped his tea again and regarded me with hooded eyes for several moments. "Are you familiar with *kintsugi*?"

"No, I do not believe I have encountered that word."

"It is the art of repairing broken pottery by mending areas of breakage with *urushi* laquer." He held up the tea bowl and, with a quick gesture, smashed it to the ground. The action startled everyone in the restaurant, and several of the men reached for something hidden beneath their jackets before they realized what had happened.

The waitress ran over to the table.

The smiling man spoke rapid Japanese to her, and she bowed and raced away.

"Many years ago, when the *chanoyu*—the tea ceremony—was performed, a vessel was broken. It was sent to China to be repaired. When it came back, it was repaired with large staples, which many found obtrusive. Japanese improved on such repairs with lacquer mixed with gold, and thus, the breaks and flaws were enhanced rather than hidden."

The waitress returned with a dustpan and began to sweep up the pieces of the bowl. The smiling man waved a hand at her. "Thus, with the repair we do not deny the history of the object but highlight and honor it. This we call *wabi sabi*—the embracing of the flawed or imperfect."

"And you tell me this, why?"

"It should be obvious even to your inferior false occidental mind that you are a flawed vessel, false man, assembled from discarded remains."

He was attempting to pray upon my doubts; I could clearly see that. Sun Tzu said, "Attack the enemy's weakness." This being who sat before me evidently knew or suspected my own internal struggle with my place in the universe.

"You seem unusually well informed."

My companion laughed, his facial tic exaggerating. "All things are visible from the Realm Between, but your motives in helping these pathetic Americans are not."

"How so?"

"I am a creature of my homeland," *Daitengu* said proudly. "But you have no allegiance to these pale weaklings. Why would you aid them?"

His sudden question took me by surprise. Why would he care for my motives? I was an enemy, and from what I had seen, he was a ruthless killer—and master of killers. Then I remembered another quote by the Chinese philosopher of war, "Appear weak when you are strong and strong when you are weak." It appeared to me that this *Daitengu* was attempting to demoralize me. If he felt I was strong enough to attempt deception, he revealed himself to be weak.

CHAPTER EIGHTEEN

"You have scruples about why I do something, *Daitengu?* I should think you would not care."

"It is wise to avoid opposition rather than invite it. When the imperial glory of Japan has taken over this decadent land, our friends will prosper, and our enemies be crushed. You would be appreciated for you, *wabi sabi*, you could have a place of honor."

Now it was my turn to laugh. "How shallow you must think everyone," I said. "The Bundists had the same low opinion of everyone not in the sway of their ideology."

The smiling man's expression darkened, and his eyes narrowed, with the pupils seeming to enlarge so no white was visible. Now his facial tic was a rapid spasm. "I will destroy all enemies in this life as I did in my one before and will begin with you." He rose, and abruptly, his skull-like features took on the aspect of a predator.

He reached across the table, but just as I was prepared to react, his hand suddenly jerked back as if he had touched a hot surface.

"*Itai!*" he exclaimed. His expression was one of confusion and then horror. "What is this?"

At the same time, I felt a surge of heat around my neck where I wore the *Koshti Bok*. For a moment, I didn't understand, and then I could not help but smile.

Thank you, little mother. You knew.

I stood prepared to take some action as the expression on the bald figure morphed into one of extreme anger, but at that moment, there was a commotion at the *maître d*'s stand by the door.

"I don't care if it's a private party, Mister Moto," the harsh voice of Detective Pettruchi said as the Italian flashed a badge. "This is police business." The short lawman, accompanied by two uniformed officers, pushed their way past the *maître d'* and took a hands-on-hips stance as he surveyed the room.

"Nobody leaves," the detective called out. The two uniformed officers took up positions at the kitchen door and fire exit to block egress. When they were in place, the detective locked his gaze on me and strode across the room to stand beside the baldheaded *Daitengu*.

"Good afternoon, Detective Pettruchi." I noticed the smiling Japanese's fixed grin and his physical manner changed, his shoulders slumping as he became abruptly less self-important looking. I noticed, as well, that the air around the Japanese was abruptly full of swirling phantom shapes as if the soul who had occupied the body before had just returned.

I saw the customers around the room at first come to attention and then work very hard to seem unmenacing. I am sure a number of weapons were secretly slipped beneath the tables.

"Why is it you are everywhere all over this case, big man?" The detective thrust his ever-present cigar in my direction, ignoring the smiling, bald Japanese.

"I just came for a meal, Officer. What case are you talking about?"

The little Italian then glanced at the kimono-wearing bald man. "And what's your story, buddy?"

The newly meek *Daitengu* bowed. "This humble one is Mako Ishita, Officer. I am the manager of this establishment. How may I help you?"

"I have a search warrant for these premises," Pettruchi sneered. "One of your employees, one Ishi Mifune, was shot yesterday at an office on Fifth Avenue. We traced him through fingerprints, and this joint was listed as his **place** of employment."

"Ishi, shot?" the bald man **asked**. "That is terrible." He wrung his hands, and his face blanched. "But how is this you are here?"

"The fingerprints of another stiff found in the river showed he worked here as well," Pettruchi said. "Robert Okino. That's one crook too many in one joint for me."

"Robert, also?"

This fact also surprised me, and the detective saw my surprise.

"That's right, Mister Paradise," Pettruchi said. "That ventilated floater turns out to be connected to you through this place." He turned to the bald Mako and held up a piece of paper.

"This warrant says I get to search this joint top to bottom, Mackie," the detective said. He turned to call out, "Okay, boys, come on in." At his call, half a dozen other uniformed officers swarmed up the stairs.

This caused some of the patrons to bolt from their chairs, with one producing a pistol, but his dining companion yelled, "*Matte!*" and slapped the gun out of his hand.

The police grabbed the gunman and roughly pushed him on the table, cuffed him, and began to pat him down.

"Everyone in this room is subject to search," Pettruchi called out. He puffed on his cigar, obviously enjoying his moment of command. He looked over at me. "That goes for you too, Mister Paradise. No matter what connections you have."

He stepped up to me, and I raised my hands to allow him to pat me down for weapons. He was particularly rough, and my shoulder wound did not enjoy his enthusiasm.

When he was done, he turned to the bald Japanese. "Okay, buddy, you got anything in that bathrobe?"

Mister Ishita bowed humbly and held his hands out in a wide, expansive gesture. "I have nothing to hide, Officer," he said. "We have a most legal business here. All paperwork is in order."

"We'll see about that," Pettruchi said. He patted down the Japanese, who smiled in my direction, but his eyes were the normal eyes of a man, and I saw none of the *Daitengu* in him.

The police confiscated the pistol that was pulled on them and roughly handled several of the men in the restaurant. After an hour of making a general nuisance of themselves, the police seemed to have accomplished nothing.

I stood the entire time, doing my best not to look smug as Pettruchi's frustration grew at finding nothing with his raid. He probed into every corner of the establishment, entering the office and kitchen. All the while, the kimono-clad Ishita stood patiently, his face fixed in a placid grin.

When the detective had exhausted all his searching, he came back to me, his ever-present cigar now a stub. "You're coming downtown with me, Mackie, we have some questions about those two employees of yours, and I'll bet the sharpshooter we arrested has a record, too."

"I will gladly go, Officer," Ishita said. "But I assure you, there is no criminality here."

"We'll see about that." Pettruchi looked at me, "You can go now, Paradise, but stay in town, this ain't over." He was apparently disappointed that he was losing his power over me. "I know you're tied into that river death."

"I will be at your disposal whenever you need me, Detective. I strive to be a good citizen at all times." As I walked past Ishita, who was removing his kimono and donning an overcoat, I exchanged a look with the bald man. For a moment, his expression seemed to change, his eyes more cunning. I touched the necklace beneath my shirt, and then, in a flash, he was the restaurant owner again.

When I left the Rising Sun Restaurant, I took myself directly to a haberdashery and bought another fedora, determined to hold onto this one. Then I returned to my office as I had a number of calls to make.

First was to Vandoma to assure myself that she and her brother were safe at home.

"Mister Paradise," she said when she picked up the receiver, "you are good?"

"Yes, little mother." I struggled with how to phrase my encounter with *Daitengu*, but once again, she proved that she was a *drukker*, a seer of things beyond the physical.

"The *beng*, Mister Paradise, he fears you. But do not think he will not attack you again."

That made it easier to tell her exactly what happened at the Japanese restaurant. When I concluded, she made a *tsking* sound.

"You said you would not take chances."

"I didn't think I was taking a chance," I said, "but at least I have seen the face of my enemy."

"You have seen one face, but such as he may wear many faces. You must beware more now that he knows how dangerous you can be to his plans."

"Yes. But it proves I am dangerous to him, and that matters, Vandoma."

She was silent for a long moment, then said, "Be watchful. I will pray."

"I appreciate it, and I will be, I assure you. I also promise to keep you appraised. I think things will come to a head soon."

"Yes," she said ominously, "I have seen darkness soon. Keep close the Luck of the Kalderash."

"I will. And make sure Nico stays close as well, this *beng* knows who I am and knows my weaknesses."

"Fear no danger, Mister Paradise." Her voice had a solemn tone. "A pure heart will win over the *marime*—the rot of this *beng*."

I could not help but smile at her comment. A pure heart? A borrowed one, a reused one, yes, but pure? I had no reason to think myself any more pure than anyone else. I tried to find a morality or core, for my life's meaning. Yet this woman had faith in me and the philosophy of her people, the *Rromano*, that were the codified pillars of the *Rromani* whose people believed in *baxt*, honor, and hope. And she believed in me.

That faith in me was reason enough to try to be the person she saw me as.

"Thank you, little mother. I will call when I have more news."

After I hung up, I went into my office—I still did not have a phone at my desk, as it was enough that Vandoma talked me into a telephone for hers—and opened my locked drawer where I kept my diary and the *Amuletae boni et mali* or *Amulets of Power; Evil and Good*. It was a rare book written in the 1700s for the Roman church to categorize and catalog the occult items that the church either feared or desired. It was in archaic Latin with both Hebrew and Old English notes in the margins as the objects were acquired or destroyed over the years. Digger had found it somewhere and gifted it to me.

The *Koshti Bok* necklace that Vandoma had entrusted to me was near the beginning of the book. It was created in 1683 to celebrate the defeat of the Ottoman Armies in the Battle of Vienna. It is rumored to have helped cause the defeat and make the wearer powerful. There was no more specific information, but it was clear from the *Daitengu's* reaction that its power was very real.

I was brooding as to my next move when the phone on Vandoma's desk rang.

"Paradise Investigations," I answered.

"I'm glad I got you in, Adam," Tommy Shane said. "I called a bit earlier expecting Vandoma to answer, but—"

"I sent her home after the affair this morning."

"A wise move. I called because I have some news."

"About?"

"The ballistics report came back on the slugs fired at us in Washington Square Park. The Tommy guns they used were the same ones that killed the gangsters in that garage in the Bronx and one of the killings in Brooklyn."

"There is no doubt?"

"None."

"Well, there is also no doubt I was the target in the park, not you, but it's better that you're out of this for a bit; it is sort of open season on me." I tried to sound light-hearted, but I'm afraid I failed.

"And something that might be related or not," he said. "A body was found decapitated in the East River the other day in Brooklyn."

"Yes, I read about it."

"Well, they found the head. It turns out it was a Japanese man."

"Really?"

"Yes, one Jiro Yagyu. And after the gunshot victim found in the river, it suddenly became more important. I've put in a call to the local precinct there if you want to head to Brooklyn to look into it tomorrow.

"Yes, I think I should."

"This thing is big, Adam. If they are connected, the extortion ring and the hits on all these different gangs, this is bigger than anything we've come across since The Great War."

"Yes, Tommy." With what I knew about the being called *Daitengu*, it was indeed big. I could not tell him about what I knew, any more than I could explain my own existence to him. "I think this is connected to a plot to destroy the United States preparedness completely."

"What do we do?" I don't think I had ever heard my friend sound so frightened, and I understood why, for no man who had ever been to war would ever wish to see another. It was said that war devours what peace accomplishes, and if the war from China spread to the United States, all the progress since The Great War would be destroyed.

"How are you feeling, Tommy?"

"Fine. The wound is sore, itching like crazy, so I guess getting better."

"That's good."

"Joan is taking good care of me, fussing like a real mother hen." His wife was a schoolteacher, and from his tales, she doted on him at all times, and I imagine more so now.

"Rest is the best thing you can do, Tommy. Let her fuss."

"It's all I can do. But listen, Adam," he continued with a sudden urgency in his voice, "I got a call about Pettruchi rousting you, and he may seem like a jerk, but he's honest. He just finds it hard to get past his own preconceptions, but he's a good cop. Don't let him bother you."

"Don't worry, Tommy. I'm used to people with chips on their shoulders picking me out as a target."

"Well, just wanted to say, if it comes down to it, he'll back your play." Tommy sounded ashamed. "I'm not gonna be much use to anybody for at least another week."

"Don't be so hard on yourself," I said. "You have Joan and Brendan to take care of. Your place is there."

"I know, but I still wish you would carry a gun."

"We've been through that. I'll be alright. But it is good to know about Pettruchi."

"I won't press it. Just keep a sharp eye out, these shooters are crazy."

"Noted," I said. "Now get some rest. I'll keep you up on what is happening."

"Okay, Adam, you're the chess player. I trust your strategy. Just watch your back."

He hung up.

Oddly enough, I abruptly felt very alone.

Sitting in the office, at Vandoma's desk, with the faint sounds of the afternoon city outside, I felt strangely isolated. More so than I had in the last years on the ice flows. Perhaps it was because the office that had been my home for three years was the center of a community that had formed, with Vandoma's desk as the epicenter of it. And now I was aware of what true aloneness was by contrast.

Being self-contained was not the same as being alone, and I was becoming more and more aware of that.

While I contemplated the whirl of circumstances, I heard footsteps ascending the stairs.

Three figures stopped before the frosted glass, and someone forcefully knocked.

"Enter," I said and prepared myself for another confrontation, but was still surprised by what I saw.

CHAPTER NINETEEN

Standing outside the open doorway was Manzetti's man, Enzo, flanked by the same two young men who accompanied him previously. The two men looked no less arrogant, but Enzo's worn face was fixed in a relaxed smile

"Good afternoon, Mister Paradise."

"Good afternoon. Come in, please do make yourself at home."

He removed his hat and stepped through the doorway, pausing to take in the room at a glance. He looked down at the bloodstain on the floor from the encounter with the two Japanese and over at the wall where the police had dug out a slug.

"I thought you might like to chat," he said after pointedly nodding toward the bullet hole.

The two men with him did not remove their hats and stood silently in the doorway.

I stepped to the entrance to the inner room. "Please come into my office." I gestured to the client chair. "Have a seat. Your two gentlemen can wait out here."

Enzo nodded, and the two soldiers remained standing uncomfortably in Vandoma's room while I and their boss went into my office.

I sat in my chair with my back to Fifth Avenue while Enzo sat in the client chair, seemingly enjoying its comfort.

"I regret I don't have anything to offer you to drink. I don't keep refreshments in the office."

"Not necessary," he **said**. "I know we were not expected." His hands were folded on his lap with his hat resting on a knee.

"Why the visit? I had planned to call you to keep you appraised of developments."

"Word was you've been busy with some visitors from the Far East on Sunday and yesterday."

"How did you get wind about my little trouble with the two Japanese **here**?"

His smile warmed. "Let's just say that Valentine didn't get everyone."

By this, he was telling me that there were still police that Manzetti or his people owned on the criminal's payroll. Crooked cops. It was another indication that the entity known as civilization was a complex organism.

I and my problems and concerns were only a small part of that vast complexity. I had come to realize there were certainly more levels to the world than I could reveal to the gangster without seeming insane. The only demon in his world was demon rum.

"Fair enough," I **said**. "Yes, I've had several encounters with the Japanese in pursuit of the solution to who killed Mister Manzetti's men in the Bronx."

"So we heard. What are the latest developments?"

"I can tell you and Mr. Manzetti that the extortion plot that has been going on in all the boroughs—I am sure he has wind of it—and the attacks on your men in the Bronx are connected as well as the attack on me Sunday."

"How?"

"The ballistics of the weapons used were the same. And at least one of the murders of other gang members in Brooklyn and Staten Island were with those guns as well. They are all connected."

"Do you know who sent the shooters Sunday?"

"Unfortunately, not yet," I **admitted**. "While we know the machine guns that were used to attack me and Detective Shane in Washington Square Park were the same ones used to kill the men in the Bronx, we have no idea who gave the thugs their orders. Both those shooters are now deceased."

"We read about that job. A lot of civilians hurt, very sloppy. They were obviously just soldiers, so yes, that would be a dead end." He seemed very knowledgeable about the subject, at least in the abstract.

"That is everything so far." I could not even begin to explain the circumstances with the Japanese demon or my speculations about *Daitengu*'s reasons for the attacks. "Except..."

"Except?"

"I'm attending an affair tomorrow night at the public library on Forty-Second Street and I suspect the same forces that tried to rob the Florence Theater last Friday will show up to harass the woman giving the speech as they did then. It all seems to be part of their grand scheme."

"Are you saying you would like some backup?"

"It wouldn't hurt to have several of your gentlemen available," I said. "If something happens it would be good to get some of these fellows alive for interrogation."

"Yes. It seems that so far when people go up against you solo, they're not around for conversation afterward."

I could not be sure, but I think he had a smirk as he spoke, though I could not dispute his conjecture. I nodded. "I would appreciate any help available."

"Call the number I gave you with the full details. I'll see that some talent will be there."

"And I will know them—?"

He gave a slight smile. "They'll introduce themselves to you, but I suspect a PI like you would be able to figure out who they were."

After he spoke, he rose, and I joined him in the outer office.

"Always a pleasure to do business," I said as he and his two underlings moved into the hall.

"Likewise." He pulled his hat on and tilted it to a jaunty angle before he headed down the stairs.

I watched them depart with a peculiar sensation of having capitulated with "the other side." On the other hand, I might as well use the resources available to me if I intended to go up against a creature like *Daitengu*.

That thought made me decide I needed to know more about my enemy, so it was time for another trip to Digger's place.

"Imagination is more important than knowledge," Digger said as I entered his shop.

"Knowledge is limited," I replied, finishing the quote from Albert Einstein. "Imagination encircles the world."

Digger laughed. "I have to try harder. What are you doing here so soon after your Sunday adventure? I thought sure you'd be in the pokey. Or the hospital."

"I zigged when the gunman zagged."

"So?"

"I wondered if you had any books on that *akuma*, demon thing, the *tengu*."

His gargoyle features lit in a wide smile. "I thought my little summary would not satisfy your thirst for information." He reached beneath the counter and produced a leather-bound book. "This is based on the culture, history, and religions of Japan."

I took the book and flipped through it.

"It's pretty complete," he said, "and talks about the political background, like when the Christians were persecuted by the shogun and all. Remember, those that believe in Shinto believe that their emperor is actually a divine being—an actual god."

"I owe you again, Digger."

"I'll add it to the tab. But don't worry me again like Sunday; when I read the paper yesterday—"

"I know. I've heard 'be careful' a lot the last two days."

"Well, listen then."

"Will do, sir. Thanks."

I had one more visit to make before night fell, so I headed back to my apartment to pick up my last suit.

When I arrived, my neighbor was relaxing on the stoop next door.

"Hi Adam, how's the shoulder?" Daniel was in their Dottie persona, wearing a green dress, a dark wig, and eye makeup, preparing to go out on a date. I always thought of either Dottie or Daniel as "they" rather than "he" or "her" simply because there was no separation in the personas in my mind. It seemed a simpler way to think of them thusly as it went back to at least the medieval references to the plural used as a singular noun in the fourteen hundreds.

The fact that they preferred the company of men romantically made them an outlier to society's attitude as to what was acceptable. It meant that for much of the time, as when being Daniel, they had to hide their true feelings and desires.

Perhaps it was why they accepted me, without question, for who I was or what I appeared to be. Dottie never asked anything more of me than my friendship and offered me only the same. We were both outsiders looking in on the rest of society with our secrets that should they be made public, might well spell destruction for us both.

"The shoulder's healing fine." I had to smile, thinking about how much getting a new hat had meant being able to "fit in" with the current style to me, and yet Dottie was brave enough to find their own style.

"I thought you were going to stay scarce for a while?"

"I just came back to grab a change of clothes. I chanced it during what's left of daylight, but I'm still too hot to be safe around at night."

"So am I, big boy," Dottie smirked, and then they recovered themselves, leaning forward with a scowl. "You've never been this dark about things, Adam, it's really that bad?"

"Yes, Dottie, there are a lot of people who don't want me breathing right now."

"That's a bit excessive," Dottie said. They looked around then added, "I have noticed several shadier than usual types around yesterday and earlier today. Asian fellows."

"That is no surprise." I looked up at my building. "Did you see any of them actually enter?"

"I haven't been here for much of the day," Dottie said. "So, no idea."

"You going out dancing?"

"That's up to the fella," Dottie grinned, "but you know what I always say; I'm ready for whatever comes."

"Yes, you do." I smiled. "I've always admired that." I headed toward my building. "Well, once more unto the breach."

"Take care, Adam," Dottie called. "It would be pretty dull around here without you."

I climbed the stairs with cautious alertness, but the hair on my doorframe was still undisturbed. I busied myself with washing up, then changed my shirt and retrieved my last suit out of the closet to take back with me.

When I looked out the window, I saw Dottie walking off down the street, arm in arm with a tall man.

"Ready for whatever comes," I repeated Dottie's words as they walked around the corner toward Seventh Avenue. A philosophy to envy.

But was I?

Dottie could retreat into their Daniel persona—however false it was to their core reality—but I was as I was for all time. I would never be able to cloak my true self more than the Adam Paradise or such similar persona I assumed. I was always outside society and humanity. But with the community—like Dottie—that "Adam" had found, I had value and a life. I would do all I could to protect that community and life.

I went back uptown to the office, checking that it had not been disturbed in my absence and settled in for the night to read up on *tengu* and Japan in general with the book from Digger.

There were also sections on the various martial cultures of Japan, the samurai with their rigid code of conduct called *budo* and the espionage agents they employed called shinobi or ninja who never allowed themselves to be captured.

That was the sort that had taken his life in the subway tunnel.

Of particular interest, deeper than the summary my friend had given me, were the facts about the Japanese demons called *tengu*. They were sometimes considered the reincarnated spirit of one who was proud and arrogant in life or ghosts imprisoned in the underworld. The book said they were the souls of Buddhists who couldn't go to hell or heaven because of the karma they created. They were also considered harbingers of war.

That checks out—that this thing would want war with the United States.

The interesting thing was that the creature was believed to have roots in a Chinese folktale. The very name *"tengu"* was derived from *Tiangou* and associated with a meteorite that fell from the sky.

It was all interesting, but nothing I found in the words gave me an idea of how I could fight a creature that could seemingly "occupy" another being.

Of interest was that there were different types of *tengu*, a sort of hierarchy with those who died with power becoming *daitengu*—a species with high intellectual ability; and the poor would become *kotengu*—the weaker species being some that could easily be deceived.

That was why it tried to bully me, to use my uncertainties against me; it was used to lording over lesser demons and tried to treat me as if I were one. So, vanity affects even demi-gods, eh?

Next time, I would have to be ready to face him demon to demon.

CHAPTER TWENTY

I woke Wednesday morning with a start to a taxi horn blaring on the avenue outside my office window. The encyclopedia lay on my lap—I was up to Q on this rereading—and my neck was stiff. Perhaps I would have to think about putting a daybed in the office if I was going to spend many more nights there.

My first order of business, after my morning ablutions, was to go to a nearby hardware store to obtain some tools and other supplies to create a hidden safe for my valuables. I had selected a spot the night before but wanted to work in daylight.

On the way back, I picked up the newspapers and breakfast.

After eating, I set to work at an uneven spot in the corner of the room near an overflowing bookcase. I was able to pry up three of the boards to expose a void space below that was between two joists.

The metal case I'd purchased fit perfectly between the floor supports where I secured it. After I was done, I slipped my diary, the book on occult talismans, and most of the cash I had in the office—a considerable amount—then refastened the boards into an ad hoc trap door.

My task completed and the area cleaned, I was satisfied that even in bright daylight, the new door was not noticeable, all the more so when I leaned a few of the overflowing books against the wall over the door. It was invisible.

I kept enough cash in my locked desk drawer to convince anyone who might break in—or if the police returned with an actual search warrant—that they had found all of my troves.

It was almost lunchtime, so I decided to treat myself to a meal at a pub I enjoyed near Penn Station. At the same time, I stopped by to see if there was any news from Leroy.

"Sure good to see you up and around, Mister P," the black man said. He went so far as to put a hand on my arm in a gesture of fellowship. "The papers had me worried about you."

"It was touch and go for a bit, I admit." I climbed up into the seat. "It has been a busy week, to say the least."

"Anything to do with what you was inquiring about with me?"

"Very much so. Things are heating up with the extortion angle just part of it."

"Well," Leroy said, "I haven't had much time to ask around, but I did find out that some guys in Brooklyn were being pushed by the same bunch. May be tied into a headless body found out by the Manhattan Bridge. All vague, but..." He shrugged.

"Makes sense with what I know, Leroy." I hopped off the chair when he finished the unnecessary shine and passed him his tip. "Keep your ears open, I think things are gonna get hopping around town in the next couple of days."

"You just watch yourself, Mister P. I need my weekly workout on your shoes to keep in shape."

It was gratifying that so many wished me well; they almost balanced out those who seemed determined to do me harm.

I spent a quiet afternoon reading, with the only other activity being a call to the number Enzo gave me to make sure he and his people had the full details of the event that evening. Then I locked up the office and headed uptown to the Main Branch of the Library and Hank's event.

The New York Public Library at Fifth Avenue and Forty-Second Street was built over a former reservoir and is a marvel of Beaux-Arts architecture. Its designer was a winner of a competition in 1911, and it was majestic, to say the least.

The Fifth Avenue side presented an imposing marble facade with ornate detailing, pseudo-Greek columns, and wide stone stairs to enter the main entrance flanked by two regal lions, which evoked the Sphinx for their placid demeanor.

The entire construction created a cathedral-like feel within, with the main reading room being almost 300 feet long with fifty-two-foot ceilings. In many ways, it was a temple to human history, learning, and the quest for knowledge.

I had spent many happy hours there, especially in my first months in the city, familiarizing myself with the history of the town and country I had decided to settle in.

I arrived almost an hour early for the lecture that Han Ku Lee was to present, a little after five o'clock.

The lecture was to be in one of the small auditoriums near the theater collection of the library. There were about fifty chairs set out for an audience of educators.

Han Ku Lee stood near the entrance to the auditorium wearing a dark green pants suit with a matching eyepatch. With her were a pair of muscular-looking Chinese men who regarded me with suspicion.

"Adam," she **said**, offering a hand to shake. "Thank you for coming."

"Hank. Are you ready for tonight?"

"I think so." Her usual bluster seemed subdued. "I've given this lecture a dozen times over."

"Circumstances outside your usual routine might make things more interesting." I told her briefly of my last two encounters with agents of *Daitengu*—though I didn't tell her anything about the more exotic aspects of the story.

These revelations were enough to give her pause.

"Then it is good Ling and Pai are here." She referred to her two companions, though she did not sound so sure.

"I also have some other help coming," I **said**. "You may proceed as you planned, and rest assured, we shall keep you safe."

"I've at least been able to arrange a meeting with the tongs." She gave a weak smile that went all the way to her green eye.

"All of them?"

"Yes, with the Jade Dragon tong acting as hosts and moderators. This Friday at the Jade Dragons' headquarters on Lispenard Street at the edge of Chinatown. I'll know the time tomorrow, but it will be in the evening."

"Hopefully, we can clear up some of the confusion that way," I **said**. "Fighting on two fronts is not easy."

"Yes. We Chinese know about that." She looked past me, and her expression darkened. I turned to see my help arriving in the form of the three gentlemen sent by Enzo.

They were led by Angelo, the soldier who accompanied Enzo on their first visit to my office. The two with him were of a similar type, dark-haired in their twenties, muscular, and dressed in expensive suits.

"No reason to worry. They are with me."

The other two stood stoically while Angelo approached me.

"You are very prompt," I **said**. "That's a good attribute."

"Enzo said to do what you asked, Paradise, but I don't have to take lip." He made a show to his compatriots of bravado in standing up to me.

"As you wish," I **said**. "I expect there may be trouble, violent trouble, in fact."

"Yeah, we kinda figured that."

"I want no gunplay," I cautioned. "If violence happens, we wish to capture any violators alive and able to talk."

"And if they don't have the same idea?" He looked to his fellows. "We supposed to talk the bullets to death?"

"Just use restraint," I **said** flatly and saw anger in his eyes. "I am sure Mister Manzetti would be anxious to listen to any stories the troublemakers might have and be upset if they couldn't talk."

Invoking the name of the gang boss cowed him somewhat and forestalled any more argument. Self-preservation would out if violence happened, ultimately, but I would hope that his fear of upsetting his boss would at least slow his regression to his baser nature.

We went into the room for Hank to set up her projector for the presentation, with her two Chinese bodyguards staying close by her. Angelo and his two did a good job of blending into the background, taking up positions near the exits while the members of the educators' conference began to filter in.

The conference attendees, who were meeting at a nearby hotel, were from universities all over the United States and Canada. They were a mixed group of men and women of various races, including a number of Americans and Canadians of Chinese heritage who had a visceral stake in the fate of their ancestral homeland.

There were dark shapes that hovered over some of the audience, but it was hard to pinpoint which individuals to whom these ill-treated spirits belonged. Their presence, however, prepared me for the occurrence of the trouble I had anticipated. The only question was how I could mitigate any disruption and if I could further the battle against the Japanese demon.

Hank's lecture this time was not just designed for a general audience to inform them on the events in Manchuria and China, but to give specific ways they could aid the relief funds and agitate to raise awareness in the American population. It was all about politically motivating America to become involved.

Hank was a powerful and passionate speaker for her cause, and I felt proud that she called me friend. The newsreel footage she showed included some of the horrible atrocities in Nanking in '37 and was graphic. There, Japanese troops raped and murdered tens of thousands of innocent Chinese civilians with impunity. The images and accounts of the experiences of individual survivors gripped the audience in rapt silence. I even heard some sobs from the watchers.

"This is why America must wake up," Hank concluded. "This is not just a problem far across the sea—no! The Japanese Empire has a hunger that devours all before it. When it has wrung the resources of China dry, it will move outward. It will collide with all the colonial powers and look with animal eyes to the East—to America."

She strode across the space before the movie screen, her gestures imploring and powerful. "Even now, after they captured Wuhan, they sent over three divisions of foot and calvary to attack the peaceful cities of Suizhuo and Zaoyang. While we speak, the battle along the Xiangyan-Huayan Highway continues in a series of bloody engagements."

"That is why I implore you, friends, now that the sleeping giant of China has been awakened, to help me wake the might of America's giant. People, not just land, are at stake. Real, living, breathing men, women, children. You may not know them, but someday, if this is ignored, it will be people you will all know. Talk to everyone to make them aware, donate—send..."

"Of course, now you ask for money." A cry came from somewhere in the hall. "It's all a money grab to line your own pockets!"

"You don't care about China!" another voice called out.

Ling and Pai came to attention then and took a step from the front of the stage to make their function clear.

Angelo's two men stayed relaxed in the shadows near the doors, their eyes on their leader, who looked to me to prompt him. I was not worried about loudmouths; rather, I kept my attention on the several members of the audience who were highly focused and just a bit too still for people who had been sitting for a lecture for over an hour.

To her credit, Hank was not thrown off her talk by the hecklers. Instead, she responded passionately.

"My heart is in China," she proclaimed. "And I would give all I have to save its people from aggression if it would be enough. It is not; it needs the other nations of the world to rise up against the ravenous monster that is Nippon—"

As she said the name, suddenly, five men rose up from the crowd as one, produced knives, and charged the stage, one of them screaming, "The On Leong tong say you lie, mongrel bitch!"

137

CHAPTER TWENTY-ONE

Ling and Pai reacted instantly to the assault, producing their own wide-bladed knives to meet the first two men who reached them. The attackers were all Orientals and brandished curved Japanese blades almost a foot long.

The four men met in the space before the stage and slashed and hacked at each other with amazingly swift, violent moves.

The other three faux-audience members continued toward the stage, but I was already racing toward Hank to intercept the knifemen. I got to the stage before them to physically block the attackers.

The first, dressed in a dark dress suit, was as broad as I and a little over five feet tall. He slashed at me with animal-quick speed and cost me yet another jacket, the blade slicing across the loose fabric to proclaim its sharpness.

Before he could return a backhand cut at me, I clamped my right hand on his forearm, my left on his shoulder, and hurled him into one of his brethren so that both men tumbled to the floor of the auditorium.

The last attacker made it past me, but Hank was ready and produced a revolver. She fired and struck the man dead center, the force of the bullet knocking him back. The thug was not wounded, however, for he clearly had some sort of bulletproof vest under his outer clothing. When he hit the stage, he made a sound of pain but moved to rise.

While this was all going on, the audience went wild, leaping to their feet with screams of distress. They attempted to race for the exits, though the confusion and chaos meant that many tripped over chairs or collided with each other in their panic.

Angelo and his men rushed toward the stage but were hampered by the terrified crowd fleeing for the exits.

I ran across the stage to stand by Hank.

"Do not use the gun again if you can help it," I called. "We must question these men."

The attacker she had shot was on his feet now. His clearly Japanese features were sharp and twisted into a mask of determination, his eyes black diamonds of focus. This **attacker** moved with a dancer's grace, the slightly curved knife he wielded flashing before him almost faster than the eye could track.

"There is no reason for this," I **said** to the knife man as I removed my ruined jacket to wrap around my left arm. "We know you are not from a tong; this will gain you nothing!"

The thug wasted no time with any reply, slashing and lunging at me with precise, practiced moves. Only the quickness of my reflexes, a gift from my creator's devotion to excellence, allowed me to evade the remarkable swiftness of the Japanese.

In the space before the stage, Ling and Pai were not faring well with the two **attackers** they fought. Pai, the taller of the Chinese bodyguards, was down and unmoving, while the man he had been fighting had now joined his compatriot to double-team Ling.

Out of the corner of my eye, I saw Ling fall to a knife slash, and then both Japanese turned to come my way.

Angelo's men intercepted not only the one who had battled the Chinese but also the two I had thrown off the stage.

The Italian gangsters acted in unison, springing on the knifemen as they swarmed the stage. Angelo's men produced leather saps and confronted the Japanese men, clearly experienced brawlers themselves, and were able to go literally toe-to-toe with the assailants.

It became a prolonged battle while the room emptied of the terrified audience.

The knifeman opposite me lunged at my left side. I blocked the blade with my wrapped arm as a shield and grabbed his face with my right hand with a claw-like grip.

Undeterred, the Japanese snapped out a low kick with his lead leg, and I felt a terrible pain in my right shin that almost caused me to fall forward. My involuntary stumble allowed him to tear free of my grasping hand and slash again at my midsection.

I twisted to avoid the point of the knife and swung my left hand, fist clenched, to collide with the shoulder of the weapon arm. The blow was hard enough that the man lost his knife, and it staggered him, but somehow, though I put all my strength into the hit, he did not go down.

The Japanese snarled and launched himself at me with multiple punches, driving me back with trip-hammer speed.

I had time to note that both his hands were deformed, bearing calloused knuckles that implied thousands of hours of impacts to distort them. The blows that hit me, which I barely managed to block with my forearms, were like hammer blows. I put the pain aside in an attempt to react, but the speed of his strikes precluded anything but defense.

I was forced to limp in retreat with the ferocity of onslaught. The adrenaline of the battle was not enough to overcome the pain in my leg; I barely managed to ignore it.

When I stumbled, my opponent pounced, driving down at me with an open hand like a falling axe. I shot my left arm up to intercept the blow, but even wrapped in my jacket, there was blinding pain. I was sure I felt it crack.

The excruciating pain spurred me to launch myself at him in anger. I drove my body into his, slamming him to the stage with my full weight pinning him down.

The Japanese exhaled violently and struggled beneath me. He obviously had grappling skills, attempting to evade me, clawing his stone-hard fingers into my side and alternately trying to drive his stiffened fingers into my throat like spear points.

The damage he had already inflicted on me caused me to lose my temper. My left hand was already beginning to swell from the blow it had sustained, so I felt no compunction to subtlety. To that end, I fastened my right hand on his face and squeezed till he screamed in pain. At the same time, I repeatedly smashed his head into the stage.

I am sure I would have taken his life in my rage if Hank had not come to rescue him from my wrath. She grabbed me by my shoulder and pulled on my shirt.

"Adam, stop, stop, you're killing him. We need him to question."

I stopped my assault and then realized the Japanese man was already unconscious.

When I climbed off the Oriental assassin, I realized the room had become quiet.

I looked up to see that all the other attackers on the floor of the lecture hall were unmoving, with Angelo's men kneeling over them. The Italians all looked disheveled, with one of them having received a bloody cut on his forehead and another whose jacket was stained deep crimson that indicated they had also been wounded.

Angelo, his own clothes askew, smiled up at me, his eyes shining with a feral light from the aftermath of the combat. "Everything's aces here, big man," he called up.

Hank jumped down off the stage and ran to the fallen Pai and Ling, both of whom were badly wounded. I used my right hand to drag the unconscious thug off the stage to drop him by the other four.

"These monkeys were not easy, big man, I'll give them that," Angelo said. His cheek was already showing bruises, and it was clear that his jaw would soon swell. "And they came prepared to play." He tore open the shirt of one of the men to show that they were wearing chain mail vests.

"That explains why the one on the stage survived Miss Lee's pistol shot," I said. Angelo grinned like a sated wolf.

"And no guns use."

"You did a great job. Enzo will be told so. Thank you."

"They are bad, Adam," Hank said from the side of the fallen Chinese. Her normal stoic manner was close to faltering; she was near tears. "We have to get them to a doctor."

I realized I might need one, as well, as my left arm was throbbing and my left hand swelling; it seemed clear that the axe-like blow might have broken my forearm. It was far beyond what Daniel could mend for me, annoying as it would mean a trip to a hospital to have it Xrayed. I was always reluctant to allow any doctors access to me for fear my lies to their questions might be found out.

At that moment, two uniformed police rushed into the room, guns drawn.

Angelo and his men stiffened, but I stood. "Easy," I said, "This time, you gentlemen are on the side of the angels."

I held up a hand. "Officers," I called, "these men defended us, and those on the ground attacked Miss Lee during her lecture. You can phone Detective Pettruchi, who dealt with the attackers last week in Chinatown."

My statement only slowed the approaching officers marginally, and they ordered everyone to face the stage, hands leaning on the edge, and they patted everyone down.

This process went on for some time, with more police and then medical personnel arriving, each layer of which needed to have the circumstance explained to them.

Hank was strident about having her Chinese assistants attended to. After giving her particulars to a responding police sergeant, she was allowed to go to the hospital with her men, accompanied by another officer.

Within a half hour of the first officers showing up, Detective Pettruchi stormed into the auditorium and marched right up to me.

"What the hell, Paradise?" the detective asked. "Do you do anything that doesn't have a body count?"

An ambulance attendant was seeing to my left arm, trying to get me to go to the hospital, as the limb was clearly swelling. One of Angelo's men had already been taken to Saint Vincent's, but the Italian gangster himself was standing nearby, enjoying my interaction with the officer.

"There seems to be a tiger whose tail I have hold of, Detective," I said. "And I am afraid this will not be the last time we interact this way."

He looked at me like he wanted to say more, but the ambulance attendant cut him off. "He really needs to go to the hospital, Officer. You can question him there."

"I promise not to run off, Detective Pettruchi," I saw his dilemma. "After all, I wouldn't want to get you in trouble with the commissioner."

His expression went from smug to angry in an eye blink. I thought for a moment he might bite his ever-present cigar in half again, but he just nodded at the attendant.

"You take one of my officers with you," Pettruchi told the ambulance worker. "I want this man watched; don't lose him."

"Kind of big to lose," the attendant said with a sly smile. Then, the white-coated worker turned to me. "Can you walk on your own, sir?"

"Yes, thank you," I said. "The leg hurts, but I can put weight on it."

As I was exiting the door from the auditorium, one of the audience members that had fled, a mousy-looking young Asian woman in a tweed skirt suit and wearing round glasses, stepped in front of me.

She looked up at me, and I saw that her eyes were blank; the black of the pupils seemed to occupy all of the eyes. The right side of her face twitched as if she were winking at me.

"You have won this battle, false man," she spoke in an oddly flat voice. "But the war will be decided after many more battles."

When she had spoken, the woman shuddered, and her whole manner changed, her eyes blinking and returning to a normal state. "Why—what?" she said, and then she fainted.

CHAPTER TWENTY-TWO

The ambulance attendant rushed to the side of the woman who'd fainted. In a few moments, she woke with no seeming ill effects from her collapse, though she was confused.

"I'm sorry," she said, "I...I guess all the excitement got to me. I was dizzy. I am alright now."

I saw the ancestral shapes that hovered over her that once again were exactly as they should be, proving her human ancestry. The *Daitengu* had "occupied" the poor woman and, having delivered his threat, left.

Detective Pettruchi stayed in the auditorium with several officers who stood over the secured and handcuffed Japanese attackers. All the captives were conscious and were, to a man, sullen and silent. Their apparent leader, the man whom Hank had shot and whom I had fought, glared at the uniforms around him with virulent hate.

"I got your number," the detective sneered at the leader of the would-be assassins. The Japanese's face was bloody and swollen, and his eyes were virtually blazing with hate. "You yellow bums think you can come into my city and kick up a fuss, that I ain't gonna stop you? Well, you got that wrong, Mister Moto."

He leaned in to stare directly into the leader's eyes, and though the prisoner had his hands cuffed behind him, the Japanese was sitting upright on the floor as if in a chair. Abruptly, the man rolled back and then jackknifed his body to spring to his feet.

The startled Pettruchi jumped back, but the Japanese snapped out a kick that connected directly to his chest, driving the detective backward to fall to the ground. Simultaneously, the Japanese leader called out in his language. The other prisoners all lashed out at the police guarding them. The bound men kicked or head-butted the officers who were caught unawares.

Angelo and his remaining "soldier" sprang to the defense of the officers, tackling two of the attackers and employing their saps again.

I spun from the doorway and ran into the room as fast as my injured leg allowed. I intercepted the leader as he moved to stomp on the fallen Pettruchi, grabbing the attacker by his shirt. I whirled and flung him with all my might into one of his other Japanese who was running at us.

By this time, Pettruchi had drawn his pistol, but with the chaos of the renewed combat, he could not find a target until one of the other Japanese broke free of the fight with Angelo and came at him.

"They're wearing armor," I called, and the detective raised his aim to fire at the man's head. The gun exploded, and the attacker died from the shot, his head a blossom of scarlet.

As the man dropped, one of the other assassins called something in Japanese, and all the survivors suddenly stopped fighting. They made a strange jerking motion as if it was choreographed, then dropped. All of them made hideous gurgling, choking sounds.

I remembered what Hank had said about the cult of warriors she called ninja. "They've bitten off their tongues to commit suicide!" I ran to the nearest fallen man in an attempt to save him.

My guess had been correct, and none of the men could be saved from drowning in their own blood—despite the efforts of the ambulance workers to clear their throats.

The events of the battle shook Pettruchi's tough demeanor, his swarthy complexion suddenly pale. He lit a fresh cigar and shook his head. "Crazy," he said. "These guys are nuts; what would make guys do that?"

"Remember, the Japanese who serve their emperor view him as a deity, Detective. They consider what they do a religious duty. And to fail is the greatest sin."

"Just crazy," Pettruchi repeated.

"There is nothing either good or bad, but thinking makes it so," I quoted. "They think the western ways are crazy."

Angelo, another bruise coloring on his cheek, walked up to me. "I'm never gonna be able to live this down."

"What do you mean?" I asked.

"Me, Angelo Ravelli, coming to the rescue of cops."

At Saint Vincent's Hospital, they insisted I have a cast put on my left forearm, though an X-ray showed it was just a fracture and not a clear break. My shin, fortunately, was only badly bruised.

I knew that the shin, like the bullet wound on my deltoid, would be only a memory in a day or so, thanks to my accelerated healing ability. The arm might take a week or more and would be an inconvenience.

I was able to convince the hospital personnel with my usual lie of having been in a car crash to explain my extensive scars, and as they were busy, they did not have much time to question me.

It was near midnight by the time I was discharged from the hospital, though I had been able to visit Hank while she kept vigil on Ling and Pai. Both men were seriously wounded, but she had been assured they would recover.

"I'll cover all costs," she told the attending physician. "See that they get the best."

I met her as she was leaving the two to their healing sleep.

"This is horrible, Adam. I should have listened to you and canceled the lecture."

"Do not chastise yourself. Not even I could have foreseen so much of an escalation."

"But you did take precautions with those gangsters—"

"Yes, but even then, I had no idea it would be on such a scale. Or that the adherents would be so fanatical."

"The *Kempeitai* have enlisted *shinobi*," she said. "The adherents of *ninjitsu* are the worst kind of fanatics. I just had no idea they were so entrenched in America."

I dared not tell her of the greater conflict, of the otherworldly demon whom I still had no idea how to defeat. And the fact that I felt there was a very specific plot, something to which the escalation of the violence was leading.

"Will you be alright?" We exited the hospital, and I hailed a taxicab for her.

"Yes. I have staff at my pool hall that will still be up. And they are a tough crowd. I have a lot to arrange to make sure Ling and Pai are taken care of."

She paused before stepping up on the running board. "What will you do?"

"Rest first," I said. "Then, I have a lead to follow up tomorrow in Brooklyn."

"Please, Adam," she said with sudden concern, "I am so sorry I got you into this, but I am ashamed to say I am also glad."

"Rest easy. We will talk tomorrow."

"Okay, I'll have a time for Friday's summit meeting by tomorrow afternoon, and we can make plans."

After she was safely on her way, I decided I was too tired to head back to the office. I was once more in need of more clothing, so I limped down Thirteenth Street to my apartment. There was no one on the street and no sign that my door had been disturbed, so I entered my place with a sense of relief.

Once inside, I locked the door behind me and, in surrendering to my sense of insecurity, slid a chair to barricade the door as an extra measure. Disrobing was an effort, and then, with no preamble, I crawled into bed, where I fell into a deep, dreamless sleep.

The sun streaming through the broad window woke me to renewed pain in my arm and shin and the memory of my confrontation with the embodied spirit called *Daitengu*. I do not believe I had quite so sore an awakening since my conflict with the polar bear in the Arctic over a hundred years before. Nor so troubled, for the encounter with the demon disguised in human form portended a paranoia I did not want to adopt.

Thomas Aquinas said, "Life is a gift from God to be loved, nurtured and lived in proper charity," yet I had taken life, albeit to preserve other life. But was my life really such a gift? My creator was a deluded man who ignored all norms and prohibitions. I had neither been nurtured nor loved, so if nothing else, Victor Frankenstein failed in his responsibility there.

Now I faced a being in *Daitengu* who, according to Japanese lore, had either been an evil human who abrogated his birthright or was never born of woman. Like me.

What made me different from him in that? He called me a false man and fought for the belief system he followed. I had no certainty of any humanity, and I, too, was fighting for a cause—the democratic principles of the country I had adopted and the safety of my chosen "family."

It seemed I could not stop the inexorable course I was on; there was no alternative but to confront and find a way to defeat the demon. Yet this being from another realm—which I now had proof that such a state existed—was elusive. If he could occupy humans as a way into this world, would it only be those of Japanese extraction, or could he be anyone?

I still did not know my enemy. Lao Tzu said, "The wise man does not display his treasure to those he does not know. And he cannot learn justice from the Ancients." So, it is likely the demon had not revealed all his weapons against me—though it seemed he had limitations for having to "use" human henchmen to do his deviltry. But I was sure that there was wisdom in those ancient secrets to help me to oppose him successfully.

I roused myself from my reflections, ready to head to the office. I only had a leather trench coat left for outerwear, so I selected it and two pairs of trousers so I could leave a spare pair at the office and a waistcoat.

After replacing my follicle alarm on the doorway, I headed off to the office. The morning newspapers already had sensationalized reports of the battle at the library, all short on facts and large on supposition, though at least there was considerable mention of the need for aid to China. Perhaps, indirectly, it might help Hank's cause.

After picking up several sandwiches and tea in the drugstore below the office, I ascended the stairs, but the sound of movement above gave me reason to pause.

I proceeded with stealth upward, keeping to the edges of the treads to minimize the squeaks, though my bulk made that almost impossible.

As I grasped the door handle, I was prepared for almost anything but what I saw when I stepped through the door.

CHAPTER TWENTY-THREE

"**M**ister Paradise," Vandoma said from behind her desk. She wore a dark blue skirt and jacket with a white, man-style shirt, her business attire. She was just rolling paper into her typewriter but stopped when she saw me and noticed my left arm. "*Dordi!* You are again injured!"

She rushed over to me, barely letting me get my trench coat off.

"It's alright, Vandoma, a doctor looked at it, and it is just a fracture."

She refused to listen to the statement that I was physically healthy and followed me into my office, where my limp gave the lie to my words. I set down the breakfast and papers I'd retrieved on my desk.

"Why are you here?" I asked. "I thought we agreed that you would stay home till all this was done."

"No. I said it was a good idea for a time, but I had vision last night. You met the *beng*, I know this!"

There was no point in lying. "Yes," I admitted. I recounted the events, trying to downplay the violence, but lingering on the moment when *Daitengu* made himself known to me. She nodded.

"Yes, the *beng* fears your power—and recognizes the *Koshti Bok* stops him from touching you physically. You must continue to wear. Why he uses men to attack you."

"I have come to believe it is so. The question still is, how do we fight him? And what is he planning?"

"Planning?"

150

"I think the fact that the attacks on Hank are out in the open, and the extortion attempts seem to have increased, lead me to believe there is some culminating event on the horizon."

"What will you do?"

"I have a lead from Tommy about an unusual death in Brooklyn that may be connected, and as I have no other avenue to pursue, so I will go there."

"We should eat breakfast first before we go," she **said**, heading back to her desk with one of the wax-paper-wrapped sandwiches I handed her.

"Wait a minute, *we* go?" I limped back out to stand in the doorway. "You were not even supposed to be here. It is too—"

"You need to have *drukker* with you. You will need me."

I made to speak again and realized there was no argument she would accept, so I switched tack. "What happened to Nico? He was supposed to keep watch on you."

She laughed. "He not watch me, I have to watch him. He come with me then goes off to do the things he does, he has sometimes still gambles, but not so bad as before."

"The idea was to keep you safe."

She held up a pistol that she produced from some secret pocket in her jacket. "I will keep me safe. And you, too. He will come back for me at the end of the day." Then, she just seemed to dismiss me and went back to her meal.

I knew when I was outmatched, so I went back into my office to eat my own breakfast.

The details of the combat at the library were scant, but other news items seemed to matter. In Europe, the Italian leader Benito Mussolini attended a celebration of a new military airfield barely twenty-five miles from the French border in what many were saying was a harbinger of dark times. King George VI and Queen Elizabeth arrived in Quebec City, Canada, at the beginning of their North American tour to promote unity in the Commonwealth and show the world a united front.

A ship of nearly a thousand refugee Jewish fled Hamburg, Germany, and the Nazis for Cuba. The Cuban government had already denied their right to land even before they sailed, but the passengers were desperate and had faith they would find a surcease.

Faith. A belief beyond reason based on hope.

Humanity had built itself a framework to hang their faith upon—be it religion, political ideology, or rational science—but I was not in that "tribe" of things human; in fact, I might be more closely akin to the demon I faced. *Daitengu* was neither alive nor truly dead.

I had to hope, to have faith, in that odd kinship being how I could defeat him. There must be something in that fact that would give me the key.

My meal and news update concluded, I returned to Vandoma in the outer office.

"We will hail a taxicab to go to Brooklyn," I said.

"It is good you do not tell me not to go."

"I recognize when argument has no value," I smile. "It is a waste of energy to oppose a Kalderash."

She returned my smile at that.

With the assurance that we would be back by the day's end to meet her brother, we set off.

The taxi driver, a portly Slavic fellow named Otto, was talkative as we headed downtown and across the Manhattan Bridge.

"I swear, folks," he said. "Seems like the whole world is changing all the time, ya know?"

"How do you mean?" I was always curious to see how those around me regard the state of the world.

"Well, the word is Durocher is gonna stay as shortstop and manage the Dodgers! Can you believe that, replacing Ruth with a shortstop?"

Vandoma kept quiet, looking especially small next to me as I was jammed into the back seat of the taxi. She knew I had little or no actual interest in sports but found the constant tribal re-bonding over sporting events fascinating.

"The way I see it, it just proves the whole world is crazy," he continued. "Like that big dust-up at the library last night? Crazy, right?"

"Yes," I agreed, "such violence is not right."

152

"Darn tootin'! People are all on edge these days. Them Chinese and Japanese scrappin' and everyone being all worried about that sauerkraut with the mustache."

"You're not worried?"

"Well, don't get me wrong," he said, "I love that Congress is spending all the money to ramp up the navy yard, and all because of that Hitler fella scaring some people, but I don't think he's a big deal."

"Why is that?" He was expressing what so many in America seemed to believe.

"I mean, there's a whole ocean to keep that jerk out of our hair."

"You don't think with planes and ships that might not be a real problem for an enemy?"

"I fought in the big war, see," he continued as he wove the cab skillfully through morning traffic. "And for all that mess over there, it didn't matter a whit over here. And that Kaiser was a real go-getter, not that little snip of a chancellor."

"You don't worry about the Nazis at all?" I was fascinated that he seemed to dismiss the looming shadows of war so easily.

"Them brown-shirted goons got their butts handed to them after that rally at the Garden back in February by LaGuardia's boys," he said. "Nah, America ain't got no stomach for that sort of nonsense." He laughed. "I mean, even the English don't think he's any real threat, or why would they send their queen to Canada on vacation? There's even talk she might come down to launch that battleship here next week. Hey, ya think she might need a cab to get to Brooklyn?"

The thought of the royal needing a taxi struck the driver so humorous that he laughed most of the rest of the way until he dropped us off in front of the Eighty-First police precinct in Brooklyn.

"Thank you for an enjoyable ride, Otto." I handed him the fare and a generous tip. He looked at the bills I had given him and smiled.

"Gee, thanks, sir," Otto said. "If you ever need a ride again, just call my dispatch and ask for Otto Korrinski. Any hour, Mister—"

"Paradise, Adam Paradise," I said, then added, "if you're not too busy driving the Queen."

He drove off laughing heartily.

"So many do not see the threat of the Nazis," Vandoma said with deep concern as we crossed the sidewalk to the police station. "I cannot see how that is so."

"People see what they want to, Vandoma. Nietzsche said, 'Sometimes people don't want to hear the truth because they don't want their illusions destroyed.' And America has an illusion of invincibility."

I sensed my companion tense as we approached the police precinct, and I stopped at the foot of the steps into the building.

"You do not have to come in with me, little mother, I know how the *baulo* put you on edge."

She looked up at me with a determined expression. "No, Mister Paradise, I am in the right, and this is the thing that must be done."

I felt a surge of pride for her strength in facing what I knew was a deep aversion and, once again, that she was my friend.

"We're here to see Captain Chino." I spoke to a ruddy-faced, distinctly Celtic-featured, older desk sergeant once we had entered the lobby of the precinct. "Detective Thomas Shane called ahead." I displayed my Private Investigator's license to the officer.

The sergeant studied the document and then looked at the two of us with barely concealed derision and considerable doubt. Still, he followed procedure and picked up the phone on his desk.

"This is O'Toole. There's…uh…a couple of people out here to see Captain Chino. Yes, a Detective Shane sent them over. Okay." He hung up and addressed us.

"You and the lady have a seat. Someone will be out to meet you in a minute and take you to the captain."

We took our place on some wooden benches along the wall while the controlled chaos of the reception area of the police station went on around us.

It was clearly a low-income area, for blue-collar individuals were the majority of those in the station lobby. I was surprised to see that a large number of those in the room were non-whites. Asians, Hindus, and Middle Eastern individuals seemed to predominate among those seeking assistance. Even some blacks.

Vandoma sat stiffly beside me, her gaze straight ahead. I could tell she was fighting a battle internally with her fears of the police and her sense of duty and loyalty to me. It made me admire her all the more.

After several minutes, a young patrolman approached us. He looked to be barely out of the academy.

"Mister Paradise?" he addressed me. "If you'll follow me, please."

We exited the lobby and were led down a dingy corridor to a beveled glass door marked "Captain K Chino." He knocked once.

"Come in," a deep voice called.

"Mister Paradise and guest," the officer announced, then stepped aside to let us in.

"You can close the door, Doyle," the occupant of the office said. "We'll be fine here."

The door closed behind us, and I found myself at a loss for words for a moment.

Captain Chino was an Oriental.

CHAPTER TWENTY-FOUR

The uniformed police captain was a distinguished-looking Asian man wearing horn-rimmed glasses. He had a touch of grey at his temples, but his broad face was unlined. He smiled when he saw my expression.

"I know, not what you expected." He rose when we entered and stepped around the desk with an extended hand.

"Good morning," he said. "Kevin Chino. I know it sounds Italian, but it is an old Japanese name. I get that surprised look all the time."

"Adam Paradise, and I apologize for falling victim to assumption."

"I'm used to it," the officer said.

"And this is my associate, Miss Vandoma Kalderash."

The officer extended his hand to her and shook it, seeming to take no notice of her physical condition or ethnicity. It made me think of how hard it must have been for a minority like himself as an officer in the New York City Police Department, let alone for him to rise in the ranks to precinct commander. It spoke of remarkable forbearance and ability.

"Please take a seat, folks. How can I help you? Tommy Shane said you were interested in talking to me about a case you're working on?"

"I understand a body was pulled from the East River recently."

He gave a wry smile. "That doesn't narrow it down much, I am afraid. We get floaters all the time because of the currents that pull them into the inlet near the Navy Yard. Three this last week."

"This one was beheaded."

"Ah, Jiro Yagyu." His expression darkened. "That is a sad case."

"How so?"

"Jiro was an old-school Japanese," the captain continued. "Came to this country with a young wife and made good as a supplier to the navy yard. Had a son here, Jamie, and a daughter, Miko. Jamie did well, a college boy, but for some reason, things went wrong."

"How so?"

"Jamie beheaded his father two days ago."

"That is terrible," Vandoma gasped.

"You have apprehended him?"

"Well," he continued, "at first, the body was dumped in the river, but when it was found and identified, and we went to the home—the son gave himself up for arrest."

"Did he confess?"

"He only says he did it, but he will not talk about it any further or explain it," Captain Chino said. "It is his right to clam up, though it doesn't really matter as this is a capital case."

"The killing of a parent is most terrible," Vandoma said. "The most of all things against the Romanipen." Which was the code of conduct for her people.

"Yes," the captain agreed. "But this is a strange one. Not quite cut and dried; I don't see any anger in the boy."

"In what way?" I could tell by his reluctance to continue that he was holding something back. I saw him look to my companion and suspected it was a grisly detail. Before I could say anything, she spoke up.

"You may say all that is, Mister Chino," she said in a quiet voice. "I will not be frightened."

He nodded to acknowledge her. "Well, the body had a massive wound to its stomach as well that happened before death. A very deliberate cut."

"And that implies?" I had a suspicion from my reading of the book Digger had given me, but the officer confirmed it.

"It was a ritualistic act," he continued. "The gutter term is *hari-kari*, which means belly slitting, but the more formal name is *seppuku*. It is actually a very reverent act of suicide."

"I do not know these words," she said.

"In old samurai families, in the old times," he said. "When a warrior had done something wrong—a crime real or imagined—he could be sentenced to take his own life. To show their stamina and honor, they would cut themselves across the stomach. The goal was to show no pain. To accept death stoically, with a calm demeanor."

"It seems an excessive act to display courage."

"Yes, well, my ancestors were very big on courage," he said. "And honor. But as it is almost impossible not to show pain, eventually the custom developed to have a trusted friend or retainer—or relative—behead them the moment before they would show pain on their face."

"This is…" Vandoma began but let her voice trail off as she could not find the words.

"Shakespeare observed, 'Our bodies are gardens, to the which our wills are gardeners.'" I said, "Human willpower can be extraordinary." I knew that my will to live had fought even my self-loathing when I walked into the cold north with the intention of ending myself. It was some spark within that always wanted one more moment, one more gust of fire. "What could have motivated such an act?"

"We don't know," the police captain said. "Once he admitted he did it, he refused to say anything else. A public defender can't even get him to talk. Even his mother—the deceased's wife—would say nothing. Old-school stoic."

We three sat in silence for a few moments. It was Vandoma who finally spoke up. "We may see this man, yes?" When I looked at her questioningly, she clarified, "It is that we should test him for the *beng*."

"*Beng?*" the captain asked.

"Uh, a suspect in our case," I said. "It would be helpful. It may be related to the attack at the library last night."

"That was you?"

"Yes, Japanese assassins called *shinobi* were involved."

"*Ninja?*" The officer's expression showed shock. "That is even more old-school than *seppuku*. Or, really, maybe just as old-school." He rose. "I can't officially interrogate him without his lawyer, but he can receive supervised visits if he wants without any officials present."

He called out, "Doyle." The door was immediately opened by the young officer who had escorted us in. "Take these people to the lock-up to see the Yagyu kid. I'll call ahead to clear it."

"Yes, sir," Officer Doyle said.

"Thank you, Captain," I said, extending a gloved hand to shake his. "I will let you know if we uncover anything useful."

"I appreciate that; stop by on the way out."

The young officer conducted us back out across the lobby and to another side corridor.

"Are you sure you want to do this?" I asked Vandoma as we walked. She noticed my limp was already less than it had been and nodded approvingly.

"We must know of the *beng*, Mister Paradise. I have feeling that this killer of his father will help."

"I trust you, Vandoma." I did, out of all proportion, perhaps, considering that I was over five times her age. Often, it seemed she was my elder, certainly in things touching on the spiritual world.

"It is good, Mister Paradise. We will do what must be done, I will know more when I see this man."

The officer led us to an ominous barred door where a second policeman greeted us.

"I will have to ask you to surrender any weapons," he said.

I held open my trench coat, "I have none." He took me at my word but did a pat down of me anyway. Then I looked to Vandoma.

The Romani reluctantly produced her hammerless .32 revolver and handed it to the officer.

When he looked back at me, I said, "It is under my license. You can check with Detective Shane."

We waited a few minutes until a policewoman could be called to pat down Vandoma, but then we were let through the gate and brought to a small windowless room divided by a wooden table and a wire screen. There were two chairs.

We sat while the officer who accompanied us stood off to one side, out of earshot. In a short time, a handsome young Japanese man in his twenties was escorted into the room by a jailer. He was dressed in prison blues but unshackled. He walked with calm and untroubled steps, though his head was down and his expression so very hopeless.

More importantly, for me, was that no dark shape hovered above him, no angry shade of a murder victim, but rather an amber form, tending toward gold. This translucent shape was more of an embracing mist in that it draped itself like a stole over his shoulders and head.

He regarded us seated on the other side of the wire with a puzzled expression.

"Do I know you?" he asked.

"No, Jamie Yagyu," I said, keeping my voice low so our words would not reach the police guards. "I am Adam Paradise. This is Vandoma Kalderash. We would like to talk to you."

"About what?" His voice was well-modulated, an educated voice that held no fear. His eyes showed great intelligence. But there was a listlessness to him, a palpable sense of hopelessness.

"Why did you feel it necessary to help your father commit *seppuku*?"

His expression hardened. "I have nothing to say."

The golden vapor that clung to the young man moved in tighter to him, almost like a hooded cloak. It was not the shade of one who died in pain or anger but one who died at peace. It seemed beyond coincidence that such an ancient ceremony happened at the same time that I was involved in this shadow war with *Daitengu*. It seemed likely, somehow, that this man and the death of his father were in some way connected to the war that I was now engaged in. It was easy enough to find out.

"Did the reason for his death have to do with a being called *Daitengu*?"

He gave a deep intake of breath, and his color blanched.

"How?" He managed to voice, his tone cold and distant. "You are not—"

"I know, I am not Japanese, yet I have learned some things," I said. "Some of them, I am not sure I wished to learn."

"Why do you ask me this?"

"You have touched the other one," Vandoma spoke up. "He who is from the Realm Between. This is so?"

His features contorted into a frightened mask. "How can you know?"

Vandoma allowed a faint smile to flit across her features. "I can see that which is unseen."

He seemed to not want to believe her; then his eyes shifted up to me. "You have no right to ask me—"

"I have a need to, sir, and no time to be subtle. I know you had no evil or violent intent toward your father—and I can tell he is grateful to you for the service you rendered."

"Grateful?" he sobbed, and his steely manner crumbled, his shoulders hunching forward. He leaned heavily on the table. "How do you know this? How could you?"

"He is a *pajivalo Martja*," Vandoma said as if all should be clear. "And I am a *drukker*, one who sees beyond. So, you must tell. It is right."

A play of conflicting emotions flashed across the man's face; he was clearly fighting an internal battle between his discretion and a need to confide in someone. I decided to offer him an outlet for his emotions.

"I am not a policeman, Jamie; I am not obligated to tell any of what you tell me to any enforcement mechanism. I only want to help. I know there is a great evil in the air. I know you did what you did out of affection for your father."

My statement seemed to give him the permission he needed to release his pent-up pain. "My father was an honorable man," he said. "He loved this country that had welcomed him, but he was loyal to The Emperor. So, when they came to him and asked him to do what they did…" His voice trailed off, and he fought back a sob.

"They? Who asked what of him?"

"Bald man, a Japanese, with eyes so black and a tic here"—he touched his right cheek—"He spoke to Father and told him that for the honor of the family, he must do this thing for The Emperor. Something bad. Against this country." He was near tears now, desperate to unburden himself. "The man said he was aware of the Yagyu line, of long service. My father, he said, was honor bound…the man said it was the Yagyu destiny to do this."

"Do what?" Vandoma asked. "This bad thing the *beng* asked."

I looked at her, wondering for a moment how she could conclude that it was the being itself that had appeared to him. I then realized the description Jaime had given was of the *maître d'* from the Rising Sun Restaurant.

"I can say no more," the boy whispered. "I honor my father." And it was clear at that point that he would tell us nothing further.

CHAPTER TWENTY-FIVE

Jaime Yagyu had reached the limit of his confession and sat in stony silence for a time before calling for the officer to bring him back to his cell. When he had left, Vandoma spoke.

"This man has not done evil," she said as if it was a decided reality. "He has faced the *beng*."

"Or at least his father did. And yes, he took his father's life as an act of mercy, that much is clear."

"What will you tell the *baulo* captain?"

"The truth is that nothing the boy said will help or hurt his case. Whether it will help us is another matter."

"There is work for us, yes?"

"Yes, Vandoma. I think we need to speak to his mother next to find out more."

"Yes," she agreed. "I think this as well. Mothers know much."

We stopped by the Japanese captain's office and indeed told him that the Yagyu had nothing useful to say but that we wished to follow up our investigation by speaking to his mother.

"Are you sure the widow is the wise thing here?" Captain Chino asked. "She is an old woman, and this is a great shock—losing her husband and her son, essentially the same time."

"We know this," Vandoma said. "But we can be gentle and even, maybe, make it better for her."

"I agree. Miss Kalderash has a very gentle touch—certainly compared to me."

This made the officer smile. "Okay," he said. "Here is her address but use kid gloves."

"Yes," I said, holding up my own hands. "Kid gloves."

The Yagyu home was a brownstone on a quiet street only a mile from the Navy Yard, not far from the river. It was a simple exterior but with a well-maintained window box with colorful flowers contrasting with a black wreath hanging on the front door.

"I think it better you lead the conversation," I said as we ascended the front steps. "I am doubly at a disadvantage as a man and, well, being what might be seen as frightening. And you are not just a *drukker* but are a *drabami*, a healer. And this family will need to be healed."

"As you say," she agreed. "But I do not know all to ask, so you will tell me when I need." This made me smile.

"Any time you seem at a loss, I promise I will offer help, but I don't think that will be much necessary."

She rang the bell, and I stood two steps below her so as not to overwhelm the occupants. After a few moments, the door was opened by an attractive Oriental girl I judged to be in her late teens. She was the feminine mirror of Jamie Yagyu and was dressed in a simple black dress. She evidenced curiosity when she saw Vandoma, but her eyes went wide with surprise when she saw me. To her credit, politeness overcame her shock, and she asked in unaccented American English, "Can I help you?"

"I am called Vandoma Kalderash. He is named Adam Paradise. We have come from talking with your brother. We wish to speak to you and your mother on a matter of importance."

The girl took a moment to register all the Romani woman had said and then stepped back into the house. "Please come in."

I had to duck to pass through the doorway into a small foyer.

"How is Jamie?" the girl asked in a breathless whisper.

"He is well, though he is very close-mouthed about recent events, his spirits seem high."

She absorbed this statement and nodded. "If you will wait here for just a moment, I will speak to Mama."

We stood somewhat chastened, not sure what to expect. I could only imagine the confusion and pain of the widow of the dead man, her son also essentially lost to her. And we were here to probe her about that death, yet it was necessary if we were to find a way to defeat the being called *Daitengu*.

Vandoma stood seemingly at ease, holding her head high and with her eyes focused on something I could not see, apparently looking to spiritual matters.

"This is right," she said in a distant tone. "*Kali Sarah* guided you to this time and place, Mister Paradise. Be at peace with this."

The *Kali Sarah* was the Roma goddess of fate and reincarnation. I had indeed felt the hand of Fate guiding me in the last week, a dark destiny perhaps for the death and destruction I had encountered, but a destiny that gave me purpose. A positive purpose that, at last, might help me expiate my early horror.

Miko Yagyu returned swiftly and led us into a parlor. It was a bright room with large bay windows out onto the street where early blooming cherry trees filtered the light to shine pink into the room.

The parlor itself was appointed with a sofa, comfortable chairs, a console radio, a small table, and a fireplace where family pictures were displayed.

There was also a small household Shinto shrine. It was on a table with incense sticks, a bowl of salt, pure water, and a number of wooden plaques with the names of family members and ancestors written on them in *kanji*—Japanese script. According to the book Digger had given me, the home shrine was known as a *soreisha*.

Above this sacred space for the Yagyu family eddied and swirled a number of amorphous forms, now blue, then indigo, then gold, as if showing generations of spirits linked to the shrine.

When the daughter saw me looking at the shrine she said, "The names of our family for many generations are written on those wooden plaques—Papa knew them all, and we learned them from an early age.

Our branch of the Yagyu clan has many famous sword masters in the past." There was deep pride in her tone, and it was clear the whole family was traditional in many ways.

The matriarch of the home, Madam Yagyu, attired in a *mofuku*, a black kimono, sat in a high-backed chair near the window, which threw a shadow across her face. She leaned forward as we entered but did not rise.

She was a petite, grey-haired woman, her features drawn and lined, the strain of her circumstance clear, with a downturn to her mouth and her eyes a bit unfocused. She turned her head toward us, and I saw no fear or surprise in her eyes. In fact, it was almost as if she had expected us. Around her hovered gold threads but no purpled mist of angry death, just a cloud of kinship, I suspected to her deceased husband.

"Mama does not see so well," Miko said, "so she asks that you come closer and in the light."

We stepped to just outside arms-length, with me letting Vandoma lead.

"We sorrow for your loss," the Romani said. "We would help you."

"How?" the older woman asked. "My husband is gone, and my son—"

"Is not lost yet," Vandoma said. "Know that death is but a separation that is temporary."

"This I also believe," Madame Yagyu said with a nod of her head. "But the nights will be cold."

"This too, I know," Vandoma said with more pain in her voice than I would have expected. "But you can help to stop others from such cold nights."

"How?"

"We seek to know of some bad people. Criminals. And Mister Paradise and I have spoken to your son about this. He does you honor."

"My son," she said as if it was a prayer. "He has done what he has done for honor, he is no criminal."

"Indeed," I ventured. "I know this." My speaking caused the widow to lean further forward to look up at me. I stepped into the shaft of light for her to see me—no sense in protecting her from my reality.

166

"You have news?" There was no fear in her question, though her voice was weak, almost a whisper. "I was told that Jaime had given himself up to the authorities, and all was set; there was no hope."

"Always, there is hope," Vandoma said. "Your son is strong with much love for his father and the honor of the family."

"Honor," the old woman said with a dark meaning. "The Yagyu Clan of my husband is old and honorable and very faithful to The Emperor. His brother Asano is even more so."

"So how is it that your husband could not do the bidding of the agent of The Emperor?" I asked, not able to keep silent any longer. When I saw her reaction to my question, I knew I had guessed correctly.

"The man who came, the one whose face always winked, he would have Jiro help him and others to do some terrible thing—"

"You do not know what that was?"

"No," the daughter spoke up. "My father would not speak of it in any detail. But it had to do with father's position at the Navy Yard, of that I am certain."

"Was it so odious a task that your husband could not just say no?" I said, "That he felt compelled to take his own life?"

"He would not tell me." The widow Yagyu said, "He felt that to reveal what they had come to him to do would be to betray The Emperor, yet he could not do what they asked for. He had come to love this country."

"My father was a man of tradition, but he was also a man who looked to the future. A man caught between." She moved to stand by her mother, putting her hand on the older Yagyu's shoulder.

As the young girl spoke, I saw the amber shapes that swirled around her mother become more active, but I also witnessed something I had not ever seen before. A silver amorphous shape now hovered over Vandoma, joining the golden shapes I had often seen swirl around her—the essence of her ancestors or those whom her healing or seeing had helped. This translucent silver shape moved to settle around the Romani woman, so to my eyes, she appeared to glow.

"These men who asked this thing of your husband," Vandoma said. "They are *marmie*, unclean, and things of the darkness. Your husband knew this, I am sure."

167

"Yes," the widow whispered. "Yet for the honor of the family, he could not reveal it while he lived…"

"I ask you then, to allow me to speak to him in the beyond so he may make right this thing."

"Speak to him?" The elder Yagyu rose now and walked on shaky legs to stand before the Romani. They were eye to eye in height, both petite in stature, yet there was a palpable sense of power that emanated from both of them, and the gold and silver of the shapes that swirled around the two spoke to me of the immense innate power the women had.

"Yes," Vandoma said. "I would look across the gulf to the other side of life and ask what was this thing that they asked of him."

I was as stunned by her statement as I am sure the Yagyu women were. I knew that Vandoma was *drukker*—a seer of things beyond. It was not a *booja*, a trick or show for the benefit of profit, but a deeper, very real ability to reach across the veil that separates the living and what comes next.

I knew now that the survival of personality—intellect—after physical death was a fact. But here she was suggesting actively seeking to talk with the dead. A séance.

Such a thing had never occurred to me to participate in. Yet, now I saw that if I were going to find out what *Daitengu* intended, the only way might be to communicate directly with Jiro Yagyu who had crossed over.

The widow spoke haltingly. "I would speak once more with my Jiro, but what you ask…the *kami* demand payment. Such things have cost."

"There are ways to pay. And I have been charged by the *Kali Sarah* to do this thing. Let us sit and speak to he who has gone on."

It was only after she had spoken that Vandoma looked up at me, her expression intense and serious but with a light in her eyes brighter than I had ever seen. I recognized that light as the power I had seen in Mother Kalderash's eyes just before she had died in my arms.

For the first time since I had known her, I realized the extraordinary nature of this hunchbacked woman who stood before me and my incredible luck to be by her side in my journey to find my destiny.

"We should do this, yes?" she asked me with a hesitancy in her voice.

I felt a surge of pride that this woman, who was wiser than I in these matters, would seek my unneeded permission.

"You are the *drukker*, Vandoma Kalderash," I said. "I will accept your will and wisdom in these things. It is a journey I will follow you on. *Latche drom.*"

Her expression stayed somber, but there was the light of joy in her eyes.

"Yes, Mister Paradise, we will make a good journey."

Then she turned back to the widow and said, "We begin!"

CHAPTER TWENTY-SIX

At Vandoma's direction, the curtains on the bay window were drawn, and chairs were pulled into a group around a small table in the center of the room. The widow Yagyu sat quietly at the table while her daughter, looking a bit confused by the whole proceedings, settled beside her.

"Mama, this is not going to help Jamie," the girl whispered before lapsing into Japanese, but the elder woman waved her off.

"*Shizuka ni kudasai*," the widow said, stopping the girl from speaking further. "This is a thing I must do, daughter. Your father sought to protect me by not telling what they wanted from him, but Jamie needs us now. And knowledge of this may help."

"I believe this is so, Madam Yagyu," I dared to say. "I know your son did what he did out of love, and if we can find and stop these evil men, we may be able to find a way to help him."

Vandoma lit a candle in the center of the table.

"We must calm ourselves," she said. "And open our minds and hearts to the power of *Kali Sarah* and the spirits of the loved ones." She placed her hands on the table and instructed the four of us to grasp the hand of the one on either side of us. "We must touch flesh to flesh to call to beyond," she added and looked down at my gloved hands.

I took her message and removed the gloves, hoping in the dim light that the two Japanese women would not notice my hands did not match in skin color or texture.

I looked down to see my own left hand, knuckles healed already from my adventure on Sunday, with my grotesque cast making it seem even larger as I enveloped Vandoma's smaller hand. The contrast was stark. And it made me once more reflect on the greater difference.

Not just a difference of race or magnitude but of species. She was a woman born naturally of a human woman, raised in a rich culture, learning to care with a family and deep spiritual beliefs.

I was born an abomination and a crime against nature, unloved and full of anger that turned to hate. I did horrible things and stole the precious gift that is life from undeserving innocents. I was a challenge to established norms, a theosophical argument made flesh.

"I think therefore I am," was Descarte's dictum, yet was it enough to simply be self-aware? There must be more purpose than consuming and surviving, at least by any being who claimed to be more than an animal. The gift—or curse—of my awareness, of my very being put on me the burden of purpose, of justifying my existence.

My return to humanity had been in an attempt to not only find my place among them but to find a way to expiate my own realized faults.

Now, to that end, I sat with the Romani woman to my left, joined in purpose to communicate with one whose life had ended. The concept of reaching across the veil from life to afterward was radical, yet if we were to help those still living and find out what the Japanese demon planned, it would be worth it.

"Focus your minds and open your hearts," Vandoma said in a quiet, reassuring voice. "In this place of peace, this sacred place of your home, wrapped in the love of family, we can reach far and with hope."

"Jiro," Madam Yagyu whispered, "talk to us."

"Mama, this is silly—"

"Quiet, Miko," the elder said, "this is right. The *kami* will understand that we must know what Papa knew."

"Be at peace," Vandoma said to the teen, whose hand she was holding to her left. "We will not violate the borders of life and death but reach across with love. Such spirits recognize intent."

She began a low rhythmic chant in Roma, the volume so low I could only make out a few words—*Kali Sarah*, fear, love and family—before the words blended together to a steady drone.

171

As she chanted, the shapes that hovered around her and Madam Yagyu became agitated, brightening to near-blinding levels and forming a tornado-like swirling mass around us. It was an eerie silent cone of light that I was aware that only I could see, though I had the sense that the three women felt that the atmosphere in the room had changed.

The widow who held my hand on my right squeezed tighter, and I heard her gasp. A vaporous shape grew out of the dancing flame of the candle. At first, an indistinct shape that was little more than a curl of smoke, the image coalesced from the flame to resolve itself into the face of an aged Asian. It was a pleasant face, though it bore a sad cast, with bushy eyebrows and a wide, expressive mouth.

"Jiro!" the widow said.

"Papa!"

"Speak, you who have passed over," Vandoma said. "We would know what it was that made you take your life."

"Akiko, my wife," the figure said. "Honor must be served."

"Why is this shade speaking in English? Would not he speak in the language of his soul, in Japanese?"

Vandoma looked to me, her eyes evidencing surprise but with no reprimand in them.

"*Nisenmono no otoko!*" the hovering face said. The features twisted into a hideous smile, the right eye blinking with a facial tick.

"Why would you say that, love?" the widow asked.

"What false man, Papa?"

I felt a chill up my spine when I heard the phrase. Daitengu had anticipated our move and somehow, from the Realm Between, taken the form of the dead man.

"What would you say to us, Daitengu, Why must you impose on the grief of this family?"

"My family is no business of yours, False Man," the vaporous face said. It wavered in the flickering flame, the visage now assuming an angry expression. "You have opposed my plans for the last time."

As he spoke, the swirling shapes around us had reached cyclonic speeds, and the brightness hurt my eyes. The sound of his voice rose to the point where I cringed from the intensity.

Suddenly, there was a burst of color and then blackness!

When my eyes opened, I found myself once more on the flat, level plane of the Realm Between, with the swirling shapes of a thousand, thousand souls, flashing across the sky above me.

I looked down at my hands before me to see no phantom shapes swirled around me. Once more, I was in that place where departed souls went. But to stay there or on their way to somewhere else, I could not say.

"False Man," the sharp voice came from behind, causing me to spin. "You task me."

There, a dozen feet from me, was the image of Jiro Yagyu, dressed in a bright, patterned kimono. His right cheek twitched, but otherwise, he stood unmoving, arms crossed before him.

"I would have it no other way." He made no move toward me, and I did not approach him. I soon grew used to the strangeness of not having my own phantoms surrounding me, and with my focus on the demon before me, I was able to ignore the banshee wails of the souls in the sky.

"You cannot interfere with what is destined, False Man," the demon in the form of Jiro Yagyu said. "Nippon will rule the world."

"It may well, but not from your hand, demon. This I have sworn and will see made so."

The features of the dead man darkened and assumed a fierce aspect. "Your challenge is the statement that proves your inferior status. Honor demands your destruction."

"Your honor is as false as the image of the man you occupy, *Daitengu*. Built on such crimes and cruelty, no empire can last."

The image of Jiro's face reddened with anger, and then he began to undergo a spasm, twisting and turning with an internal struggle. In moments, the figure of Jiro split physically with a red-faced, hawk-beaked being literally tearing itself out of the chest of the old Japanese.

As I stood aghast, the demon assumed its true form as a separate thing from the human being. In moments, the two stood side by side, complete and unconnected.

The shade of Jiro was confused, his eyes darting around in near panic, but the demon-made-solid stood proud and defiant, black wings spread.

The beaked being, dressed in a crimson kimono, his black wings flapping behind him, laughed at the expression I must have displayed.

I was truly stunned at witnessing this transformation. It waved its wings in what I assume was delight.

"You are weak, False Man, with no center upon which to draw strength. My Emperor is the wellspring of all and divine in inspiration."

"You justify crimes by recourse to religion like so many have," I countered. "All wars and the vilest of crimes have been justified by deep passions of spiritual beliefs."

This statement brought a laugh from the beaked beast. He advanced on me but halted several feet away, apparently unable or unwilling to lay hands on me directly. Even in this non-corporeal form, I felt the heat of the *Koshti Bok* on my chest and knew that was the reason he did not manhandle me.

"Why have I been called to this nether world where unclean spirits reside? This *Yomotsu-kuni* is a place of horror," the old man said. "My death was honorable."

This statement caused the demon to laugh again, and the old Japanese turned to it, his confusion having given way to anger.

"You, *goryou*," Jiro Yagyu's shade said, "You would twist family honor and cause suffering."

"You were weak and could not fulfill obligations of the blood," the demon said. "And aligned yourself with this False Man and his mongrel country in opposition to our sacred homeland."

"This country was good to me," Jiro's image said. "I could not betray it nor take a life as you ask. It is wrong."

"Wrong is determined by the winners. Weakness never wins."

"The great warrior said, 'The truth is not what you want it to be,'" I quoted. "It is what it is. And you must bend to its power or live with a lie."

The hawk-faced creature snarled at me, his wings flapping in agitation. "Just what mongrel races would say."

"It is your own champion, Musashi, I quote," I said. "And I add that kindness is not weakness; it takes more strength. You would pervert all the principles of that code of honor you purport to adhere to."

"You *magatsuhi-no-kami* would spoil our family honor to expiate your sins in life," Jiro said. "It is why I chose *seppuku*."

"You are a coward," *Daitengu* hissed.

"No, he is braver than you have ever been."

I addressed myself to the shade of Jiro. "Your son has been charged with your murder."

"How is that," the old man asked. "We did what we did at night, by the river."

"The river gave up its secret quickly," I said. "And the police know their business. He will not speak to the deed and will suffer for it. What is it this creature asked of you?"

"They would have had me help them cause death in the Navy Yard; we had word that there would be important guests this Sunday."

"You will not stop the plans of The Emperor!" The *Daitengu* lunged for the shade of Jiro and I sprang forward to physically block him.

The demon stopped a foot from me, repulsed by the power of the *Koshti Bok*. He staggered back with a serpentine hiss.

"False Man," he snarled as he hovered above the ground with his wings flapping. "I will crush you."

At that moment, I saw another figure walking slowly from the distance toward us. At first indistinct, the figure faded in from nothing to a solid form like a heat mirage. When it resolved itself into a full form, it was a familiar one, Mother Kalderash.

"Fear not from this *beng*, Adam Paradise." She moved to my side and looked up at me with wide, caring eyes. Then her body and face transformed, and she was Vandoma.

175

The Romani daughter's face was drawn in concern. "Return from this place, Mister Paradise. It is time for Mister Jiro to pass on to the land beyond."

She turned to the elderly Japanese. "Know you do your family honor, and we will help your son in any way we can. Be at peace."

Jiro Yagyu nodded, his face settling into a gentle smile, and as he did, he began to fade. "Tell Akiko I will wait for her and Miko that…" Then he was gone.

"Vandoma, I—" I began, and then all went black.

My head snapped up, and I was seated in the parlor of the Yagyu family. The three women were looking at me with startled expressions. I was confused.

"Vandoma, what?"

"You were called to the Realm Between," she said. "The forces reached through and pulled you to them, Mister Paradise."

"Yes, I…I saw your mother. For a moment."

The Romani nodded. "Yes. It was she who called to me to bring you back."

"You saw Papa?" Miko asked.

"Yes. And he spoke of both of you. He said he would wait for you, Madam Yagyu."

The elderly woman sobbed quietly. "Thank you, sir."

"Did you learn much in such a place?" Vandoma asked me.

"I don't know," I said honestly.

The younger Yagyu opened the curtains, and the room was filled with light once more.

"Jiro spoke some words," I said, "*magatsuhi-no-kami* and *goryou*, he called *Daitengu* both things."

There was a gasp from the elder Yagyu. She clapped her hands together several times, which I understood to be how she prayed.

"I know those words," Miko said, stepping to her mother's side. "*A magatsuhi-no-kami* is malevolent and destructive spirit who was a human. They are sometimes venerated as *kami* or ancestral figures."

"And the term *goryou*?"

"*Goryou* are vengeful spirits," Madam Yagyu said. "Those who died violently and without appropriate funerary rites."

"They inflict suffering on the living. Mama would threaten me with a *goryou* when I was bad as a toddler." Her mother grabbed her hand and kissed the back of it.

"Those spirits must be pacified," the older woman said. "Usually through holy rites but sometimes through enshrining them as a *kami*." As she spoke, she glanced toward the family shrine.

"And the name you said before," the daughter added, "that is a title, not a name; a leader of demons."

I looked to Vandoma, whose expression was intense. I could see she was focused beyond the room again, to something she saw at the edge of our physical reality. She, too, cast her eyes to the shrine in the alcove of the room.

"Jiro spoke of 'our family honor to expiate your sins in life,'" I commented. "And this *Daitengu* spoke of 'my family' and his blood." I rose on shaky legs and moved to look close up at the family shrine. "Do you know, madam, the names of each of these venerated ones?"

"Yes," she said.

"Then, I think I need to learn them all from you."

CHAPTER TWENTY-SEVEN

We assured the Yagyu women that if there was anything to be done for Jaime, we would do it, then took our leave of them.

Vandoma and I were still somewhat stunned by our experience after the séance and stood in silence on the street until I was able to hail a taxicab to return to Manhattan. It was a long ride through heavier-than-usual afternoon traffic.

As we passed over the span of the Manhattan Bridge, I was once more struck by the material accomplishments of mankind and how their morals and philosophy lagged so far behind the technical development of the species. They could cooperate to build such massive structures to create the stone canyons of Manhattan itself, yet they created artificial and arbitrary divisions of skin color, culture, and ideology.

National boundaries were manufactured differences that magnified the tribalism of the species and fed the hatred of "the other" for the power of a few individuals at the top of the national structures. The Nazis and the Japanese racists fueled their hatred with this concept, and while they were the most extreme examples of that othering, everyday people harbored such feelings deep in their beings. "They are from another block." "They wear their hair differently." "They eat different food."

I saw it every day. I constantly found those differences fascinating, but I was a creature outside, so I was no bellwether to judge by.

I looked to the petite woman who sat beside me in the cab. She was an example of what humanity could be—herself born to disadvantage with her physical deformity and her racial group persecuted and derided, yet she was open and accepting. She had accepted the others she had encountered with Dottie, the Yagyu women, and their religion, even Enzo and his ilk and me. She saw the world from a distance, as it were, with a larger perception of the reality that we were in. Perhaps that was what true spiritual certainty brought: wisdom and acceptance, an awareness of the transitory nature of so much, and recognition of what really mattered.

And the society she lived in, this place called America, allowed that to occur, if not encouraged it. For that reason alone, I felt I owed it my allegiance and best effort to preserve it.

"We are here, Mister Paradise." She broke through my reverie. I had become so absorbed in my musings that I had not noticed we pulled up before the building that housed my office.

I paid the taxi driver.

"I will pick us up some lunch," I said to her as we exited. "You head up to the office."

"Yes, this is good, I am more hungry than I thought."

"Tea?"

"Yes, please."

She went up while I went into the drugstore that occupied the ground floor of the building. I purchased some sandwiches at the lunch counter and got two hot teas to go. It was still a bit strange with Sydney, the new proprietor, waving to me, thinking me just another tenant.

I had purchased the building through a dummy corporation after the previous owner died. He was a man who I had believed to be my friend and who betrayed me. I had thought long and hard about having given him my trust and not seeing the signs of his betrayal. I could have closed myself off to new relationships and friendships but concluded that would be self-destructive and poison my view of the world.

Still, I had to be cautious with my history and my background, for perhaps justifiably, I would be feared and reviled for what and who I was. Only Vandoma, her brother, and her late mother knew my true story.

179

I was surprised to hear Vandoma already typing as I ascended the stairs, and more so when I opened the door to find her brother Nico sitting in a chair across from her desk. It was clear that the locked door had not been an impediment to him; he had a wide and unusual skill set.

"Good afternoon, Nico."

He rose to acknowledge me as I set the lunch down on his sister's desk. "I'm sorry. I did not know you were here or would have brought food."

"Thank you, Adam Paradise, but I have eaten already. I came early because I had news."

"About?"

"The men who would ask for money," he said. "I have spoken to two of my tribe who have heard rumors."

"Rumors?"

"Yes. They say that something is supposed to happen this Sunday."

"Do you know what?"

"They did not say," Nico said. "But there is the sense that there will be much disruption. Those who whispered of it said that it would be a time for many crimes to happen."

I digested this information. It certainly seemed that the death of Jiro Yagyu and his connection to the Navy Yard had something to do with *Daitengu*'s plans.

"Thank you, Nico, this confirms some things we have been learning."

Vandoma's fingers were flying on the type keys while we spoke but stopped to add, "I can finish this story of *The Void* and deliver it today on the way home."

"Well, have your tea, at least, while it is still hot."

"I will do so." She took the cup. "You should eat as well."

"Yes, little mother. If you will excuse me, Nico, I will go into my office and dine."

I closed the door to my inner office, sat, and enjoyed my food and tea while I filled my journal with the recent events. It was a process that allowed me to examine my actions, somewhat from a distance, to gain perspective. I also read more from the Japanese cultural book to confirm my suspicions from the events at the séance.

This absorbed me for some time, and before I realized it, there was a knock on the door.

"Come in."

"I am done this story," Vandoma said. "I would bring it to the publisher."

"Good. You might as well go home afterward. I will not be long here. I guess I'll go home myself tonight."

"You will take care?"

I laughed. "Yes, little mother. You do the same. Nico, you keep an eye on her."

"Always, Adam Paradise," he said, flashing a wide smile. "Kalderash protects Kalderash."

"As it should be. Thank you."

The two left, locking the outer door behind them, and I was alone, with only the sound of the city filtering into the office.

I had spent most of my existence alone, much of it lonely and longing for connection as much as purpose. Now, in that office with the Romani siblings' steps fading away, I no longer felt that. The thought made me smile.

I finished my notes, returned my journal to the hidden safe, and pondered my next move.

It seemed clear that the Japanese demon planned some sort of event for the coming weekend, perhaps as the climax of the campaign it had been waging against the United States. But not knowing what, even if I knew where—possibly—what could I do with that information? Who could I tell?

I went to the telephone on Vandoma's desk. I was not fond of the instrument, but the Romani had convinced me it was useful. My fingers, even with my gloves off, were too large to work the holes easily, so I used a pencil to dial my friend Tommy Shane.

"Hi, Tommy," I said when he picked up, "how are you doing?"

"Going a bit crazy sitting around doing nothing," he said.

"Much pain?"

"Not really, just sore. It's good to hear from you. What's the news?"

My arm beneath my cast was itching, so I worked a pencil under it to scratch. "I think that the extortion ring we feared has taken a darker turn." I went on to explain that I suspected something might happen on Sunday at the Navy Yard, though not the details of how I found out or any mention of *Daitengu*.

"Damn, Adam," he said. "That was supposed to be a close secret, that the king and queen were coming to christen a new cargo ship."

"Not so close a secret, Tommy. I heard rumor of it from a cab driver."

He cursed again. "This is serious. If anything happens to them, the repercussions will be a disaster."

"That may be the reason. Any sort of incident could be terrible publicity. All the more if it could be made to appear that it was somehow related to the situation in China."

"Can you find out anything more on this, Adam?"

"I will continue to probe, but you should inform whoever is in charge of the security for the royal visit to be extra vigilant."

"I'll do that as soon as we get off the phone."

"Good. I will be heading home to get a good night's sleep, but will call you in the morning."

"Watch your back, buddy; these people are monsters. They'll stop at nothing."

"Yes, monsters," I said, aware of the irony. "I'll be careful. Night"

I went back into my office, turned off the light, and started to leave just as the phone rang.

"Paradise Investigations," I answered, doing my best to imitate Vandoma's phone manner.

"Adam, I'm glad I got you." It was Hank. "The plan is to meet at the Jade Dragons' headquarters tomorrow night at eight. Can you make it?"

"Of course," I answered. "Do you want me to meet you before?"

"No," she said. "It is better if I go in first; I don't want to appear to be storming the place, you know?"

"I'm that scary?"

She laughed. "You can be, big guy, but the whole reason for this is to de-escalate the situation."

"Yes. But let me tell you what may come to bear on the situation." I told her my suspicions about Sunday.

"I heard that the ship being christened was owned by an Anglo-Chinese company," she said. "So just that fact alone would make the public backlash against my fundraising horrible."

"My suspicion as well."

"Okay, Adam, I have things to do to get ready for tomorrow night. I'll see you then."

"Good night."

As I set the receiver down, I felt as if all the events of the previous week were coming to a head.

I donned my leather trench coat, exited the office, and locked the door. Afterward, feeling not only hungry for food but for a clarity of purpose, I went to a small Japanese restaurant I had heard of in the East Village.

I had read of a delicacy called chicken teriyaki and was determined to try it. It seemed a good time to broaden my culinary tastes and to remind myself that it was not the culture nor people of Japan that I opposed, but the militant structure of its government—and the very specific demon who called himself *Daitengu*.

The eatery was small, a mere hole-in-the-wall, run by a husband who cooked and wife who served. The food was good, and the woman could not help giggling at my size and enthusiasm as I ate.

I left after the meal with my hunger satisfied and my sense that the tribalism of humanity was indeed pointless.

I walked home, conscious that somewhere out in the night was an enemy whose resources were limitless and whose methods were ruthless.

Fortunately, my journey was uneventful, and I soon found myself settling into my bed for a long and untroubled sleep.

CHAPTER TWENTY-EIGHT

I woke Friday with a renewed sense of purpose. It was an overcast, cold day, so wearing my trench coat did not make me stand out more than my usual appearance. I made my regular stop at the drugstore below my office and got the papers, plus tea and breakfast for Vandoma and me.

Her type keys were singing as I ascended the stairs, and the sound gave me a comforting sense of normalcy.

"*Jo reggelt*, Vandoma."

"*Jo reggelt*, Mister Paradise." She paused in her typing to smile up at me. "They had another story for me yesterday, so I came in early to begin, they wish it today."

"Then it is lucky I brought breakfast for us both." I set the teas and sandwiches down on her desk and took a chair across from her. The last week had been an exceptional one, so to just sit calmly with her was a welcome relief from the pressures of our adventures.

"How is your arm?" she asked, sipping her tea.

"It itches, so I know it is healing well enough."

"What have you decided to do about the *beng*, Mister Paradise?"

"All I can do is be alert, little mother. I have a thought but must do more research. I will go to Digger today to look up some things."

"This is good. Knowledge is the most powerful weapon." She took a bite of the sandwich and looked pensive. After a time, she said, "You will be careful, yes?"

"I will be. I like the way things are around here, so I won't jeopardize it." I spoke at first meaning to placate her, but then I realized I meant it. Here, sitting and breaking bread with her, I felt not only calm and comfortable but accepted—as I did playing chess with Tommy or chatting with Digger or Leroy. Accepted, for once, not an outsider. It settled over me as a strange, almost alien feeling. It made me smile, then laugh.

"You find funny that I say this?" Her voice sounded hurt.

"No, far from it, Vandoma. No, I was reflecting how very good this is, this moment."

She beamed. "Yes, it is good to eat with friend."

We finished our meals in companionable silence, and then I went into my office to read the morning papers while I planned my day.

There was no news in the papers of George VI and Queen Elizabeth coming down from Canada, but Tommy implied it was a close secret, so that was no surprise. Elsewhere in the world, Moxie Donovan had a column on the riots in Jerusalem as Jews protested the British White Paper on Palestine, setting immigration quotas that would limit them to one-third of the region's total population. The reporter prophesized that the region would be a powder keg in the near future, especially with the Jewish persecutions going on in Germany.

Not a lot of positive images of the human race in general in the tabloid pages, but then I thought back to my breakfast and felt better about it all.

After a time, I thought it would be late enough for Digger to be in his shop, so I gathered myself to head over.

"Lock the door after me. I hope Nico will be back soon?"

"Yes, Mister Paradise, he will be back by afternoon."

"Good. If you finish that manuscript before the end of the day, you might as well take it to the publisher and head home."

"You will be back?"

"At some point, but I have a couple of errands to run, so I might not see you before you go home."

"Tomorrow?"

185

"I think you might as well take tomorrow off," I said. Her expression darkened, so I added, "After all, we're both working Sunday, right? At the Navy Yard."

"Yes," she said. "You will call me to tell time?"

"As soon as I hear from Tommy when the event is, yes. I hope to talk to him tomorrow. Tonight, I have the meeting with the tongs."

"The Chinese lady?"

"Yes."

"There will be trouble?"

"I don't think so," I said. "Miss Lee has considerable influence and the point of logic on her side, but…"

"Always careful, yes?"

"Yes."

I waved goodbye and headed out to walk over to the Tome Tomb.

"I charge there to return, and change thy shape; thou art too ugly to attend on me. Go, and return an old Franciscan friar; The holy shapes becomes a devil best." Digger grinned at me from behind his counter like a church gargoyle waterspout, hunched forward. The effect was blunted when his glasses slipped down his nose, and he had to adjust them.

I laughed, thinking how apropos the quote. "Marlowe's Faust, at the first meeting."

"Darn, I can't get you," he said.

"Try this," I replied. "If we say that we have no sin, we deceive ourselves, and there's no truth in us."

He looked perplexed for a moment, then laughed. "Almost got me; it's a trick question. It's also from *Doctor Faustus*!"

"Got me."

"How can I help you, Adam?"

"I wondered if you had anything more specific on the *tengu* of Japan. And anything on the samurai family, Yagyu?"

His expression became intense, his eyes rolling up in his head, and I could almost see him reading the index of his mind. After a few moments, he said, "Back in the alcove, two shelves up from the bottom. There should be two books there, one a list of the major families."

I had to maneuver to fit my bulk into the narrow space without collapsing stacks of books but managed to find the books exactly where he said they were. The book on Japanese spirituality was thin, but the one that was essentially the Japanese list of major families was quite substantial.

"You never fail," I said as I stood back up and dusted off my trouser knees.

Digger noticed my cast for the first time. "What happened?"

"Just clumsy. Nothing catastrophic."

"Big feet, eh?"

"Or else I would fall forward." I paid him for the books and bid him a goodbye.

The weather was good enough that I went to a park on Twenty-Third Street off Fifth Avenue to sit and read the new acquisitions.

This reading took me till almost dusk when I decided I deserved a good meal before heading down to Chinatown to the tong meeting. And since I was only ten blocks from the little Japanese restaurant I'd eaten at the night before, I stopped there. I had really enjoyed the chicken teriyaki.

The same kimono-clad waitress came to my table, and I ordered my teriyaki. I also ordered the warm saki again, which I quite enjoyed with my meal.

Even the fortune cookie was benevolent: "*You are about to have an eventful meeting.*"

"Prophetic," I said aloud.

I paid my bill with a smile and left the restaurant to walk to a phone booth at the corner drugstore. I called Tommy for an update on the Navy Yard.

"I'm glad you called, Adam," he said, his words breathless with excitement. "I tried your office—"

"I've been out most of the day. What's the news?"

"You were right that this thing with the tongs might be connected to the Navy Yard. The ship being launched is the *Empress of China*, Chinese registry, but it is an Anglo-Chinese company, so the king and queen are making a side trip—unannounced officially—to meet the Chinese ambassador and christen it."

"That would have an enormous effect on public opinion if something threatens those monarchs on American soil."

"Exactly, though how they think that would be positive..."

"I imagine if violence occurs, it would make the isolationist's argument to stay out of the conflict stronger."

"Possibly. It would certainly make us look weak for not being able to protect a foreign leader on our soil." He was quiet for a moment, then added, "I took the liberty of telling the Secret Service agent in charge of security, Rex Bennet, where my tip came from. I hope you don't mind."

"Not at all. I will report to him when I get there Sunday. What time is the event?"

"The christening is scheduled for two."

"I will be there early and speak to him. And I'll talk to you tomorrow to see if there are any updates. I'm going with Miss Lee to talk to the tongs tonight to attempt to take them out of the equation."

"Be—"

"I know, Tommy, be careful."

"I will. Give my best to Mary."

I walked away from the call with a new sense of urgency. It was even more important to remove the menace of a tong war from the mix while I tried to find a way to fight the Japanese demon.

At Twenty-Third Street, I boarded a train for downtown. I seldom rode the underground rail as I felt particularly cramped, especially in the cars with fans in the ceilings.

The train was not crowded, so I easily found a seat on the wicker bench at the end. I rode without incident to Canal Street and then walked the few blocks to my destination on Lispenard Street. It was off Broadway at the edge of Chinatown.

The summit with the tongs had been arranged for the evening at the headquarters of the Jade Dragon Benevolent Society, a former bank that had gone out of business in the crash.

When I arrived at the converted bank, there were a number of young Chinese men standing in front of the building, doing their best to both look tough and nonchalant at the same time. I noted that there seemed to be three separate groups of them, as the suspicious looks of each cluster of men indicated to me that all was not rosy in the tong world.

When I made to move toward the front door of the building, a well-dressed middle-aged Chinese man stepped in front of me.

"Sorry, no tourists," he said politely in unaccented English.

"Understandable," I said in Cantonese, "but I am not a tourist. I am with Miss Han Ku Lee. We were invited."

He registered surprise but recovered quickly. "Come."

He gestured and then proceeded me through the double door into the foyer of the building. There were two guards inside the foyer to whom my guide spoke quickly in Chinese, and then I was ushered into the main room of the former bank. A number of chairs had been arraigned in a wide semi-circle in the center of the marble floor.

There were half a dozen elderly Chinese gentlemen seated in the chairs with their backs to me and a younger, fit Chinese standing behind each of them, obvious bodyguards.

Hank stood in the apex of the semi-circle, looking relaxed and defiant at the same time. Next to her stood a muscular Chinese in his twenties whom I assumed from her description was Leo Chung, leader of the Jade Dragon Benevolent Society, who had arranged the summit.

When I entered the high-ceilinged main room, all eyes turned toward me. Hank said something to Chung, and then she motioned for me to come forward.

I removed my hat and walked through the circle of chairs to stand beside Hank.

"Apologies for my tardiness. It was unavoidable with the trains."

"You do like 'em big, don't you, sister," Chung said, referring to her regular guy, Chadeaux. The tong leader was dressed in flashy teal suit in the latest style, an expensive red silk shirt, yellow tie and had a pencil mustache over full lips. It was clear that, though dressed like a dandy, he was a very physical man. His stance told me he was a fighter.

"Honorable fathers," Hank said, "This is the one I spoke of, Adam Paradise."

I stepped into the center of the chairs feeling much like a gladiator in an ancient Roman colosseum might have.

CHAPTER TWENTY-NINE

All those seated in the chairs were leaders important in their communities and clearly knew it. Most of the men were dressed in traditional Chinese attire, but two wore expensive but conservative Western suits.

"So chicky here says you got something to say, high pockets," Leo Chung said. He had assumed a cocky contrapposto position in an attempt to appear casual, but I could detect a tightness in his jaw that told me he felt himself as much on display as Hank and I were. This was possibly his moment to impress the council of the tong leaders.

I nodded to his introduction and turned to Hank.

"I've told them what we've guessed so far," she said to me, "but—"

"I know," I said quietly. "You are a woman, so they don't take you seriously." Her tight lips and quick head nod told me my surmise was correct.

"Gentle uncles," I said, addressing the summit in Cantonese first, then switching to English as my grasp of their language was not so extensive. "Miss Lee has informed you that there is a clear plot afoot to pit you against each other—and to discredit her efforts to help the people of Manchuria and China. And thus aide the Japanese cause."

"She has given us no proof of this," a bearded man in a traditional gown said. "The Hip Sing tong must have proof."

"The honorable Lo Ping knows we cannot provide that," Hank said. "Because the men who did the attack at the Florence are either dead or escaped."

"And the men who killed people at Washington Square Park and the library," I added, "also died. They took their own lives in a traditional shinobi way. So, there is no proof we can offer."

"Then how is it for us to make decisions based on will-o-the-wisp suspicions?" A second tong leader, a clean-shaven older Chinese in a suit, said. "On Leong tong deals with facts."

"These criminals are clever chameleons," I said. "They have taken the names of your tongs—and the Jade Dragons—and used them to cover their crimes and cast suspicion on you."

I fixed my eyes on the tong leader, Lo Ping, and his wizened face twisted into an impish grin. He returned my gaze with a stealthy stare, yet he kept the right side of his face turned away from me.

"You have no proof then," Lo Ping said. "So, you would have us believe in this mystery man when it might well be this upstart Jade Dragon who creates this story to gain our trust?"

"I have done no such thing, Uncle Lo," Leo Chung insisted. "We come before you with truth. The Jade Dragons have been blamed for what these criminals have done as well."

"You bring us this woman and this big *gweilo* and expect us to stake the future of our tongs on stories?"

"These are not stories," Hank insisted. "There is a concerted attempt to destroy my Manchurian relief efforts. This will help the Japanese."

"You are a hysterical woman." Lo Ping gave a snort of laughter. "You prove your words are not wise." That infuriated the Chinese woman, who stamped her foot.

"I will not be dismissed like this by a fool who will not listen to reality," she moved toward the old man with balled fists. I put a hand on Hank's shoulder to stop her.

The bodyguards behind Lo Ping stepped forward, but Lo Ping put a hand up to stop them. "You would prove you cannot be trusted."

I found myself stunned by their refusal to understand the situation. I knew that humans had an amazing capacity to deny even obvious realities based on their own biases. Still, with the multiple reports of these tong-based robberies and the attack at the park, this seemed absurd.

I studied the seated elders with new eyes. Wu Fang of the Hip Sing had a sour expression and adjusted his glasses even though they didn't need it. He gave a sidelong glance to the complaining Lo Ping, who returned the look with a shake of his head.

Lo Ping had a satisfied expression on his thin face. When he saw me studying him with new eyes, his grin widened, and I realized something I had not noted before.

Shades that floated over most of the elders told me that they had been responsible for or connected to numerous deaths. The thugs who stood behind the leaders all had at least one shade of a departed soul hovering over them that told me they had all killed.

Except for Lo Ping. The bearded man had a curious lack of swirling forms over him. Neither the ancestral shades, whose translucent forms seemed to reflect blood ties and hovered over almost all humans, nor the dark shades of those that had died violently and were connected to their killers.

The space above the tong leader was singularly devoid of any shapes. The swirling blobs of color were everywhere else in the room. But no shapes moved over Lo Ping. None.

"You are wasting the time of all of us," Lo Ping said. "And it is offending the dignity of our tong to bring such absurd claims..."

"Absurd!" Hank exploded, and I had to pull her back from charging at the old man. "People have died, and all this is stopping funds going to China..."

"We are concerned with here," Lo Ping said. "Your—"

"Wait," I said, stepping in front of Hank so swiftly that the bodyguards of the tong leaders reached into their jackets to produce knives. I remembered Vandoma's warning to me on Sunday afternoon to beware of the *szelhamos ordog*, the impostor devil.

"Adam, no!" Hank tried to push past me, but I stopped her.

"No, Hank." I raised my voice but stood still, hands held up to stop the guards.

"Listen, all of you." I looked directly at Lo Ping. "This is not your leader."

Leo Chung snorted behind me, and Hank gasped.

"I know what you are," I said. I saw the image of Lo Ping give a feral smile, the twitch of the right side of his face now clear.

"Your *gweilo* desperation will not dictate to this council," Lo Ping said. "Throw this interloper out of here."

The bodyguards moved toward me, brandishing their knives.

"Adam, no!" Hank yelled again.

The first of the guards got to within arm's length of me, and I took the most expedient means to dispatch him—I slapped him in the side of the head with my open hand, hard. He flew into a second man, and they both tumbled to the ground.

"Stop it!" Hank cried and tried to grab me, but I shook her off as a third guard lunged at me on my left. I dodged the thrust and stiff-armed the Chinese with my injured arm, hard enough to knock him off his feet.

The other elders had jumped from their chairs to escape the violence, but Lo Ping sat unmoving with the same feral grin.

I moved straight for him.

For the first time, I saw fear on the old man's face as he tried to back away from me but slammed into a wall.

When I reached the old man's form, I wrapped my arms around him.

"I know your name, one-eye," I whispered.

The form of Lo Ping screamed, a high-pitched wail that started out as one of an old man's terror but morphed into a squawk that was more animal than human.

The other around me froze at the bizarre cry, more so when the figure before me began to change. The old man squirmed and wriggled but then the winged figure of the demon rose from him as the power of the *Koshti Bok* repelled him from the physical form of the old Chinese.

Those around me all gasped at the fantastical sight they witnessed.

The demon flew above the room, hovering in the cathedral-like space, its red face an emblem of rage, its black eyes mirrors of terror. "I will destroy you, False Man," it proclaimed. "And all you care for!"

Then, the creature flew straight up and vanished before it reached the ceiling.

There was deadly silence from everyone for several moments until Leo Chung exclaimed, "Well, butter my buns, now I've seen it all."

Suddenly, everyone began to talk at once, using a mix of English and Cantonese.

I addressed myself directly to Lo Ping.

"I apologize, Uncle, for laying hands on you, but—"

"No," he said. "I felt that...that *devil*...in me, was aware of what it did but could do nothing."

"What did we just see, Adam?" Hank's good, green eye widened with disbelief.

"Yes," Chung said. "What the hell just happened?"

Here was a new problem. How did I explain the demon I had just chased away without revealing my own strange history?

Everyone in the room looked at me for an answer, but it was Lo Ping who saved me.

"It was a Japanese demon who imposed itself on me," the old Asian said. "A creature of evil who wants to destroy our homeland across the ocean and here, in America."

He went on to tell how he was readying himself to leave home to come to the conclave, and the spirit had come upon him, robbing him of the control of his body. It said it was like he had been trapped in a car racing toward a cliff that he had no control over—he was aware of what was happening but could do nothing to stop it.

"I do not know how this man knew," Lo Ping concluded, "but I am grateful."

"It was this, a Romani talisman," I said, opening my shirt to show the *Koshti Bok*. "I took to wearing it when I first encountered that monster."

Hank looked at me with an odd expression. "You are a ball of surprises, big guy. What else you got under your hat?"

I only replied with a wry grin.

"I say we swear here to work with all our Chinese brothers," Leo Chung said, taking the focus of the gathering. "It is clear to me that we must work as one to protect our tongs and, maybe even, our homeland."

All the other tong heads, though firmly in the twentieth century, were connected to the superstitions of their past—so they accepted the evidence of their eyes that they had indeed seen a demon.

Everyone celebrated a new dedication to unity with wine, and they all agreed to meet again to plan ways to work together afterward.

They thanked me again for revealing *Daitengu* and even apologized to Hank for their suspicion of her. I found this later the most amazing development of the entire experience. It gave me hope.

As we were leaving, Hank pulled me aside. "All right, big guy," she said before she climbed into her roadster to head back to Harlem. "Tell me how you did it."

"What do you mean?"

"Oh, come on, I don't believe any of that hogwash about ghosts and stuff. Look, you can't fool me. What was the trick? Anton was a stage magician."

Her boyfriend had been a stage performer before his career as a troubleshooter, so she was sure I had used illusion to create the spectacle she had witnessed. This woman of the rational world would not believe the superstitions of her homeland, even though she certainly had more than enough reason to, but there was no way I could fully explain it to her.

I just nodded.

"All right." She saw my reluctance to comment on the phenomena she had witnessed but misinterpreted it for my benefit. "He'll never tell me how he does his magic tricks either," she said. "That magician's code. Doesn't matter, though, it was brilliant. They're all working together now. You're smart, big guy."

My silence seemed to confirm her hypothesis that it was all planned, and I let her believe the fiction. "What's next for you?" she asked.

"I have something to do on Sunday that may tangentially concern this at the Navy Yard."

"That's funny because, on Sunday, I'm meeting with the Chinese ambassador at the Brooklyn Navy Yard for a boat launch." I imagine it was with relief that the summit had worked out so well. "It really is a small world. I would hope that the Chinese ambassador will be well protected, though, and so it will be a pleasure. I guess I'll see you Sunday. Thanks again a lot. Adam."

"Well, stay alert, Hank; I really have a feeling we are not out of the woods yet."

She flashed me a dismissive smile and then drove off.

If she didn't believe this. she certainly wasn't going to believe anything that might occur Sunday.

CHAPTER THIRTY

I decided to walk uptown to my apartment, enjoying the crispness in the air and the activity of the city's nightlife. I felt like I was washing myself in the normalcy of it, the lives lived as they had been for millennia. Couples on dates, people rushing to or from a show, or on their way home from a hard day at work.

All these people living their lives with no thought that a demon from across the sea was attempting to destroy their whole way of life. And none of them were aware that I, a creature from the abyss, was walking among them who hoped to thwart that demon.

The stroll helped me clear my thoughts about the events I had just witnessed and helped me form a plan for the confrontation I was sure would happen on Sunday. I was certain *Daitengu* would try once more to spread chaos at the Navy Yard; he would not be able to resist the challenge of facing me once more and flaunting his deeply felt superiority to me. Another demonstration of his culture's triumph over the decadent West.

I also knew now that the demon did feel challenged by me, his boasting a hollow attempt to show strength, but it revealed that he feared me, and I was homing in on his secret, his weakness.

I was at my apartment before I realized it.

My ascent up the stairs was cautious as I had the sense that the demon would take no chances with me and might already be sending minions to assault me. My fear was unfounded, as the guardian hair was still on the doorjamb.

In the sanctum of my room, I relaxed, though still slipped a chair under the doorknob for insurance.

Once I disrobed, I washed and, though tired, settled down to read. I chose Sun Tzu and his *The Art of War*. "Know the enemy and you know yourself; in a hundred battles you will never be in peril. When you are ignorant of the enemy but know yourself, your chances of winning or losing are equal. If ignorant of your enemy and of yourself, you are certain in every battle to be in peril."

This passage resonated with me particularly as it seemed my confrontation with *Daitengu* had devolved into a journey into the mirror, facing my own weaknesses and discovering my own strengths.

"But either way, peril awaits on Sunday," I said aloud as I closed the book. I went to bed with the thought of peril echoing in my mind, peril to those I cared for and the society I was integrating into. And a very real fear that I was not up to the battle; even though I had some plan for my way to oppose the demon, the stakes were almost overwhelming.

For the first time in as long as I could remember, I felt fear. Not for myself, for I had no expectation of survival for me, not like a naturally born being—but for those whose lives I had now made myself responsible for.

Sleep came with difficulty, but it eventually did, and I rested.

I decided to give myself a quiet day on Saturday. I rose, dressed, went out for breakfast at a nearby diner, and then called Tommy for any updates on the event Sunday. There were none, so I picked up the papers and returned home for a leisurely day.

Once more, the news was not encouraging but also not surprising. Europe continued to move toward some sort of confrontation, with the German chancellor pushing hard against his neighbors.

No news at all about the English monarchs or their plans, so it did seem the visit was officially a secret, but clearly not much of one.

I spent the day alternately reading and painting, took myself out to dinner, and made a phone call to the Yagyu family to ask a question and make an appointment to stop by them the next day before the trip to the Navy Yard.

"Tomorrow at one in the afternoon," I told Vandoma when I called her after speaking to the Yagyu women. "I will meet you at the Cumberland Street gate."

Her voice was strangely reserved. "There is much darkness in the cards as I have read."

"The cards? Tarot cards?"

"Yes. I have seen death tomorrow, darkness, Mister Paradise."

She sounded more frightened than I had ever heard her.

"Don't fear, Vandoma. You know we are in the right, the *beng* is a vile thing."

"Yet evil is strong. You will continue to wear the *Koshti Bok*?"

"Yes, whenever I go out, I wear it."

"This is good." I could hear relief in her voice. "And you will wear it tomorrow?"

"Yes, little mother, but you better tell Nico not to bring his gun—you either—there will be Secret Service there. They will certainly search everyone near the viewing stand."

"How then to protect us?"

"If there is shooting, we'd best leave it to the professionals; they have been warned, so security will be good. I am hoping to spot the *beng* before he can act."

"I will pray this night. And look at the cards again."

"Let us hope they will give you a different result. I'll see you tomorrow."

I was uneasy when I hung up. For all my bravado in speaking to her, the dark cast of our conversation shook my confidence. She was a *drukker*; she could see beyond the physical, and if she saw darkness and death, there would be both the next day. The question became, could we control who died?

After Vandoma's prediction, I thought it expeditious to take the precaution of calling the number Enzo gave me to request some more of his special brand of security—I was not sure the official forces would be up to the level of decision to be made if the shinobi attacked. They would be bound by official rules.

I was somewhat stunned that Enzo picked up the phone himself.

"You are a very busy man, Mister Paradise. I wondered if you would call after Friday night."

"As ever, you are well informed."

"We only heard that you convinced the tongs to smoke the peace pipe, but that's impressive. It seems you kept your word."

"Thank you, but I am afraid those who troubled Mister Manzetti are still active. I think they may show up at the ship launch at the Navy Yard tomorrow. There might be some trouble with the visiting king and queen of England."

"Not very confident in the police?"

"Not really," I admitted. "They sometimes are too...uh...restrained in their response for the sort of enemy we face."

He was quiet for a moment, then said simply, "Understood. There will be backup."

"Thank you, sir. And thank Mister Manzetti for all his help on this."

After I hung up, I felt a bit better about the prospects for the next day. Still, in order to give myself some mental rest from worry, I went to a double-bill film showing at a local theater. There was an epic western, *Man of Conquest*, about the founding of Texas. A second feature came along with it, *Three Texas Steers*, and the concluding chapter of the serial *The Lone Ranger Rides Again*, based on a popular radio program. There were a number of shorts and news reels. They were morality plays in black and white, simple fare, but exactly what I needed to take my mind from the stakes of the day to come.

Motion pictures not only allowed me to see the world in a way that others might but also to see the society-approved morals and attitudes, at least as seen by the mythmakers of Hollywood cinema.

It allowed me to indulge myself in the illusion, at least momentarily, that I was just one of the crowd, an audience member. We all enjoyed the triumphs of the heroes and the vanquishing of the villains with egalitarian comradery. It put me in mind of Plato's shadows on the cave wall from his *Republic*.

Socrates spoke to Plato of people chained for their whole lives in a cave who see only shadows on a cave wall, never to see the real world. They have to interpret the silhouettes and thus never see what they really are. Socrates says the philosopher is like a freed prisoner who can see the real shapes of the world as they are.

For me, cinema served the reverse purpose, as I was outside all the time. The analogy amused me, and the time in the theater did its job of relaxing me and preparing me for the day ahead.

I had dinner at an Italian restaurant, returned home, and went to bed early.

Unfortunately, despite a pleasant time at the motion pictures, Vandoma's words and dire prediction for the day to come were the last thoughts that passed through my mind before I dropped off to sleep.

I woke at first light on Sunday, feeling little rested for all the time in bed, I suspect because of dreams or nightmares I did not remember.

My arm under the cast was itching considerably, but I felt it had healed sufficiently for me to remove the plaster. I had the tools to do so, so I spent some time cutting the cast off.

It felt good. I washed the arm and flexed my fingers with no discomfort. I wrapped the forearm in an elastic bandage and decided to get on with my day.

I dressed to head to breakfast at a local diner, my mind still dwelling on Vandoma's prognostications of darkness. When I departed my apartment, I saw Dottie coming down the block, heading for their apartment next door.

"You're out early, Adam," Dottie said.

"So are you."

Dottie adjusted their wig and smiled sheepishly. "Actually, out late. Why are you hurrying off with such a glum expression?"

I hadn't realized my dark thoughts were so clear. "Nothing particular," I lied. "I am going to Brooklyn for a ship launching today."

"Going to Brooklyn makes me feel that way too," they joked. "But seriously, is there something I can help with? Is this connected to the reason you were making yourself scarce at the beginning of the week?"

"It is, thank you, Dottie," I said. "But I have it handled. Things will work out today, one way or the other."

"Well, remember, Adam, ready for whatever comes."

"Absolutely," I said with a wave. And oddly, I felt better for simply saying it.

I took a taxicab to the home of the Yagyu family, where I secured something I hoped would help me in any confrontation with *Daitengu*, and then to the main gate of the Brooklyn Navy Yard. I promised the women once more that I would try to find a way to help Jaime, though I had no idea exactly how I could.

President John Adams authorized the Brooklyn Navy Yard in 1801. It was located on the East River in Wallabout Bay by a semicircular bend of the river across from Manhattan. It was a massive complex of dozens of structures with Admirals Row, a grouping of officers' residences at the west end of the yard, and the Naval Hospital, a full medical complex on the east side of the site.

The yard was a forest of tall metal structures as if leviathans had set them down haphazardly on the same scale as the bridge that loomed large behind us. There were drydocks for the shipway capacity, several structures such as large machine shops, and an administration building, all on the same gargantuan scale.

After the election of 1933, aware of fraying relations with Germany, Italy, and Japan, FDR had stepped up shipbuilding activities, making sure that America's allies were supplied with ships. On any given weekday, there were 4,000 workers in the yard.

I arrived just before one o'clock to find Vandoma and Nico both waiting for me outside the Cumberland Street gate.

"*Jo reggelt*, Mister Paradise," Vandoma said. Her greeting was cheerful, but her expression was serious, even glum. It seemed that her predictions prayed on her mind as well.

"And to you and Nico. I hope you are well."

"We are well," she said. "But the cards still portend darkness, Mister Paradise. A blind eye will be opened and there will be death."

"The die is cast, Vandoma," I said after a long moment. "We do what must be done."

"Yes, but there will cost, Mister Paradise. I have seen this." Her voice was as subdued as her manner as if a dark cloud hung over her.

"Today, we must confront this *beng*. You yourself once said that the cards only tell what might be, that we still could control our own fate."

"True, Mister Paradise," she admitted, working to give me a smile. "We must follow our destiny."

"So be it. Now let's find that Secret Service fellow Bennet and introduce ourselves."

CHAPTER THIRTY-ONE

Special Agent Rex Bennet of the Secret Service might well have been cast by Hollywood. He was over six feet tall, dark-haired, handsome in a well-tailored, dark suit, and had the air of easy authority. My private investigator license got us ushered into his presence in one of the guard shacks that he was using as a central base to coordinate security.

"I'm still not sure how you could have stumbled onto the arrival of the royals, Mister Paradise."

"Stumbled is the word for it, Mister Bennet. First from a cab driver but then from someone on an unrelated case. Only a rumor until I spoke to Detective Shane."

"Yes," he said, waving for Vandoma and me to take a seat in the Spartan shack. Nico had decided he would wait outside, his aversion to authority taking precedence over his curiosity. "Do you have any more specifics?"

"No. But the individuals who could be involved are highly motivated." I proceeded to tell him about the attack last Sunday and the library assault, assuming he had already been informed but would want to hear my version of events. When I was done, the man nodded.

"Detective Shane mentioned both incidents, and I've talked to the commissioner about you as well. What do you suggest?"

"Miss Kalderash and I can mingle in the crowd and look for any of these men," I said. "Her brother—who is outside, will stay with her. I am hoping we can detect any of them before they can act."

"That sounds good. We have men around on high vantage points and in the crowd. And, of course, the city police in uniform. I should introduce you to the police liaison as well."

Just at that moment, the door to the shack opened, and Detective Pettruchi stepped in. "What is that Gypsy doing standing out—" he began but froze when he saw me.

"Good afternoon, detective," I said. His expression flashed from anger to annoyance in a heartbeat, but I saw him rein in his emotions.

"Mister Paradise," Pettruchi said through gritted teeth. He looked to the special agent.

"He was the tip that alerted us to possible trouble, detective," Bennet said.

"Of course," Pettruchi sighed.

Bennet went on to tell him what I had learned and what our part in the day would be. He listened and grudgingly said, "Whatever you say, Mister Bennet. I've got my men deployed, and we're ready to let the crowd in. There are a lot already here for the boat launch, not just the workers' families. Bunch of Chinese dignitaries."

We left the shack with Pettruchi. Once we stepped outside, the detective turned to me.

"Listen up, Paradise, I may have to kowtow in front of the powers that be, but if you think I'll put up with your shenanigans, you can forget it."

"I really don't intend to—"

"Just shut up," he said. "I got exiled to this babysitting job because of you, so I don't have any patience for you left." He was red-faced, and his fists balled with suppressed anger. "I don't need another bloodbath."

"I'm sorry you feel that way, detective, but I am here in hopes of stopping violence."

"Your moll still packing a gun?" he sneered.

It took all my control to keep from striking Pettruchi. He saw my mood change and backed away from me.

"Mind your tongue, detective." My voice was a low growl. "Manners matter!"

The policeman said nothing more but moved off toward the site of the viewing stand that had been set up at the drydock where the ship was to be launched.

"*Baulo* always yell," Vandoma said flatly. She looked up at me with a gentle smile. "Do not let him upset you, Mister Paradise."

"We Roma are used such insults," Nico said. "We have grown thick skins. And long memories." He flashed a quick grin. "For friends our as well."

Once more, I found myself reflecting on my luck in having encountered these two for the quality of the humans that they were. Their friendship honored me.

"Let us go to the opposite ends of the stands," I suggested, "and keep an eye for any of *Daitengu's* men. If you see them, tell a policeman. And signal me."

"As you say," Vandoma said. Then she did something she had not done before but moved her hand in a warding sign, which I knew was a protection against evil. "Go with care."

"And you."

My mind was still on Vandoma's predictions of disaster, but I had to dismiss that to keep my mind on the task at hand.

There were two wooden bleachers set up at slight angles to a raised wooden platform at the bow of the *Empress of China* that loomed overall. The massive cargo vessel was easily many stories high and once more caused me to marvel at mankind's physical accomplishments.

The flags of China, England, and the United States hung from the front of the reviewing stand, which had a dozen seats facing bleachers.

Hank was on the stand already, chatting with a well-dressed Chinese gentleman I assumed to be the ambassador. The half dozen other dignitaries on the stage were all well-heeled sorts, but I thought it quite telling that the Chinese woman was as much at ease with them as she was with the criminal element. Perhaps there was little difference...

There were uniformed police officers in the front of the bleachers; all seemed alert and earnest, but I doubted they could detect the minions of the demon. Certainly, they would not see *Daitengu* before I or Vandoma did.

I went to the extreme right side of the bleacher and stood in the shadow of the structure, where I could see across the seats. Half the faces were Orientals, with the rest being working-class Caucasians who were most likely the yard workers on a busman's holiday.

It did not take me long to spot the men Enzo had sent, as their type and the black shades that hovered over most of them were clear. What surprised me was when Enzo himself walked over to me.

"Good afternoon," I said.

"Hey," he said. "Nice day."

"I'm surprised to see you here yourself."

"I ain't ever seen a king," he said with a slight smile. "Seemed a good chance."

"Much appreciated; I hope it stays as pleasant a day as this."

He shrugged and then walked off to take a seat on the bleachers. I noticed Angelo beyond him, looking annoyed but alert.

Hail hail, the gang's all here.

The crowd was jovial and enjoying the salt air. Several food sellers moved among them as if it were a sporting event. Nothing happened for a considerable amount of time, and I began to feel that I had been wrong with my predictions, but then I remembered that Vandoma had also seen danger in the day, and I had considerable faith in her abilities.

Just as I despaired of anything happening, there was a murmur that rippled through the crowd, and the British royals appeared in an open-topped limousine, preceded by two motorcycle officers.

The crowd cheered, and the monarchs stood and waved, which brought about a round of applause.

That was when I saw *Daitengu.*

The demon was in the baldheaded man from the Rising Sun Restaurant. He was dressed in a longshoreman's peacoat and wearing a watch cap pulled down over his ears. The man was seated in the center of the bleacher near a bottom tier, with Asian men on either side of him who had dark shades floating over them.

He had not seen me, as far as I could determine. The question was how to deal with him and those around him without exciting a panic.

I saw Detective Pettruchi and moved to catch his eye with a small wave of my hand but thought better of it. He would certainly overreact, his attitude toward me coloring his judgment.

The king and queen ascended to the platform to meet with the other dignitaries, greeting all, including Hank.

I moved back under the bleachers and went to the other side, looking to make eye contact with Vandoma or Nico. Both were at the far end of their bleacher. I did catch Enzo's eye and indicated the three Asians with gestures. He followed my gaze and nodded.

On the platform, speeches began, with the commander of the Navy Yard welcoming everyone.

I saw Vandoma but also saw several men in the crowd by her with dark shades above them, rough types that did not fit with the rest of the crowd, but what was surprising was that they were blond Caucasians.

Like at the extortions, they have allied themselves with Bund members to help them blend in.

I reached into my coat pocket for what I'd brought from the Yagyu home: a small wooden plaque.

Vandoma knew that names had power, and I had guessed that this was the name of the demon who called himself by the title of *Daitengu* when he was human. His plaque was from the family shrine, which is why he had sought out Jiro to aid him.

The widow had told me of the family legend of one of her ancestors with a facial deformity—not quite the one-eyed hero Yagyu Jubei, who was famous. A lesser ancestor with a vague suspicion of criminality or shame. One whose nickname was after a one-eyed demon, a *hitotsume-nyuudou.*

The books I'd read said such people could indeed become minor deities, worshiped in the family shrine as a way to appease their restless spirits. This one had risen through the ranks of demons, I suspected, to be what he was.

Nico saw my gaze, and I pointed to the three blonds. He indicated he understood, and I saw him move surreptitiously behind the men.

Now, I looked once more for Pettruchi.

I saw the detective talking with one of his uniformed men and walked over to him with as casual a movement as possible. My hope was that *Daitengu* had not seen me yet and that we might be able to contain his forces before they could act.

"What do you want?" the Italian said. His cigar was glowing red hot and enveloped him in a noxious cloud of smoke.

"I have spotted two groups of criminals," I said, then proceeded to describe the clusters.

To his credit, Pettruchi listened to me and then dispatched the uniformed man to the other bleacher.

On the stage, the Chinese ambassador stepped up the microphone and began his remarks.

Pettruchi and I went back under the bleacher, where the detective summoned four others of his officers.

"You stay out of this, Paradise," he said. "This is police business."

There was no point in arguing or trying to explain who or what he was facing, so I said nothing. I just stood back as the phalanx of unformed men went out front, around both sides of the grandstand.

The officers approached the three Japanese from either side just as King Edward stepped up to the microphone.

At that same moment, the police by the blonds stepped up to those three men who, seeing the officers, pulled handguns and opened fire.

Simultaneously, *Daitengu* yelled, "*Shingeki!*"

That was the signal for half a dozen other men in the crowd to draw weapons, and a gunfight began.

CHAPTER THIRTY-TWO

The men with *Daitengu* also drew guns and fired, felling two approaching officers immediately.

At the first shots, the crowd erupted into chaos with screams of terror as the attackers charged toward the raised platform, yelling, "Pay tribute to the On Leon tong!"

The police were restrained from firing in the direction of the crowd, but *Daitengu*'s men had no such prohibition and were indiscriminate with their gunfire.

This was where bringing in Enzo and Manzetti's men paid off. The Italian "soldiers" in the crowd were able to stop some of the attackers from making it to the reviewing stand with superbly targeted marksmanship.

Detective Petrucci fell in the first fuselage of shots, but to his credit, he died as he jumped in front of one of his own fallen men and tried to return fire.

On the other bleacher, I saw Nico and Vandoma dodging down as bullets licked up the bleachers around them. I almost ran toward them, but the crowd went mad, scrambling from the seats and falling over themselves to avoid the lead death. I realized I could best save them by dealing with the shooters.

Enzo, Angelo, and Manzetti's men were hampered by the terrified audience but were not so gentle as the police and shoved their way through the crowd to fire down on the demon's forces.

The police, though not completely caught flat-footed, lacked any real leadership in the chaos with Detective Petrucci down. Many officers went down in the first barrage, targets of the attackers. The demon's men, still on their feet, charged the reviewing stand, but the Secret Service men on the platform got the king, queen, ambassador, and several other celebrities out of harm's way, acting with smooth professionalism.

Hank produced her own pistol and began blazing away at the attacking Japanese and blonds, refusing to duck behind the agents who were blocking the celebrities with their bodies.

I took the wooden plaque, which I had soaked in coal oil earlier, and struck a match to it. I screamed out, "*Katame*," which was the name on it. It was the nickname of a one-eyed demon, a *hitotsume-nyuudou*.

Daitengu heard me over the gunfire and turned toward me. I could see now that the human face he had donned had the same violent tick on the right side, which was apparently the reason for his original human body's nickname. It was not a complimentary name in his time and still seemed to upset him.

He screamed a monstrous yell as he changed direction and charged me.

At that moment, one of the demon's men pulled a gun and fired at me and struck my left arm right where the break had been. The pain was intense and caused me to drop the flaming plaque.

I tried to ignore the pain and scooped up the burning religious object from the ground, then ran at *Daitengu*—*Katame*—at full speed. My path carried me past Enzo, who was shooting at one of the demon's men.

As the talisman in my hand burned, the monster screamed as if its own body were on fire, writhing where it stood, in place.

I intended to physically overwhelm him as I had in the tong headquarters. This time, the plan was to drive him permanently from the human host, but as I prepared to close with him, I saw another one of *Daitengu*'s men turn from the platform to draw a bead on an unsuspecting Enzo.

There was no time to warn Enzo, so I swerved to shove him out of the way. The bullet meant for the Italian hit me in my right leg, high in

212

my thigh. The impact of the projectile spun me around, and I yelled involuntarily, stumbling but managed to keep from falling. I recovered and continued forward, limping toward the demon with the flaming plaque held before me like the weapon it was.

When I reached *Daitengu*, his screams increased as his claw-like hands reached for me. His hands once more wrapped around my throat with steel band strength, squeezing the air from me. His eyes were blazing pits of black fire, with his hate for me, for life, for all that I was fighting for visible to me.

The hate I saw in him fueled me, for I knew what I was fighting for even more clearly than before. My right to be, my purpose in a cruel world that was colder than the Arctic, yet with warm, bright spots of the community I had found. This was the purpose that Mother Kalderash had seen for me. There was no cost too high to end this monster.

The image of Vandoma avoiding bullets, the thought that this being before me had endangered her, caused me to roar with fury and push forward to jam the plaque into his chest.

When the burning wood touched his flesh, *Daitengu's* body rippled as if in a strong wind. It hissed like steam as the flaming wood melted into his chest and sunk into him as if he were a stick of butter.

His shriek of agony was a new horror, but the plaque continued to sink into him when I let go of it. At the same time, he fell to the ground, releasing his hands from my throat as he clawed at the flaming wood.

In the madness of the gunfight, I may have been the only one who noticed, but the bird-like shape appeared like a superimposed image over the fallen bald Japanese. It gave a squawk that was eclipsed by the noise of the gunfire; then, the otherworldly demon image was gone in a puff of smoke. The body of the bald man lay still, the strain of the monster's departure apparently too much for his human heart to stand.

I stood for a moment to recover my breath, the pain in my thigh and left arm flaring back at me with sudden force. All around me, the battle was raging, but it seemed as if it were a hundred miles away and muffled.

I managed to look over at the bleacher where Nico and Vandoma were crouching. I felt a momentary sense of triumph that she was still well but then saw one of the demon's men between us pull a hand grenade. He made as if to throw it at the grandstand.

I jumped at him, landing on him and trying to wrestle the weapon away from him. We both tumbled to the ground. I wrapped my hand around his to keep him from throwing the explosive, but he fought me. He threw powerful punches at my face and head, trying to wrestle the grenade away from me.

Out of the corner of my eye, I saw Nico and Vandoma running toward me to help.

"Stay back," I yelled. Both our hands slipped off the grenade, and it fell to the ground.

There was no time to do anything else, so I threw myself on the grenade just as it exploded!

A searing, hot pain ripped through my body, and I felt myself propelled into the air. It was a blazing light show of reds and whites, and then I was slammed to the ground on my side so hard the air was driven out of me. For a moment, I almost blacked out.

Suddenly, as quickly as violence began, it was all over.

The police and Secret Service, with the ruthless assistance of Manzetti's men, had stopped all of the attackers. The few who were not outright killed once again took their own lives, even the Caucasians, though they died by biting a poison false tooth rather than through their tongues.

The crowd had fled, but by a miracle, without any loss of life, though several civilians were injured. At least five policemen died on site, and a number of others were seriously wounded. The dignitaries had been rushed off the platform safely by the Secret Service.

That, at least, was the silver lining in the horror of the violence.

For myself, I lay in a pool of blood, unable to move. My body felt on fire and cold at the same time. This was worse than the fight I had with the polar bear on the ice so long ago. Much worse.

The grenade man lay a few feet from me, his eyes wide and staring into the great beyond, his body riddled with shrapnel from the explosion.

Enzo ran to kneel at my side; his expression told me he knew how serious my condition was.

"You saved me," he said in a hoarse whisper. "Thank you." He seemed to struggle even to say those words, and it told me how hideous my wounds truly looked to him.

I glanced down to see my intestines spilled on the ground beside me. There was no doubt in my mind what fate awaited me.

"A favor," I managed to whisper, for looking at the body of the bald man, I knew I had a way to help Jaime Yagyu.

"Anything."

I told him what I had in mind, and he allowed a faint smile to touch his lips.

"Done." He said, then moved off to round up his men—I assumed to get them away from the authorities.

Vandoma, Nico, and Hank all appeared kneeling at my side, their faces white with fear.

"Adam," Hank began, but I raised a hand to pat her leg.

"'Tis not so deep as a well nor so wide as a church door, but 'tis enough, 'twill serve'" I quoted, attempting to smile.

Vandoma seemed to be struggling to breathe.

I reached up to my neck, fumbling with clumsy fingers to unfasten the latch to the necklace I wore.

"I return to you the luck of the Kalderash," I said with effort. "It has served me well."

It was hard for me to keep my eyes open. The pain and fire that I felt in my stomach and chest was beginning to fade, and I suspected my time was limited. Vandoma knelt beside me, her face framed by her wild hair, streaks of tears marking her cheeks.

I could no longer feel my legs. Vandoma attempted to project hope with her gentle, pleasant features, but I could tell there was none.

"Be calm, little mother, admit it, you saw this, didn't you?"

She nodded and the tears began again. "I hoped..."

"It is alright, Vandoma. My life was not in vain. Their plot is foiled, the demon is done, and most of all, you are safe."

I coughed and felt a shudder run through my body. "I told Enzo to have two of his bought police swear that one of the dead attackers confessed to killing Jiro Yagyu; a deathbed confession will hold up in court. Jaime will go free."

215

"Mister Paradise," she sobbed. "This is not fair."

"You know life is not." I had trouble keeping my eyes open, the lids feeling heavy. "But it is a gift, and it is good. All of it. I had this brief time, and I have tried to use it well. You should live the best you can."

I was sad that I would not be able to spend more time with this kind, wise soul, and even a little fearful for the undiscovered country that was after, but I remembered Dottie's motto, "ready for whatever comes" and the fear leaked out of me like my blood.

Out, out brief candle...

"Adam," she cried.

"Vandoma," I managed with all the effort I had left. "It has been a pleasure to know you. I will wait for you. *Latcho drom.*"

"*Latcho drom*, Adam Paradise. I lov—"

And then darkness.

I was dead. That is, if I had ever truly lived, for I was assembled from the bodies of dead men.

Now, there was only darkness. Yet, I was aware of it.

How could that be?

Hell hath no limits, nor is circumscribed
In one self place, for where we are is hell,
And where hell is there must we ever be.

(Christopher Marlowe,
The Tragedie of Doctor Faustus, act 2, scene 1)

216

Adam will return in
Paradise Investigations III:
The Undiscovered Country

ABOUT THE AUTHOR

Teel James Glenn traveled the world for forty-plus years as a stuntman, swordmaster, storyteller, bodyguard, actor, and haunted house barker before turning to writing.

He has several dozen novels published and his novel *A Cowboy in Carpathia: A Bob Howard Adventure* won best novel 2021 in the Pulp Factory Award. He is also the winner of the 2012 Pulp Ark Award for Best Author.

His short stories have been printed in over two hundred magazines including *Weird Tales, Mystery, Pulp Adventures, Cirsova, Silverblade, Heroic Fantasy, Blazing Adventures* and *Sherlock Holmes Mystery*.

His website is: TheUrbanSwashbuckler.com
Facebook: Teel James Glenn
Bsky: @Teelglenn

Bibliography

<u>**Novels and Novellas**</u>
A Cowboy in Carpathia
A Year of Shadows
Bayou Sinistre
Bloodstone Confidential

Britannia Occultus
Callback for a Corpse
Chronicles of the Skullmask
Cultists Always Ring Twice
Deadly Shadows
Dragonthroat
Fae Well, My Lovely
Fear the Reaper
Gaslight Magick
Ghostmaker Inc.
Journey to Stormrest
Killing Shadows
Not Born of Woman
Semper Occultus
The Clockwork Nutcracker
The Cowboy & The Conqueror
The Cowboy and the Contest

Curious about other Crossroad Press books? Stop by our website:
http://crossroadpress.com
We offer quality writing
in digital, audio, and print formats.

Subscribe to our newsletter on the website homepage and receive a
free eBook.

www.ingramcontent.com/pod-product-compliance
Lightning Source LLC
Chambersburg PA
CBHW030305200626
46816CB00002BA/767